TIMING'S EVERYTHING

A NOVEL

CONNIE WESALA

Connie Wesala
2016

Copyright © 2015 Connie Wesala
All rights reserved.
ISBN-13: 978-1539335245
ISBN-10: 1539335240

Cover design, photography and layout by: Michael W. Wesala

For Michelle and Michael
Thanks for the wonderful travels we have experienced together and for all your support and love. Mike, our trip to Oxford shows throughout this book and I see your lovelyphotographs in each and every scene. Michelle, thank you for your loving suggestions throughout the writing of this novel.

Chapter 1

"Wellies packed?" my best friend, Jennifer, asked.

"I can't fit them in." I sighed loudly. I'd spent $75.00 on a pair of cute rain boots and waited six weeks for them to arrive. "I'll buy a cheap pair when I get there," I said.

The expense of this trip was adding up quickly. With the dollar to pound conversion, I was in sticker shock, and I wasn't even across the pond yet.

"Maybe it won't rain," Jennifer teased. Her broad smile was intended to lighten my mood, and I knew it. I threw a rolled-up pair of athletic socks across the bed where she lay sprawled, watching me cram the last of my items into the corners of my suitcase and the outside pockets.

Book, passport, wallet, cell phone. I was done.

"Sit on this," I said. I pointed to my bag on the floor, lid closed but bulging and fighting my attempts to zip it shut.

Jennifer shot from the bed and plopped her butt dead center, pressing all of her weight against the obstinate case. I started zipping slowly but surely, pushing items further inside with my fingers as I worked it inch by inch around the large bag. Once I turned the last corner, it slid with ease, and Jennifer clapped her hands.

"Well done," she said. She clambered from the floor and stood directly in front of me. She placed her hands on my shoulders, her face inches from mine. "Amy, you are going to have a great time."

As assuring as that sounded, I was not convinced. But I was leaving my best friend for a month, and I wanted our last visit to be positive and upbeat. I had taken roughly a quarter of my packed clothing from the suitcase last night. Each piece remained rolled and in a pile on my bed. As much as I wanted to grab a second bag and stuff it all inside, I knew that was ridiculous. I probably wouldn't wear half of what I'd packed anyway.

"You need a coffee," Jennifer said. "Now!"

At the Starbucks a half-mile from my house, we ordered our favorites—chai latte for me, vanilla for her—and took a table toward the back. It was already too hot in Phoenix to sit outdoors. Everyone was complaining about the hottest June on record with 110 becoming our norm.

I sipped my iced drink and felt myself begin to relax just a little.

"You deserve this trip, you know," Jennifer said.

"It's costing me an arm and a leg. I hope you're right. But I must admit, I'm getting pretty danged excited!" I knew I was grinning from ear to ear. I had wanted to attend a conference like this for several years and to have it be in Oxford, England was icing on the cake. Or whipping cream on the latte, as it were.

"You're going to miss me," she said and grinned.

I crinkled my nose and frowned. "I know."

"Well, we can email and text," she said, "Just don't be waking me at 3:00 a.m."

I laughed. I was still uncertain how the time thing went. I had read it a dozen times. I'd figure it out later.

"OK, I promise; but keep the phone close by just in case," I teased.

"Your flight leaves at 10:00?" she asked.

I nodded. "Pick me up around 7:30 I guess. Stupid international flights."

That evening I talked to both kids on speaker phone while I cleaned out the refrigerator and double checked litter and food for my seven-year-old cat Hermione.

Sarah, my eldest, age twenty-six, said insistently, "Make sure you text or Facebook every evening, O.K?"

"Get a SIM card as soon as you can, Mom," my son reminded me once again. Chris was twenty-four and had spent the last few weeks teaching me more about cell phones, computers, GPS and Google Earth than I could absorb.

"Have a great time," my daughter yelled, speaking over her brother.

The hardest part was leaving the two of them—and of course, Hermione, my black and white all-American cat.

The kids had been thrilled at the opportunity and, in fact, had been the deciding factor in my decision. As for the cat, she would probably hate me for a good six months, but she'd get over it. I was the only one having second thoughts at this point. Was I too old? Would I be able to keep up? Were the topics going to be over my head?

At 9:00 I turned off the lights—too late for any of that.

Chapter 2

At two a.m. I woke in a cold sweat from a dream about Luke. I hadn't seen him in a year and a half. Our relationship was one I couldn't seem to walk away from. I managed to fall back to sleep around three, and the alarm buzzed harshly at five-thirty.

Jennifer stopped her Honda Civic at the curb by International Departures around eight o'clock, and I retrieved my large suitcase and carry-on from her trunk. I gave her a long hug before she closed the driver's door, and she waved a final good-bye as she pulled away from the curb.

I had a two-and-a-half hour wait; then a one-hour layover in Dallas. Hell, I'd have one of my two novels read by the time I even landed at London Heathrow.

Once on the long leg of the journey, I was able to settle into my seat, dislodge a book, my iPod, lumbar pillow and socks from my carry-on and relax. I smiled politely at the gentleman in the center seat and was grateful for the aisle. I'd been bruised numerous times in the past by food carts, but it was better than being crammed against the window where I had to beg to stand up or scramble over seat-mates to get to the bathroom. The center seat was the worst, because both the aisle and window people inevitably felt they owned both arm rests.

I shoved my earbuds into my ears and turned on some country music, read a few pages and zoned out. My thoughts turned to Jennifer. She'd had a difficult year with a breast cancer scare and a divorce from hell. I hoped I'd been as good a friend as she had the past sixteen years. I wouldn't have survived my divorce thirteen years ago or my break-up with Luke without her; I knew that. We'd met as high school administrators, and our differences made for an unlikely friendship but one that had grown stronger over time. She was right; I would miss her.

The conference I was attending had been on my wish list for years. After retiring early from education, I had decided to study creative writing and try my hand at a new career. That had proved more difficult than it sounded, but my first novel was out on Amazon, my short stories had won a few awards, and I was well into my second book.

Writing had kept me busy and filled a huge void. After twenty-five years as a teacher, counselor and administrator, I had been at loose ends without a 50 hour work-week plus I really missed the students.

I was fortunate. With retirement from the state plus my ex-husband's social security (and an ugly divorce from Bruce with a not-so-ugly settlement), I was doing alright financially. So I had treated myself to a month at the Rothmere American Institute, part of the University of Oxford, taking an interdisciplinary master class with scholars from the fields of poetry, drama, music and visual and performing arts. The list of Who's Who on the faculty was impressive, and for the next five weeks I was going to immerse myself in Shakespeare, Jane Austen, Virginia Woolf, T.S. Eliot, Joni Mitchell and Tom Waits among others.

I was on a high just thinking about it. I had no idea what to expect as far as the background or age of the other participants. But I had declined the dorm room with a twin bed and found a basement apartment a short bus ride from campus. It was a little pricey, but I'd have privacy, a queen bed, shower of my own; plus be able to cook and relax in the evenings. It was well out of my budget, but after a year of grieving Luke, it was time to simply put money and energy into myself. I ordered a glass of chardonnay and found some snacks in my purse.

Chapter 3

Thirteen hours later, I waited at the carousels to retrieve my luggage; then schlepped it through customs before following the over-head signs to the outside bus terminal. After shooting a quick text message to Jennifer and both kids, I stepped out into a warm sunny day, quickly spotted the bus to Oxford and slid into line behind a half dozen other travelers, most of whom looked as disheveled and jet-lagged as I did. I hadn't slept on the plane as planned, but no way was I closing my eyes for my first ride through English countryside.

I smiled at the woman ahead of me and wound up taking the seat beside her in the third row from the front. She was tall and lithe and wore a black jersey sleeveless dress with a large amulet necklace. I noted she was wearing heels and carried a stunning designer handbag. I felt like a slouch but introduced myself. Her name was Susan, and she was returning home from Paris.

I watched as English villages slid past the window. After living in the desert for so long, the intensity of color made my eyes tear. The thick foliage was a lush green. I wanted to take pictures, but all I had was my cell phone. As I bent over my over-sized leather purse to look for a breath mint, I caught sight of two men across the aisle and behind me in my peripheral vision. I turned slightly and observed their interest in me. Both were staring at my overnight bag which was tucked under the seat in front of me; then shifted to the purse in my lap. I felt the discomfort in my gut.

I had been told to dress down and not wear jewelry. An American woman traveling alone drew attention. There were pick pockets everywhere according to the research I'd done, but I thought that was surely in the large cities like London. I looked forward for a moment or two; then glanced back again. They continued to look my way as they whispered to each other.

I talked with Susan for a bit to try to stay awake. I admitted to being American and told her about my plans. "Do you live here?" I asked.

"For the past seven years," she said. "Came to Oxford with my husband to study for two years and didn't go back when he returned." She cocked her head as if to say, it happens. "Where are you staying?" she asked.

"St. Margaret's Road," I said. "Found it online, and the owner seems quite nice, at least on the computer."

"That's a beautiful area," she said. "Big old Victorian homes, but many of them have been turned into rentals the past few years. Just too much upkeep on them."

"The apartment looked nice in the photos, but of course you never know …" I had been worried about that for a week or so. The place almost looked too new, too nice on their website. I just hoped the garden patio looked as lovely as the photograph.

An hour later, we pulled into the Oxford bus terminal, a large outdoor area with a dozen buses in queue around the perimeter. Gloucester Square. I'd been taught how to pronounce it so I didn't sound like an American. Glos-ter. Got that down at least.

I gathered my overnight bag and my purse from under the seat and pushed the straps onto my left shoulder. As I did, I turned enough to see the two men. They seemed edgy, nervous, but they made no eye contact with me.

I turned to Susan and whispered. "Would you mind walking with me to get our luggage? I'm suddenly rather uncomfortable."

"Of course," she agreed. "I'll help you get a taxi as well."

I followed her and waited to retrieve my large suitcase. The driver was busy pulling bags from under the bus and literally throwing them behind him as he went. I grabbed mine, and it rolled with difficulty along the cobbled street. My short heels turned on the roundness of the stones, and I suddenly wished for sneakers and comfortable clothes and to be settled in the apartment.

Susan followed me with her one Tumi bag slung over her shoulder. I felt foolish and way over-packed. It was all I could do to handle the suitcase, my overnight bag and my large purse. Talk about looking like an obvious tourist. I spotted the two men just outside the ticket office; one smoked a cigarette and the other kept glancing my way; then down to the ground.

A few moments later, Susan hailed a cab and gave the driver the address.

"Thanks so much," I said as I settled into the rear seat.

I watched the city slide past, and within ten minutes he pulled sharply to the curb. He walked my things to the side door of the old house and waved good-bye as he left me. "Enjoy your visit," he called.

I glanced around. The street was pleasant and shaded with thirty-foot trees in each front yard. The houses were a blend of graceful Victorian and Gothic architecture set on very narrow lots. No porches ... I noticed with interest. Susan was right. The cars parked along the street and in each driveway made it obvious this section of town had been turned into rentals, but it was pleasant enough.

14A was a red brick three-story with white trim. The front yard consisted of patches of dirt and grass. I could see into a large bay window as I walked up the drive-way past several large trash bins and spotted a side door. I rang the bell and waited for the owner to answer.

"Mary Madden?" I asked when she opened the door.

"Yes, you must be Amy," she said. "Let me grab the key, and we'll get you settled."

I followed her just a bit further along the drive to the rear of the house, through a wooden gate, and down a short but steep flight of cement steps to what would be home for the next five weeks. She struggled with the key for a moment, then stepped aside to let me enter. Just inside the front door was a tiny landing, then an additional four steps into the basement apartment. I walked into the kitchen; then turned left into a large room that served as both living and eating area. Mary followed, talking quickly and explaining where things were located before I had time to really absorb what she was saying.

As I surveyed the living space, she took a sharp right into the bedroom. It was larger than I'd expected with a queen size bed and an overstuffed duvet. Along the back of the room to my left was a wall of built-in shelves, cabinets and drawers. At the front of the house was a triple bay window, though I'd be looking up to the front yard.

The small bath had been renovated with modern fixtures—a tiny one person shower, pedestal sink and no toilet. Where was I to put my toiletries I wondered? I looked at Mary, and she must have read my mind.

"The second bath has the toilet," she said. "And you can place some of your items inside this cart with the bath towels." She pointed to a white metal shelving cart on wheels. She turned and walked out the bedroom door.

I followed her as we retraced our steps through the kitchen and down a short hallway. The full bath was to the left with a second bedroom beyond it. I would use that as my office, and I hoped the outdoor patio area would be a tempting place to write each day.

Mary showed me how to use the range and dishwasher and opened the cabinets to point out pots and pans, cooking utensils and dishware. The refrigerator was small but would be fine for one person. I didn't intend to cook a lot anyway.

"I'll be on campus all day and probably get back around 5:30 each evening," I told her. She nodded.

"My cell number is on the bookcase there. Call me anytime. Want you to be comfortable," she said.

"Thanks."

"Oh, one last thing," Mary said. "Make sure you lock the door anytime you are inside. It's a safe neighborhood, but you never know."

She explained where to catch the Number 6 bus the next morning. It would take me to city center where I would get off on St. Giles; campus would be directly to my left.

I locked the door behind her, rolled my suitcase into the living area, kicked off my shoes, and lay down on the sofa. I was asleep within seconds.

I had no idea what time it was when I awoke. England was eight hours ahead of the U.S., and it would take a day or so to adjust. I was too tired to unpack. I moved to the bed, closed my eyes and died for the next three hours.

When I woke up around four o'clock, I grabbed my phone; then realized I could get no cell service in the basement apartment. Once I stepped outside and up the six steps to ground level, my screen lit up with message alerts. For a moment, I let my frustration get the best of me. It was going to be inconvenient for sure, but there was nothing I could do about it. A walk around the block helped my legs, my back and my mood.

The damp British air felt like a warm towel on my face—better than a facial at any fancy salon in the states. As I walked along, my eyes soaked in the color of the city—verdant green everywhere with blankets of yellow, pink, magenta, blue and purple. The vibrant colors popped from tiny front-yard gardens, hanging baskets and window boxes.

I was in love. Love at first sight. The only other time I'd fallen so quickly had ended eight years later as Luke walked out my front door and disappeared. Well, if I could love England for eight years that would be fine. I relaxed into the feeling and let it overtake me.

At the end of St. Margaret's Road, I turned to my right, past a church;

then walked a block or two further. There, on the corner was a traditional neighborhood pub made of lime-stone from the 1800's with a heavy oak door that I had to push hard against to open. I walked through the restaurant portion, past the heavily detailed carved bar and out onto a small garden patio with wood and iron tables and chairs. I smiled and nodded at an older couple in the corner, took a seat and ordered my first pot of English tea ... with milk and sugar, of course.

Chapter 4

That night I fell into bed and slept until I felt the light from the open bedroom window. Great, I had forgotten to even close the drapes. I'd get organized this morning and make it to campus for the 10:00 a.m. registration meeting.

As I rummaged in the kitchen I found things the previous renters had left in the refrigerator and cabinets. There was enough coffee to brew a pot. A café press sat on the counter, and an electric kettle would heat the water quickly. I made a short list of things to purchase at the store and found a printed page of directions and recommendations from Mary. There was a small market on the corner—the one I'd passed yesterday on Kingston— and a larger grocer a half mile up the road. I suddenly felt energized with excitement. I was here in England, at the University of Oxford with scholars and fellow authors, and how lucky can one person be?

I took my coffee into the living area and opened the curtains that covered the sliding glass door to the patio. There were several moss-covered concrete steps up to a grassy yard, and spiders hung from the adjacent trees and shrubs. The lovely flowered tablecloth from the on-line photograph was nowhere to be found, and the round wrought iron table and chairs could have been from Walmart. Darn! Trees covered the entire area and the dampness from overnight dripped onto the entire brick patio. The seats were too wet to sit on, so I returned to the dining table in the living room. Darn! My second disappointment.

I sighed, drank my coffee and headed to the shower, with a quick stop in the hallway bathroom to pee. This could be very inconvenient, I thought. But I put it aside. This was going to be a wonderful trip, I reminded myself. No complaining!

As I stood at the registration desk shortly before ten o'clock, a young woman waited in line just ahead of me. She turned and smiled.

"Hi," I said as I held out my hand. She was about twenty, decades younger than me, and most of the other students seemed to be that age. I looked around to see if there were any other gray-heads. Not that I allowed any of mine to show. I spotted one man who appeared to be late 40's like me, and an older woman maybe in her late 60's. "I'm Amy," I said.

"Shannon," she said. Her British accent was strong to my American ears.

"American?" she asked.

"I guess it's obvious, huh?" I grinned. "Your accent sounds British," I said. "Are you from around here?"

"Born here but living in France. Have been for a couple of years."

"How wonderful," I said. Before we could talk further, the registration staff asked her to move forward. By the time I was finished completing my paperwork, she'd slipped into the building where the seminars would be held each day.

The campus was lovely—just as I'd anticipated. I couldn't wait to leave the seminar at lunch and walk across to the main university buildings. The University of Oxford, as I'd learned, is basically the City of Oxford. Just after noon, I walked past Mansfield College, and after just a few more blocks, crossed Broad Street, circled past Radcliffe Camera and the Bodleian Library and exited next to the History of Science Museum.

Every step or two, an immense stone head loomed above me. Strange, ugly sculptures that looked like animated cartoon figures. Every street and side-walk was cobblestone, and I knew I'd be living in my sneakers and flats. Stone guttering ran the length of each building with a carved gargoyle on each corner. Between them, glaring down on passersby, hung creatures called grotesques. I had learned the difference from a brochure at the apartment. Gargoyles were actually designed to release water from the gutters.

Grotesques were simply decorative and, as their name suggested, most were extremely grotesque. I understood now where we got the adjective. Some seemed to shoot from the honey-colored stone in which they were embedded. Within twenty minutes I'd walked around a few blocks and finished my sandwich and Coke. So much more to see and do. I was tired from the long exhausting flight, but too energized to feel it.

The afternoon was packed with informational meetings and our first introduction to the world renowned professors who would be leading the seminar. I was awe-stuck, and Shannon, who sat beside me in the large lecture hall, appeared to feel the same.

At our mid-afternoon break, I walked out with her, but a few people she'd met earlier in the day called for her attention. Much younger I realized. I approached the man I'd spotted earlier in the day and hoped I hadn't misjudged his age. Forty, I was guessing.

"Are you enjoying the seminar so far?" I asked.

"Oh, yes, absolutely wonderful," he said. He reached out his hand for me to shake. "Tom—Tom Bradford."

"Amy Crawford," I offered. "You're from the states?" I posed it as a question as I wasn't really certain.

He nodded. "Boston," he said. "And you?"

"Phoenix ... well, a suburb of Phoenix," I said.

"You here alone?" he said, then blushed bright pink. "That was presumptuous of me," he said. "Good grief."

"It's fine," I said, and I laughed to put him at ease. His blond hair glowed in the dappled sunlight filtered by the leaves of the chestnut trees; his green eyes were clear and bright.

"Well, I mean ..." He tried again. "My wife is with me but holed up in a small room we rented for the month. I just thought I'd ask in case you wanted to get together."

"I'd love to meet her," I said. Part of me was a tinge disappointed. He was a good looking man, not too tall, stocky with broad shoulders, and was no doubt a writer.

Tom glanced to his right and waved at someone. He turned to me and waved her over. "Have you met Miriam?" he asked.

I nodded at the woman as she joined us. "Hi, Amy Crawford," I said and extended my hand.

"Miriam McConnell," she said. "Nice to meet you. So glad there are at least three of us 'mature' people here, aren't you?"

I agreed and told her we'd have to stick together. "I like 'mature'," I said. "Much better than 'old'." We laughed.

Just then a chime reminded us to return to the lecture hall, so we said good-bye, and I took my seat inside and penciled notes the remainder of the afternoon.

The presenter today was the woman in charge of the conference—Dr. Elizabeth Montrose, and much of the information being disseminated was of a logistical nature. But the last half hour, she introduced the speaker for the following day, a woman I'd never heard of but with credentials that filled a page. Before we broke for the day, Dr. Montrose gave us an assignment, and my heart soared. This was why I was here; I couldn't wait to get back to the apartment to start. I quickly planned a simple dinner in my head, grabbed my bag and found a large grocery store across the street and steps from the bus stop. I was already getting the hang of this #6 bus.

As I rode back to the apartment, I read emails from Jennifer and Sarah and typed a quick response to each. That evening I closed the curtains and turned on the small stereo. From the fridge, I pulled out humus and pita bread, a jar of olives, and a wedge of cheese. I sliced an apple and poured myself a glass of white wine. I had already slipped into pj's even though it was barely six o'clock, and I took out my brand new red spiral notebook and my favorite pen and settled at the round dining table in the living area.

For the next two hours, I became Jane Austen as I philosophized about the state of women authors in the twenty-first century compared to the 1800's. My eyes began to close around 8:30, and even though the sun hadn't set, my body would not let me continue. I pushed the heavy duvet to the floor and crawled under the sheets. Jet lag; surely it would subside in the next day or so.

Chapter 5

Within two days I'd acquainted myself with the neighborhood, the local markets and the restaurants near-by. I had also established a morning coffee routine at a corner Java and Co. café not far from campus. On Wednesday morning as I stood at the glass-front counter, I fumbled with the change in my hand and tried to count out three pound, fifty. The young cashier was the age of a university student. I opened my palm, and she picked out five coins and smiled. As I turned to find a seat, I balanced a plate with a tomato, egg and cheese sandwich, a hot drink and my notebooks, plus the purse on my left shoulder which immediately slid down my arm, making it impossible to handle it all.

"May I help you?" A thick male voice spoke from behind me. I turned enough to smile as he reached for the heavy plate and took it from my hands. I nodded at the nearest table, and he slid my sandwich onto it and pulled out the heavy wrought iron chair as I pulled my purse back onto my shoulder and stuck out my right hand.

"Amy," I said. "And thank you."

He shook my hand, and I noticed his 6'5" frame towering over my 5'3".

"Roger," he said. His blue eyes sparkled in the sunlight as it glinted off the east windows and his smile, like a George Clooney clone, tipped up just slightly on his right.

I needed to sit down or say "good-bye and thanks again" or do something—anything besides standing dumbfounded like a fool. But I couldn't seem to move either direction. Luckily Roger picked up where I'd left off.

"You're welcome," he said, and I sat down quickly so he could push my chair forward.

I expected him to say "nice to meet you" and head for the door. Instead he stepped to my right and continued to speak. "Are you visiting?" he said. He had an easy unhurried manner about him which calmed me.

I explained my five weeks at a literary conference, shared how long I'd been in Oxford and asked if he lived in the city. My breakfast sat uneaten, the crust growing hard and the egg congealing. I could not escape his eyes long enough to end the conversation. So I finally nodded to the seat across from me and asked if he'd care to join me.

Thankfully he placed his leather satchel on the opposite chair and said he'd be right back. I watched him order a pastry and coffee. The few minutes allowed me to straighten my belongings, tuck my hair behind my ears, check my make-up in the reflection of the window and place my napkin onto my lap. I sipped my coffee and pushed my plate to center it.

When he sat down and was more at eye level, I was able to further assess his features and his British accent. Over the next half hour I managed an adult non-crazy conversation about jobs and backgrounds, single status and the weather. He was a grad student at Oxford. How much younger was he? I wondered. At least six years I guessed. Did it matter? We were having a one-time casual breakfast. I reminded myself more than once that he was not Luke. He was not short and stocky or brown-eyed and caramel skinned— definitely not Luke.

I finally glanced at my watch and noted the lateness. I began to gather up my belongings, placed my napkin on my plate and sent the nonverbal message that I was about to leave.

"It was so nice to …"

"It was nice…" We both spoke at once. We laughed and stood at the same moment. I got to the door first; he opened it by reaching around me for the handle. I had seconds, very few seconds. Was I letting him just walk away with a slight nod good-bye? Was I going to let him turn the corner and disappear? I stepped through the doorway and onto the sidewalk. It was cobblestoned for a few feet each side of the café, and as I turned to face him and to make the decision, my left foot caught the slightest edge of the rounded stone, and I was suddenly plunging forward. Roger's right arm grabbed my waist and held me upright.

There was nothing more to say. I'm a klutz? I'm actually a drunk? I need someone to take care of me? Instead I started laughing, body shaking laughter that turned to crying eyes laughter, and he joined me.

As we both contained our outburst, he shook his head. "May I walk you to wherever you're headed?" he said.

"Oh, so you think I'm incapable of getting from point A to point B without harming myself?" I asked. I smiled to let him know I was teasing.

"Well, it sort of appears that way," he said and grinned.

"I'm fine," I added, "just headed to class across the street." I pointed toward the RAI building. "But you're welcome to join me."

We continued to talk as we walked along. I needed to rush to make it on time, so we said good-bye quickly, but not before discussing the current King Tut exhibit at the Ashmolean Museum.

"I've been meaning to go, myself," Roger said, "unless you prefer going alone." He was giving me an "out".

I felt myself warm to a glow. Did we always assume an "out"? I had, for over a year. Since the break-up. I glanced at his jeans, turtleneck and cable sweater. *Not a "perv"*, I told myself.

"I'd like that." It was my voice, though it surprised me.

"I'll call you," he said. He typed my cell number into his phone, and we waved good-bye.

As I made dinner in the tiny kitchen that night, a song kept winding its way through my head. "White Lace and Promises." Carole King and James Taylor—from the '60's or '70's? *Was that sung at my wedding?* Definitely at some one's. Maybe if Bruce and I had stayed married, I'd have remembered! I'd forgotten or blocked so many thousands of facts. In some ways it made me sad. And yet … would I change it? No children, or at least not the darling ones I had been blessed with. So even if the marriage had been a mistake, the outcome had not. And I'd spent years paying for that mistake.

That's the story of my life, I thought. Paying for foolish decisions. Actions and consequences. I had moved recently and found a box crammed full of journals. I had ripped out the worst pages. No reason for my kids to know any of that. *Maybe that's the story of every one's life,* I had said out loud and slammed shut yet another notebook full of crap.

Journaling was just another way of avoiding living. And right now, I was headed to a garden patio in Oxford, England to eat a home-made dinner, and it was time to start living. As I sat down on the wrought iron chair, I arched my back and raised my face to the heavens. The sun was low in the sky, but it peeked through some heavy clouds and showered the patio with its warmth.

Chapter 6

I noticed Tom Brady standing alone the next morning and approached him. He smiled warmly when I spoke, and once again I couldn't help but wish there were no Mrs. Brady. At 48 I was becoming a hussy. I laughed at that thought.

"You seem to be enjoying the conference," he said.

I nodded. "I feel old this week," I admitted. "The topics sound so broad and yet so intense."

Tom nodded in agreement. "It's almost too … what's the word? … esoteric?"

"Mind boggling," I said, and I laughed. "That's what I call it."

"These young people seem to be eating it up," he said.

"I know. I've been in education forever, but not in a philosophy class in thirty years."

Just then, Shannon joined us with two other young students. I observed their easy going demeanor, their laughter and light-heartedness. Had I ever been like that? Even in college, I had been anxious and unsure of myself. Working night and day for A's, over-studying for every quiz or test—filling blue book after blue book. Always trying too hard.

I was exhausted by junior year and in the hospital with mono that spring. Nerves—they called it back then. There was always a tension to be perfect, to be accepted, to prove myself. I was a ball of nervous energy bouncing through life.

Shannon was vivacious and outgoing; her red curls were unkempt, and her lack of make-up gave her a natural, healthy look. We were divided into study groups on the second day, and I pleaded silently to be with the other two 'over-40s,' but it was not to be. Tom, Miriam and I were split between the four groups assigned to meet every other day.

My group consisted of three young women in their mid-20s and two young men slightly older. While I tried to shine during lectures, I grew quiet in group—waiting for others to take the lead and adding comments only when I felt certain of my analysis. My writing, I knew, was probably superior to theirs. Written assignments didn't require thinking on your feet. I had time to sort out my thoughts—outline if I needed; scratch out, delete, re-word. We weren't graded. This was an experiential course of study intended to make you think, analyze, conjecture, compare and contrast. I suddenly felt a hundred years old, and I hated it.

In the lecture hall I worried that I raised my hand too often. Each time I felt my right arm rise, I watched to see how people were responding to my need to know—a trait Luke had criticized during our years together. "Can you not just accept not knowing?" he had asked many times. It was not in my nature. Knowing gave me control; it gave me pride, as well as acceptance. "Why wouldn't I want to know?" I had asked him. "Why do *you* have to keep everything secret? You keep everyone guessing and wondering. You force me to ask." The arguments escalated into our entire relationship instead of focusing on whatever situation we were discussing at the time.

By 4:00 that afternoon, my brain was exhausted, but my body needed to move. I gathered my belongings and slid from the lecture hall seat. I was impressed at the comfort of the padded chairs and the retractable arm tables. I had been worried that sitting for eight hours would make my already sore back seize up. Middle-age was so much fun. I waved good-bye to Shannon as she scurried out the rear door. I hesitated long enough to catch Dr. Montrose, the director, on her way out. She saw me and smiled.

"Ms. Crawford," she said, "so nice to see you."

I was a bit surprised that she recognized me. "Thanks. I'm glad to have a chance to say how much I appreciate you accepting me for the program."

"Oh, my goodness, dear," she said. "The pleasure is all ours. To have you come from America . . . and someone more mature and experienced. It's wonderful to have you."

If I were a blusher, I'd have blushed.

"Well, thank you for that," I said. "I just hope I can keep up with these young people." I gave a laugh. "They're half my age at most."

"Have you met Dave Bradford or Miriam McConnell?"

I nodded. "Yes, at registration. I'll get together with them soon."

She turned to her right to exit, but I stopped her.

"Dr. Montrose, is it far to Christ Church? I thought I might take a walk and look for signs of famous authors."

She gave a slight laugh. "Well, you've come to the right place for that," she said. "The campus is open, of course, but you won't be able to tour at this hour. It's about a twenty-minute walk."

She gave more specific directions and said, "Stop into Alice's Shop across the street—you don't want to miss that."

I thanked her and crossed Broad Street to Cornmarket; then turned left and south to St. Aldate's. A block away I spotted the high spires of Christ Church Cathedral and the famous bell tower built by Christopher Wren in 1682. Wrought iron fencing surrounded the campus. Alice's Shop sat directly across from the main entrance into the memorial gardens.

The heavy iron gates were tall with gold ornamentation at the top and a large coat of arms in the middle of each. Just inside, laid out on the graveled walk, was a circular memorial that caught my eye. The sword embedded into the stone and quote surrounding it brought a lump to my throat. It started to drizzle as I reached the gardens, and everyone fumbled for their umbrellas.

The gardens bloomed in a fusion of purple, orange, pink and blue with a backdrop of honey colored stone buildings. The simplicity of the gardens took my breath away. Holy cow. I was standing in the very spot where Lewis Carroll, a.k.a. Charles Dodgson, walked to classes. I remembered my college British Lit course. Carroll wrote Alice in Wonderland for the dean's daughter, Alice Liddell. It is said that on a boat ride on the Cherwell River with the three Liddell children, he outlined the book within a few hours. It is known that Alice and her siblings loved Carroll and spent hours listening to his stories. What isn't known for sure is what his feelings were for the eleven-year-old girl.

I wandered further into campus, up the dirt path between Merkel College and Christ Church. Long-horn cattle stood under the tall Sycamore trees in the meadow to escape the rain. I stood for a few minutes soaking in the hazy rural beauty of gardens and meadow and rivers. The Cherwell and the Thames Rivers outline Christ Church meadow making it a triangle of beauty. Further on, a dozen soccer fields were chalk marked for play.

I turned left and pushed through a turnstile onto the grounds of the Meadow Building. As Dr. Montrose had said, the entrance to Christ Church was closed. From the pages of Alice to those of Harry Potter—I felt I'd been here a hundred times.

As I left, a large tour bus pulled up to the curb to load its passengers. I detoured around it and crossed the street. Large poster signs of Alice and the Mad Hatter greeted me. I walked through the door and down a few steps into the shop. Just as advertised – Alice everything. Tea cups and pots, calendars, dish towels, pencils, note-books—something for every budget. For several hundred pound you could purchase a lovely pocket watch. I went directly to the book display and chose a miniature copy of the famous tale and three bookmarks for friends. I ignored the price and didn't try to convert to dollars. I just couldn't, or I'd never spend a penny

I spoke to the sales woman as she ran my card. "So this was a candy store originally?" I asked.

"Your first visit?" she said. "American?"

"It's the accent."

She laughed. "Yes, Alice bought candy here often. It was The Old Sheep Shop back then. Lewis Carroll loved her, you know." Then she whispered, "More of a slight crush I think."

"Ahh, yes … urban legend stuff."

She nodded. "But all true—all true."

I thanked her and left the shop; the little bell on the door tinkled behind me, and I realized the sky had somewhat cleared. I backtracked to Cornmarket, passed a large indoor mall, then smaller shops along the pedestrian-only street. Just past Debenham's Department Store, I ducked into the Primark to grab a few grocery items and a pre-cooked frozen dinner.

An hour later I was settled in front of BBC news waiting for the oven timer to go off. A glass of Pinot Grigio sat on the coffee table in front of me alongside a small plate of crusty bread and cheeses. Heaven! It didn't take long to complete the evening's assigned writing; then I showered and took my journal to the desk in the second bedroom and jotted a few notes about my day.

I shot off a quick Gmail to Sarah and told her about Alice in a few short sentences. I attached a picture of the shop from my phone.

In the Oxford guide I'd picked up, I studied the pubs I wanted to visit soon: the Eagle and Child where C. S. Lewis and J. R. R. Tolkien once gathered to write and drink. Turf Tavern tucked down an alleyway just under the Bridge of Sighs. It claimed to be the oldest. The Bear Inn discredits that. It was built in 1242—sounded pretty old to me. Their claim to fame was that Thomas Hardy wrote Jude the Obscure there.

I looked at the lengthy list of tourist attractions and knew I'd have to pick and choose. With seminars each day, it left only weekends and late afternoons to explore. I took my pen and marked them by priority. Writers first; political figures and philosophers second, and then the rest: museums, castles, palaces, etc.

The Bodleian Library was first on the list—the largest in the world with nine million books. Lots of Harry Potter sightings at The Bodleian as well as Christ Church.

As I washed my face and stared in the mirror, I saw fatigue but also sparkles in my eyes that I hadn't seen in ages. And not one thought of Luke since I'd arrived four days ago. The relief had relaxed me along with the wine, and I was sleeping more soundly than I had in years.

As I climbed into bed, I checked the screen on my phone for messages. Roger had texted to confirm our meeting place the following afternoon. I quickly typed, "C u there." A lightness spread inside me. I leaped from bed, walked to the front door and up two of the outdoor steps so it would send.

We agreed to meet outside the museum entrance on Beaumont Street at 4:00. I passed it every day. The Greek architecture with large marble columns was impressive yet somewhat out of place.

Chapter 7

The next day it was difficult to focus on the workshops. In part because the historian who was speaking that day was boring as hell, but I also kept thinking how little I knew about this man. Was I a foolish woman, meeting someone I barely knew? Still … it was during the day at a museum. What was I worried about? Besides, I refused to call it a date.

Roger was standing just outside the main doors when I arrived. Professorial popped into my mind, and I smiled. A stray beam of sunshine fell onto the narrow street and in the two seconds it struck, I saw silver strands mixed in his dark hair. He was either graying early, or he was older than I'd guessed. People went to grad school at any age, I reminded myself. I also quickly reminded myself that if I could see him, he could see me, and sure enough, at that moment, he waved.

Oh, my God, this *was* a date. His broad smile welcomed me; we said hello, and he held out two tickets. "Oh, goodness. I didn't mean for you to pay," I said.

"No worry." Then he grinned. "You can pay for dinner later." His voice was teasing.

After seeing Tut, we wandered in the area of art and antiquities and an excellent Egyptian exhibit. The Ashmolean housed the world's largest collection of astrolabes—Roger's favorite area. I was partial to the Greek pottery. It was near closing when we wandered back downstairs and out of the three-story building. The sun was hidden from view by the tall buildings across the street, and the museum was shadowed by the Randolph Hotel and the Oxford Playhouse. We crossed the street, and I wondered if I should mention dinner or assume this was the end of our day. I waited to see what he'd offer.

He took my arm as we quickly hopped out of the way of a tour bus and up onto the curb. "I'm sorry I can't have dinner tonight," he said.

I felt a release of tension. *Good*, I thought. Don't want to make this into a "thing".

"I'll tell you what," he said, "Have you been to the Cotswolds?"

"Not yet, but they're on my list for sure," I said.

"Great. I have a car I seldom use, but I'll pick you up tomorrow morning. The weather is perfect for a drive."

He was right. Oxford had just enjoyed several glorious days of rare English sunshine, and it was supposed to continue. I had no classes until Monday.

"Are you sure? That's a lot of trouble."

He waved me off. "You OK to take the bus back? Give me your address."

I gave him directions and told him I'd be out front waiting at eight.

"Wear comfortable shoes," he called as he turned and headed in the opposite direction.

Do not go home and journal, I said as I boarded the bus and tapped my pass card against the driver's magnetic pad. This is *living*, I reminded myself.

At five to eight the following morning, I waited on the sidewalk in jeans, a red long-sleeved V-neck that hit at just the right spot above my cleavage, my new ugly European walking shoes, with my cell phone and wallet in a small shoulder bag. I was nervous. Was this a bad decision? A man I barely knew—out of town and most likely no cell phone service. I'd let no one know where I was going. I gulped as he pulled to a quick stop, hopped out and held the passenger door open for me. Way too fast to change my mind.

As we drove north out of the city, Roger gave a running account of what we were seeing.

"Jericho—where you're staying—is for the wealthy. As we drive out of the city, you'll see areas where younger families and the rest of us can possibly afford to buy."

We passed a few industrial complexes, and then he took a round-about onto the four-lane highway and headed northeast.

"It's over sixty miles to circle the Cotswolds and takes forever, so we'll just drive through a few small villages and head back."

"Sounds great."

Within a few miles we were off the highway and back on narrow winding paved roads. There were spots where two cars could barely maneuver, and more than once we slowed and pulled over to let on-coming traffic have the right-of-way. I laughed.

"I could never drive here," I said.

"Especially on the wrong side of the road," he teased.

"Exactly."

"You Americans. Tell me when you want to stop." Within a half mile, I did.

"Sheep," I called out.

Roger turned sharply to the right, narrowly missing an oncoming car which startled me; then onto a rutted dirt road, stopping on the grass shoulder.

I jumped from the car with cell phone camera turned on, took a deep breath of fresh air and rural smells, and sighed.

Roger smiled down at me. "You look …" He hesitated.

"Content? Happy?" I laughed. "All of the above, I confess."

He reached for my phone. "Go stand over by the fence," he said.

I complied and posed in front of the flock.

We passed through two tiny towns, Bufford and Bourton-on-the-Water, stopping to take pictures, pick blackberries and walk around the picturesque villages. Their charm was straight out of the tour books. The rolling verdant green hills were broken by stands of trees. Dark-pink blossomed Hawthorne, Horse Chestnut, Wych Elms and Yew.

At the base of the trees spread a vast display of yellow celandine, yellow marsh marigolds, anemones, bluebells and daffodils. Hedgerows broke up the pastures, and Roger pointed out 14th century outcroppings of limestone. We followed along miles of low stone walls that separated the highway from the grazing land. After a quick lunch, we made an ice cream stop in Stow-on-the-Wold; then drove through lower and upper Slaughter, past a tiny post office and a few shops.

On the return trip, Roger slowed the car, and his hand slipped from the gear shift onto mine. For the next hour, we shared our personal histories interrupted only by mile after mile of perfect postcard scenery.

Roger had, in fact, been married. "We were too young," he said, "but I suppose every divorced person says that."

I smiled. "Well, that's my line," I admitted. "So you were in college when you married?"

"Yes," he said, "Met at Cambridge, dated eight months, married … together the requisite seven years while we both got our Master's degrees, started jobs and lived on love and soup. They both grew stale after a while." He glanced over at me. "Your turn …."

"Pretty similar. Married just before senior year in college. Then a year in a university town while Bruce got his masters; two more during my masters while he worked. An almost affair with a professor, a reconciliation baby—my first child—at twenty-three."

Roger's question mark eyebrows asked for more.

I sighed deeply. "Second born—my son—when I was twenty-five, a few years later a divorce. I don't like to talk about it. But the best thing—I had two great kids.

"You taught all those years?" he asked.

"Only a year or so after Sarah was born. High school counselor for fifteen and a few years as an assistant principal."

He nodded. "Enough for now," he said. "Let's go grab an ale."

"Whoa," I said, "Not so fast. Did you ever marry again?"

He shook his head. I let it go.

Back in Bufford, he turned right, down a winding lane lined with Yew trees, over the stiles and onto the gravel parking lot of a small pub. "Off the beaten path," he said. "Best kind."

We crossed a footbridge where old Willows hung low over a tiny stream. The tiny stone building had low ceilings crisscrossed with heavy oak beams. We spent an hour drinking stout ale and chatting about nothing in particular.

When he dropped me off back in Oxford around 9:30, he walked me just to the steps and gave me a quick hug. I said good-night and headed down the steps to the apartment while he waited for me to get inside and lock up.

Before I went to bed I journaled what I'd learned that day. Roger was 43—not as bad as I thought. Five years, though I hadn't shared that I was 48. Of course, once he realized my kids' ages, he'd figure it out. Divorced for many years. Getting a second master's degree in Business Management by end of summer. Considering opportunities in London.

He'd seemed impressed that I'd been published and was working on a second novel, though I assured him it had been pure luck. I put down my pen and notebook and shut off the light. I couldn't help but wonder why he hadn't kissed me after such a lovely day.

Chapter 8

Sunday was a day of laundry and errands in the morning. I should have been working on revisions for my editor, but by noon I couldn't wait to get to town and immerse myself in history. Oxford, according to the tourist guide I'd purchased earlier in the week, had produced thirteen prime ministers and many cabinet members, bishops, and civil servants. William Gladstone, in fact, had been PM four times.

Albert Einstein had studied here in the 1930's. The names of the famous sounded like a British history book. John Locke, John Wesley, William Penn, and W.H. Auden. Not to mention American Rhode Scholars including Bill Clinton, Susan Rice and surprising to me, Kris Kristopherson.

The presence of Henry VIII was everywhere in Oxford, and particularly in Christ Church. In 1529 when Cardinal Woolsey fell out with the king, Henry turned the Christ Church monastery into a cathedral and, as head of the Church of England, made it his own.

I passed through the Meadow Gate main entrance into the cloisters where I stood in awe of the architecture and shot photos of the fan-vaulted ceiling. The detail of the carved wood was stunning. As I entered the Great Hall, I was amazed at the size of Harry Potter's dining room: actually the daily dining hall for Christ Church students. I clicked off shot after shot as did my fellow tourists.

The covered walkway took me along to the Cathedral. As I stepped up to the doorway, I remembered the scene where Professor McGonagall stood on this staircase welcoming Harry and his friends to Hogwarts. I couldn't help but smile.

Inside, the sun lit the stain glass. I searched for the Alice Window. Sure enough, fifth window on the left, I spotted the March Hare and the Mock Turtle. I followed a crowd into Tom Quad just as the clouds moved in and gazed up at Tom Tower. The six-ton bell which hangs in the tower is sounded 101 times each night and is the loudest bell in England. A statue of the winged Roman god, Mercury, stands in the fishpond at the center of the courtyard.

Connie Wesala

I toured Christ Church for nearly two hours, then walked back toward town, stopping at Carfax Tower to take a peek inside. Tourists were lining the stairs to the top, and I quickly decided to forego the view, at least for today. Just as I was walking into the mall, Sarah's ring tone piped loudly. With an excited voice, I almost cried into the phone. "Honey, why are you calling instead of emailing? Is everything OK? Is your brother ..."

"Mom, everything is fine," she said. "I just thought I'd try to catch you and hear your voice."

"Ah, how sweet," I said. "Guess what? I'm headed into a mall; imagine that."

She laughed. Our favorite diversion was shopping together every other Saturday. "What are you buying me?"

"Who said I was buying you anything?" I teased. "What do you want me to bring you back? A big hat?"

"That would be fun ... but, no, those things give me a headache. I don't care—you pick."

I sat on a bench and talked to her for ten minutes; crowds of people swarmed the pedestrian-only street. A few times I had to ask her to repeat.

"So you're doing OK?" I asked.

"Yeah, fine, but I want to hear about Oxford."

So I tried to describe the city of spires, but it was impossible to put into words. "I'll just have to send you pictures," I said. "I can't do it justice. Suffice it to say it's one of the most beautiful places I've ever been."

"Oh, I'm so glad, and classes?"

I told her briefly how old I felt and how young the other students were. "I'm trying to not sound so damned old," I said. "I think they all may resent me sometimes."

"I'm sure that's not true," she said.

"I'm not so sure, but I don't know how to change it. I *am* freakin' old."

"Mom, you're one of the youngest forty-eight year olds I know. Don't let that bother you. Just be yourself."

Where had I heard that before? "I know. I miss you," I said.

"I miss you too—come home!"

"See you in a few weeks. Email me," I said.

The noise was making it difficult to hear. I think she said, "Send pictures!"

We hung up, and I sat for a moment feeling a rush of sadness. For the next hour I walked through stores that did not appeal to me, and I left after buying one small item for Chris. I wanted to be outdoors. I took time to browse through the bookstore on the corner and picked up a new novel on the British must-read list.

Not wanting to go home just yet, I walked north and east and wound up in the University Park gardens—seventy acres of nature right smack in the city. I sat on a bench to rest and almost dozed off. I sensed clouds gathering even though I had my eyes closed. The breeze shifted and a cool wind brushed my cheeks, and darkness showed through my eyelids. Just then a raindrop hit my face, and when I opened my eyes, the sky had turned the gardens a vivid deep oil painting, unlike the pastels that had been there earlier. I scrambled for the umbrella inside my purse, and by the time I got it out and opened, the droplets hit like pellets. I was nearly drenched by the time I walked the four blocks back to the bus stop.

Just as I walked onto the drive-way of Mary's house, my cell phone rang again. I glanced at the screen. Roger. A smile stretched my lips heavenward into a grin.

"Hi," I said. "It's raining!"

"Imagine that, in England of all places." he teased.

"Alright, I get it."

"Want to grab a bite of dinner? I can bring something over instead, if you don't want to be out in the rain."

"I don't think I'll melt," I said. My voice sounded high pitched to me, and I didn't like the excitement I was feeling. Slow down, I told myself.

"OK, then, I'll take the bus and meet you at your place. We can walk in the rain like ducks into Jericho for a beer and burger. I know just the place."

Once home, I dried off and reapplied make-up; then decided to change into warmer clothes. Jeans with a long sleeved white blouse and a blue and white striped pull-over sweater for warmth.

The doorbell rang sooner than I expected. I grabbed my umbrella, and we headed out.

"Are we going to get lost?" I said, as we wound our way two blocks east, then north, and then west onto curved narrow roads that seemed to go nowhere.

"I promise I know where I'm going," he said. "Trust me."

Trust him … hmm. Did I? I wasn't sure.

We walked uphill for another block or two, turned onto a street with no signage and there at the circular turn-around sat a tiny stone building with a lovely grass patio area—lovely if it hadn't been so wet. I closed the umbrella and shook it before stepping up the three stone steps. The entire pub held 50 people max and was broken into a half dozen tiny rooms with benches and bar tables and stools. Geraniums filled the window boxes. One young man handled the counter area; dispensing pints of ale, taking orders and money, and serving tables. I ordered a quarter pound cheeseburger and a light ale; Roger asked for a steak sandwich and a beer.

"With chips," he said.

I smiled. French fries—yum.

"Tomato sauce on the table; mustard as well," said the young bartender.

I walked toward the back of the pub, down a small hallway and into a room that looked like an artist studio. The walls were covered with drawings, pastels, and oil paintings—mostly scenic, and all of them of Oxford.

Roger joined me after he paid and placed our beers on the square wood table between us. "Nice, huh?"

"You are a wonder," I said and smiled. "You know this city like the back of your hand."

He nodded. "Well, not every street but enough."

I tilted my head toward the side wall at a painting that had drawn my eye. All of Oxford's spires glistening in oil.

He looked where I was pointing. "City of Spires, just as the brochures say. It's very nice, isn't it?"

I agreed. We ate and talked for an hour or so and on our way out, I stopped at the painting to check the price. $250.00—out of my range unfortunately. But I stood and soaked it in one more time. I'd come back again if I could possibly remember all the twists and turns that got us here.

"I don't think I could get home if you weren't here," I told Roger.

He took my right hand in his left and led me down the puddled path toward the paved road. "Good, I like to keep you guessing."

I turned and frowned at him but just for a second. I could see he was joking. "Yeah, well, that can go both ways, you know."

We slowly made our way back to St. Margaret's Road. The rain had stopped, and it was simply damp and getting cold. I was glad I had worn the sweater. I glanced at Roger every block or so. He seemed deep in thought, so I didn't interrupt with chatter as I usually did. The silence actually felt quite comfortable. Just as we turned onto my street, he pulled me to him and under a dripping oak tree, he lifted my chin and kissed me softly and gently. Nothing urgent or physical; just warm and loving, and I felt myself melt a little inside.

He left around 8:30, and I worked on an assignment that I'd put off. I had to re-write every other sentence as I was totally distracted. Luckily this was a no-grade assignment. I had no idea what I had written when I finally turned off the lights at 11:00.

Chapter 9

The next two days were hectic with morning and afternoon seminars, and Roger's semester was winding down which meant putting finishing touches on his paper, preparing for oral exams, and defending his thesis. A few quick phone calls were all we could manage.

Monday's morning session had consisted of a performance in the gardens of the institute. A talented writer and actress performed a selection from her story, Testament, which "explored the continued imprint of Biblical narratives on the southern psyche." I walked to lunch with Tom Bradford and Miriam McConnell. Shannon waved as she headed off with a group of younger students.

"Whew," Tom said, as we crossed St. Giles Street, through the ancient cemetery beside Martyr's Memorial, and looked both ways before scurrying across Magdalen to a small café.

I hadn't gotten acquainted with Miriam, though Tom and I had spoken again about getting together for dinner with his wife. Miriam looked to be a good fifteen years my senior, a tall, white haired British woman one would call striking, if not beautiful. She wore simple below-the-knee shift dresses with lovely bright silk scarves—a different one every day. What impressed me most was her obvious grasp of every difficult topic we explored. Her understanding showed on her calm face, her slight nods of approval, and her clear concise questions. I felt somewhat intimidated by her obvious intellect as well as her ability to tie scarves in a dozen different styles. After we ordered, I shared my amazement at her way with knots. She laughed.

"Oh, my dear," she said. "It's not a talent really—just a lot of practice."

"I have a short neck, and when I try I simply look like a be-headed wife of King Henry with fabric keeping my head attached to my body. Certainly not flattering."

"Nonsense," she said. "I'll teach you before you leave. Bring one tomorrow, and I'll show you a simple one."

I glanced at Tom and laughed.

"Don't mind me—I'm married—I'm used to listening."

"To think we moved from Biblical influences to scarf tying in a matter of minutes."

"Something I can actually understand," Tom said sheepishly.

"Miriam, you seem to be soaking all of this in as if you knew it already," I said.

She waited as the server placed our lunches in front of us and poured more water.

"My background is in British Literature," she explained. "I'm a professor of linguistics at Newcastle University."

I nodded. "And you're British so you're probably familiar with many of the presenters."

"Yes, she said, "plus I attended the conference last summer as well."

"Well, I'm a writer and researcher with a few years of literature under my belt, but I was ill-prepared for the intellectual level of today's speaker."

Miriam smiled. "Don't feel intimidated. Just soak in what you can and enjoy yourself."

Good advice, I thought. Relax and let life happen—my new mantra.

"Besides," Miriam said, "this afternoon is musical."

"Yeah," Tom said. "A recital of T.S. Elliott's poems? Nice and light."

We all three laughed aloud.

"Well, Tom," I said, "maybe they'll throw in a little Beatles here and there."

We returned to campus refreshed and light-hearted and spent the afternoon listening to Dave Matthew's evocative musical setting of Marina.

Tuesday morning was more of the same, only we had a two hour discussion group where we shared, discussed and broke things down to a comprehensible level.

Shannon led the group to which I'd been assigned. I spoke up today and raised several questions, pleased that I was finally comfortable enough to participate. I'd been an administrator, a counselor and a teacher of kids not much younger than these. While Miriam intimidated me, there was no reason to let these young people do the same.

That afternoon as I turned the corner, I saw a gray car cruising slowly past the house, stopping for just seconds, long enough for me to see the flash of a camera aimed at the building. The owner, Mary, had talked of selling the big old house—all that upkeep—maybe she'd hired a realtor or an appraiser. I put it aside.

But the next afternoon I watched again as the gray sedan slowed for several houses before picking up speed. I rang the bell to the main house, but no one answered. I'd call her later. My cell chirped as I walked down the steps to my basement apartment. I stopped before I lost the cell signal. Roger's number showed on the screen.

"Hi, how are you?" he said.

"OK, I think, but the oddest thing just happened." I described the car and the drivers' actions. There was concern in Roger's voice.

"Sounds very suspicious. Are you there alone? Where's your landlady?"

"She mentioned going into London for work, but I'm not sure if that's this week or next. But I just tried the bell, and no one responded."

"I'm coming by," he said without waiting for me to approve or disagree.

I descended the stairs carefully, said hello to the spider who had taken up residence just outside the door, and let myself into the apartment. I lost reception as I stepped inside. "Damn."

I locked the door, dropped my belongings and turned on the electric tea kettle. Within twenty minutes, I heard a knock on the door and Roger's voice telling me it was him. I opened the door wide, and he frowned.

"Dead bolt?" he asked. It was hanging by its chain, and I shrugged.

"Tea?" I asked.

He declined, and once again I went over each detail though there were few. I still hadn't seen the face of the driver or the passenger. I described the car by color and style. No way did I know European cars by make. In fact, a Ford in England barely resembled one in the states.

"Same time of day?"

"Yes, a bus ride from campus each afternoon. So roughly 4:30 … 5:00. Just as I stepped off the bus and headed toward the house."

"Odd," he said, "but also worrisome. A lot of crime these days, even in these old neighborhoods."

I nodded.

"If they see the main house dark and empty, they may not even know you're here."

I shivered with the thought of being alone during a break-in. Even if I was safely locked inside the basement apartment, the sliding glass door was an easy entry, and it wouldn't take much to break the chain lock on the old door.

I saw Roger's eyes asking me the question I was thinking. As if he could read my mind, he said, "I'll either stay here, or you can come with me until we reach the owner."

"Police?" I asked.

"Not much for them to go on I'm afraid, but let's ask her if she wants us to report."

I thought for a moment. Which felt better? Being in my own surroundings with Roger just outside my bedroom door on the sofa? Or packing a bag and going to his place? It felt uncomfortable either way, but I opted to leave the house and apartment to the stalkers for tonight. As I packed an overnight bag, Roger found a broom the length of the sliding door and secured it into place along the slider. He closed all the draperies, turned on outside lights and turned on the TV and an inside lamp. I smiled as he reached for my bag.

"Pretty good," I said.

"Jewelry? Computer?" he asked

I patted the bag. "Nothing very valuable anyway, but I grabbed it."

Roger settled me into his one bedroom as I knew he'd insist on, and then he began a meal in the kitchen while I tried to phone again. This time Mary answered on the third ring. She agreed calling the police would be a waste and said she'd be back tomorrow on the 2:00 p.m. train.

Roger retreated to his thesis after dinner, and I to an assigned manuscript for the remainder of the evening. At ten o'clock, he walked into the bedroom and stretched before grabbing a pillow and blanket from the bed. I was torn. So was this truly just a friend kind of set-up? No romantic feelings on his part? But if he did reach out, what would I do? Probably decline. It was too early, right? My next thoughts flip flopped again. It's 2010; we're adults. Nothing? Nothing?

I gave a long sigh. "Tired?" he asked. He walked to me and put his arms around me. His arms felt comfortable and protective. As I lay my head on his chest, the smell of maleness hit my nostrils, and I felt an urgency I hadn't felt in a long time. But as I pulled back a little, he pecked my nose with a slight kiss and said good-night.

Connie Wesala

Chapter 10

I lay in the dark wide awake for some time. Roger's light snoring finally lulled me to sleep. He was showered and dressed when I awoke around 6:30 the next morning.

"Hate to rush off," he said. "I made coffee, and there's cereal in the cupboard and milk in the fridge. I have an eight o'clock meeting with my thesis advisor."

He once again kissed me on my nose; then grabbed his leather satchel – the one I'd seen the first day we'd met in the café. "Seriously, make yourself at home."

"Thanks," I said. "And thanks for letting me stay last night."

"You're welcome. I'll see you later?"

I answered his question with a nod. I knew he was as busy as I was, but I was suddenly feeling just a little neglected. Maybe he wasn't interested in anything more than friendship. Then I reminded myself, once again, that I had no business making it anything more than that either. I would be leaving soon; there was no reason to make things complicated.

I walked around the apartment checking out personal items, but the apartment was practically sterile. A pair of reading glasses and the newspaper sat on the ottoman; books lined the bookshelves, both academic and a great deal of fiction. One 4"x6" framed photograph of himself with an older couple beside a lake. A typical guy's apartment and just a rental for the semester. Noting the time, I poured a glass of orange juice and a cup of coffee and took both into the bathroom to get ready for the day.

That afternoon I left campus at 4:10 and walked toward the bus stop. Roger was standing directly under the large blue sign in jeans and a black button-down that was fast becoming my favorite outfit. Did he know that already? He smiled when he saw me.

"Riding the bus today?" I asked, knowing well and good his apartment was the opposite direction.

He shifted the strap of his satchel to the other shoulder.

"Guilty as charged. Gas is too expensive."

I laughed. "Well, you're going the wrong way."

The bus pulled to the curb, and we stepped onboard quickly and scanned our pass cards. The short bus ride was a treat. We shared our daily news and were at my corner right on schedule at 4:30. Like two private eyes, we turned the corner, and half way down the block we spotted the vehicle—this time parked in a drive-way two doors from the house and across the street; engine running; two men in the front seat. Today, the passenger was holding binoculars while the driver fiddled with something on the dash.

"Wait here," Roger said. He crossed the street which would put him behind the vehicle. Then he nonchalantly strode toward the car. One house before my rental, he turned right as if to walk to the front stoop of a duplex, but I saw his cell phone camera aimed behind him.

The driver must have been nervous as he immediately pulled onto the street and toward me. I kept my head down and walked crisply toward the apartment. Roger was still standing on the stoop of the near-by house, but he caught up with me just as the two men turned the corner toward town.

He was checking the photos he'd just shot—eight in all. Two blurry. One too far away. But five zoomed closely on the license plate, the driver and the back of the passenger's head; no faces, but clear enough to get hair color and length, and approximate sitting height.

We rang the side bell, and Mary answered quickly. As we stepped inside, I introduced Roger, and he showed her the photos. Together we called the Oxford police. The two officers dispatched arrived in ten minutes, took our statements and asked for Roger's photos which he downloaded to their own phones in seconds.

"Do you have any suspicions?" I asked Mary. "Any idea about the car or the men?"

She shook her head. "No one I know," she said.

Most of their questions seemed directed at me. Were these the same men I had mentioned from the airport bus? Could I be certain? Was there anyone from back home who might be having me followed? Did I have any expensive electronics or jewelry?

I answered each question. "Yes, I thought they were the same men." "No, I couldn't be certain." "No, no one from home would do this," and a definite "No" to the expensive jewelry.

The officers gave each of us business cards with personal cell numbers and said they'd cruise the street about once an hour till their shift ended at midnight.

Roger walked me down to the apartment and hugged me good-bye with concern. "I don't like that you have no cell service down here."

I didn't disagree. It was a thorn in my side, and I hated it. "I'll be fine," I assured him. If I stepped out the sliding door to the rear yard, I could make an occasional call, and I promised I'd try him before going to bed, around 11:00.

After he left, I walked outside to check my phone. 13 messages and 2 Gmail. Jennifer had tried twice and left a voice message. I listened to her voice and immediately felt sad. On my fingers I tried to figure out the time back home—too early. I waited till 9:30 and figured again. 9:30 minus 8 … just after 1:00 p.m. I grabbed a jacket as the temperature had dropped considerably with the clouds and wind moving in from the north. I went out the front door to the street. Standing in the bright light of the motion-sensor spot-light, I dialed her number, hoping the international card was working. I kept an eye on the street.

She answered on the third ring. "Amy, how are you?" she screeched.

"Oh, my God, I am fantastic. I can't begin to tell …"

"Tell me everything," she said.

So for the next fifteen minutes I summarized the past four days, mentioning Roger but playing down our day at the museum, the Cotswold drive and the feelings beginning to surface. I also left out the topic of stalkers.

"I wish you were here," I said and surprised myself by how much I truly meant it. I did wish she were here to share all this.

I went back inside and sat in the nearly dark living room—the glow from one table lamp in the bedroom cast shadows on the walls around me. Missing someone meant you thought about them, wondered what they might be doing, considered how they were. It wasn't something that came natural to me, though I didn't know why.

I enjoyed people—loved people—but there was a clearly defined line I didn't cross. I enjoyed being alone and never understood people who claimed to be lonely and yearned for companionship. Weeks would go by before it dawned on me to pick up the phone to call and arrange a lunch or movie. I was a great listener, a sympathetic, caring person and a good conversationalist.

I even had a dry sense of humor most people found appealing. But I went through life pretty much alone. I realized that I wasn't so different than Luke in this regard. As much as I resented when he pulled back and even disappeared for periods of time, I had to admit I did the same.

In college I'd been an active participant in university life, joined clubs, ran for office, and pledged a sorority. But even in the midst of frat parties, I was the one holding someone's hair out of her face to puke; the one who shushed the group as we sneaked in after curfew. I attended the numerous formal dances and had a date, arranged by a sorority sister or with my best guy buddy, but even then I watched from the sidelines most of the evening.

As a kid, I hated school picture day. Home-permed hair, glasses, hand-made dresses sewn by my mother. Even after I got contact lenses at the end of high school, discovered heated hair curlers and bought matching Bobby Brooks wool skirts and sweater sets with my summer earnings, the reflection in the mirror continued to be one of a homely little girl from the wrong side of the tracks.

Luke often spoke of his home town in that same way, adding that there were more dogs on the streets than people. We were not so very different, I reminded myself again.

I forced myself to return to the present, stretched with a long sigh, and went to bed.

Chapter 11

On Thursday—nothing. No sign of the car anywhere. Roger met me on the corner of St. Giles and Broad after class, and we took the bus to my apartment; then a short walk to Jericho for an early dinner and hugs that turned into slow warm kisses. As he listened to me double lock the door on the other side, I called out, "Say good-bye to Spidey."

I turned on BBC news and curled up on the couch to read through my seminar notes. Classes were interesting and exciting, but challenging for my older brain. Discussions around "the role of conversation and dialogue" and "the relationship between literature and drama and the fields of anthropology, journalism and film" required intense concentration, and my brain was fried by the end of each day.

I had met Roger a week ago, and I was falling hard and knew it. But we were moving slowly—both of us tentative about a relationship it seemed. I still didn't understand the lack of passion. Perhaps I didn't understand men at all. I'd always heard that "men want one thing." Not that I actually believed that, but I did know it was usually on their mind. If he continued to hold back, I could only assume one thing –that we were only going to be friends.

Friday morning I rang the side bell to check on Mary. No sign of them, she assured me. Odd. I couldn't let go of the questions their presence had created. Anything unanswered bugged me. It wasn't my most becoming quality. I hoped it wouldn't drive Roger away as it had Luke.

I was determined to be my real self this time though. After nearly eight years of trying to please Luke, trying to be who he wanted, I had been so exhausted it took me a year to gain back my energy and my own persona.

That afternoon I stood outside the college, saying good-bye to Shannon. I had just asked what she was doing over the weekend, when I glanced to my left. I must have felt it before I saw it. Gray, square, dirty, dark windows cruising at a very slow speed; even slower as they passed me. Two men. Did I see binoculars or just imagine them?

Shannon noticed my concern. "What is it?"

"Probably nothing, but could I ask a favor?"

She quickly agreed to walk me to the bus stop and insisted on seeing me onto the # 6 headed north. Roger was calling later to finalize plans for a British movie. "No sub titles," he had teased, referring to my difficulty with British accents and idioms. I left a quick voice message and then dialed Mary. She was home, and I let out a loud sigh of relief. She would watch from the front window ... no, she would walk to the corner to meet me. I didn't argue. Of course, it wasn't necessary.

Roger waited for me at the curb at 7:00, and he drove toward town as I repeated what I'd already told him.

"So you think this is about you? Not Mary or the house?"

"I have no idea, but obviously they know where I am during the day, and they wanted me to see them."

I watched Roger divert his eyes, and a flutter inside me made me question why. It lasted only a second, and I let it go as I listened to his voice rise with concern.

"But who? Why? You don't know anyone here, right? Thousands of miles from home. I mean ... it makes no sense, Amy."

"I know," I said. "I've gone over every detail since I arrived. The plane to London, the bus ride to Oxford, the first cabbie who took me to the apartment. Lunches, walks, the library, classes—nothing—absolutely nothing out of the ordinary. Of course, you can always miss a small clue. American, female, alone, single, dressed well, attending Oxford ... but if it was about money, wouldn't they simply find me on an empty street and rob me?"

It didn't add up. Just thinking about it again made me nauseous with anxiety. I looked at Roger and shook my head. "I'm not up for a movie," I said. "I'm sorry. Just take me home."

He reached over. His hand was soft, but his grip was firm. He took the first right turn and parked on the street. His arms went around me, and he pulled me tight against his chest. When he bent to kiss me, I met his warm, wet half-open lips and found his tongue for a brief moment. We settled into the sensation, and let the kiss linger. When I finally pulled away, I knew that we had only started the evening and that a long night lay ahead.

We made it into the apartment, through the narrow kitchen and into the living room before removing the first pieces of clothing. I opened the bedroom door, and we fell on to the mattress together enjoying touching

Connie Wesala

each other's skin, wanting more but not rushing it.

When he rolled off me and lay beside me, I turned to face him.

"Should we be doing this?" I asked. "I have less than three weeks left—and then …" I let the word slide slowly. *Did there have to be a then?* I wondered. *"Can't there just be a NOW?"*

Roger started to speak, but I placed two fingers to his lips to quiet him. He looked at me with surprise in his eyes, but they twinkled. Even in the darkened bedroom, draperies drawn, his eyes glistened, and I lifted myself onto him and let his hands explore. We made love for an hour, fell asleep for another, and woke to find each other again. I slept from two a.m. to seven the next morning.

When I opened my eyes he was gone, and I felt a sharp pain and hunger. Ah, well, I thought. "Just as well." I got up to go to the bathroom and grabbed my pink and white striped satin robe. Looked in the mirror, brushed my teeth and ran my fingers through my hair. I opened the bedroom door and was greeted by the smell of bacon and coffee, and felt a lightness fill my body.

He was standing at the stove with his back to me, humming a current song. He had on jeans but no shirt, and his broad muscular shoulders made me smile. The coffee pot was full of brown heaven, and an open pastry bag sat on the counter. He'd been to the store and back while I slept. I silently crept toward him and reached both arms around his waist. He smelled clean and fresh, and I pushed my face into the back of his white T-shirt and sniffed. The smell of a man. It had been a long time.

He turned to me and pulled me into a kiss, and I was glad I'd taken time to brush my teeth. He released me quickly and returned to the eggs frying in the skillet and turned them with the spatula.

"I got juice if you want to pour it, and grab that bag of calories there." He laughed and pointed the spatula at the pastries.

"You better believe it," I said. "I am famished."

"Gee, I wonder why you have such an appetite," he said with a broad grin.

"Yeah, well, I also need a lot of that caffeine."

We brought the plates and glasses to the table, and I poured coffee and put the croissants and scones onto a plate.

I settled into my chair and sipped the hot coffee as I drank him in with my eyes. *Don't talk*, I told myself.

Over breakfast we checked the weather report for the day, even though it rarely changed. Morning clouds, possible showers till noon, sunshine till evening. It was Saturday. Nowhere to be.

"Hum, what can we do till the rain stops?" he teased.

"Man, I don't know," I said, but I let my robe open slightly to show cleavage.

He placed his cup on the round table; took mine from my hands and placed it there as well. Then he lifted me from the chair and pulled me to him. My robe fell to the floor. In the bedroom it was delicious and quick. Then we slowed and took more pleasure and wasted time till the sun peeked through the clouds.

After we showered together—close quarters in that tiny area—I spent a half hour with hair and make-up and clothes for a hike around the meadow. It had been Roger's suggestion as soon as he toweled off and saw the sun peeking through the bedroom window. "I'm craving nature," he teased.

As I bent to tie the laces of my walking shoes, I heard him speaking in a whisper in the living room. I leaned in to listen but could not make out the words. His voice sounded serious, even intense. At that moment a sense of reality took over, and I admitted to myself how little I really knew about Roger. Or he about me, I added.

He clicked off when I entered the room.

"Do I need a jacket or umbrella?" I asked nonchalantly.

"Always appropriate in jolly wet England," he said. "But no—if we get wet, we get wet. Here, give me your ID or whatever you need—don't even bother with a purse."

I complied, and we set out for a long walk in the meadow. Port Meadow consisted of miles of countryside right smack in the city and just blocks from the apartment. It was a popular spot for the locals. People walked for miles along the paths that circled the grazing land, throwing Frisbees for their dogs. It was a pastime to spot the herd of wild horses that grazed there. If you were lucky and it didn't take hours to reach them, the horses were amenable to being petted. Couples and families sat on blankets with lunch baskets or walked along the river where a dozen sailboats slipped silently downstream.

To the west I could see acres of white fencing where horses and cattle grazed; their houses too far off to see clearly. Geese, and even a few swans, took advantage of the sunshine and floated about at river's edge. A few people fished off the bridge where bikers crossed the narrow Isis River that turned into the Thames as it flowed and broadened.

I soaked up nature as one would a cold drink on a hot, dry summer afternoon back home, and I realized once again how much I missed green and the colors of flowers, tree blossoms and the fragrance of the wild flowers and the grass.

I didn't realize tears were on my cheeks until Roger reached over and wiped them away. "What's wrong?" he said. "Are you homesick?"

"Quite the opposite. In fact I was just thinking how much I don't miss it."

He looked surprised. "Let's sit." He pointed to a bench overlooking the water amidst a dense stand of tall shade trees. I leaned back into his arm which rested along the seat-back behind me, and we were quiet for a while longer.

"Come winter, you might feel differently," he said. He smiled. "Although the snow is a beautiful scene in Oxford, the cold bites hard."

"Sounds lovely to me. I miss seasons," I said.

I turned to Roger and sat up straight and faced him.

"Tell me about your ex-wife," I said. "I want to know."

He tried to decline, but I gently prodded. "And the other women since then. There have to be a few women since then," I added.

He straightened a bit, then bent forward, allowing his elbows to rest on his knees, and he gazed down through the water below.

"Name, rank and serial number, huh?" He scratched his hairline and turned to make eye contact. "Melissa. Psychology major. 42 years old. Lives in Cambridge. No children. Unmarried. Crazy."

The last word startled me. "Crazy … how?"

"Crazy as in nuts, psychotic, certifiable."

I was all ears with a hundred questions or more.

"Was that during the marriage or since the divorce?" I asked.

"Both, only I hear it's gotten worse the past year or so."

"Heard? From whom?"

"My ex-mother-in-law keeps in touch," he said.

"Really? Often?"

"Once every month or two. She's not hospitalized. It's not like that. Though at times she probably should be."

I listened and waited.

"Two years into the marriage it started—the paranoia, the jealousy, the out of touch with reality stuff." He grew silent.

I waited.

He shook his head. "It's tough to talk about, Amy. I feel like I'm being disloyal or something, you know? I was exaggerating about psychosis. Not voices or hallucinations—just delusional I guess best describes it."

"I'm sorry for pushing. If it's too hard …"

"No, it's ok. I want you to know. I managed for seven years, and then I just couldn't take it anymore, and I told her I wanted out.

"And do you see her … Now I mean?"

He shook his head. "Not now. I did for a year or two—took the train up to visit for a day, but even that didn't work well. She accused me of cheating, of lying, of all kinds of horrible things."

"I'm sorry, Roger," I said, "How horrible."

He puffed air into his cheeks making him look like a frog, then released it audibly. He took my hand. I could tell there was more he wanted to say, so I kept silent.

After a moment he looked directly into my eyes. "This past week—with the car and all—well, I can't say that I haven't questioned it being Melissa's doing."

My mouth fell open in surprise. "Really?" I said. "She's capable … you think she might … really?"

Roger reassured me by saying he didn't really think she was capable of that, but now he had put the question in my mind. "But, Roger, don't you see? That may very well be what's going on. Paranoid? Jealous? A new woman in your life. It only makes sense."

"Maybe," he said, "and yet even I'm not sure she'd ever go that far."

I was certainly ready to believe she would. It was the only logical explanation we'd found. No one else even knew or cared that I was here.

"You have to call her parents, Roger. We have to know. My God. She may want to hurt you more than me," I insisted.

I knew he was getting ready to argue, so I cut him off. "No, seriously, you need to call. Now."

I walked a short way down the well-worn path to give him privacy. What I needed right now was to talk to Jennifer, but it was the middle of the night in the states. So I got on Facebook and sent a personal note along with a picture of the lovely landscape around me.

When I glanced back, Roger was sitting idly with his cell phone in his lap, so I returned to the bench and asked how things had gone.

"Nothing new. She's doing well on this new medication. In fact, seems remarkably better and stable."

I must have displayed my feelings of disbelief as he repeated the conversation in more detail. "No signs of her old behaviors or paranoia, doing quite well, even considering returning to work."

A comment literally hung in my throat but wouldn't release. Who was I to question? I didn't know any of these people. *In fact*, I reminded myself yet again, *I don't really know this man either. Obviously*, I added. So I let the comment die on my tongue and simply said, "Well, that's good ... I guess, although it still leaves us with two men in a car following me around Oxford."

I didn't like what I was feeling—which was a lot of anger. And suddenly, even though less than thirty minutes ago I had said I didn't miss home, at that moment all I wanted was to talk to someone back home right now.

As we walked back to the apartment, I knew I was too quiet, but I couldn't risk saying cruel and hurtful things. I just wanted to be alone. I just wanted to call my kids. God knew; if someone killed me over here in the UK, they would kill me a second time. *How old are you?* I asked myself. *Too old for this stupidity and naiveté*, I answered.

We reached the drive way. Roger's car had been parked at the curb since last evening. A clear announcement to my landlord that he'd slept over. Oh, well. I stopped by the driver's side door and turned to Roger, gave him a big hug and lied. "I'm exhausted and need a nap. Call me in a few hours?"

His mouth opened, but just as I had been moments ago, he seemed tongue-tied. "OK," he said after a long pause. "Yeah, I agree—let's get some rest. We were up half the night." He pulled his keys from his pocket; then reached for me and hugged me hard. He looked into my eyes when I stepped away. I knew without a doubt he wanted to kiss me, wanted to stay—maybe even talk more about this. But I knew he knew my mood had shifted. I gave him a peck and walked to the curb where I blew him a kiss and waved goodbye.

Sleep was not an option, and I lay on the couch with BBC on the *telly* and old 50's music on the radio at the same time. Neither could drown out my own voices. My thoughts were all over the place. He was sweet and kind and smart and sexy. He was a businessman and a grad student and a great guy. But maybe he was also naïve and stupid with an ex ready to have me killed.

He knew I had no cell service. I waited till 8 o'clock, stepped out to the rear patio to get reception and found three missed calls from him. The proverbial ball was in my court. I walked back into the apartment without returning them.

The next morning I woke refreshed after ten hours of sleep, and two cups of coffee later, I took a brisk walk around the block. Everything was quiet on the tree-lined street. The church on the corner would fill with noise in a few hours, but for now it was a silent sentry watching over the neighborhood. My anger had dissipated during the night. I'd wanted to believe we'd found an answer when obviously we hadn't.

It had been three days since the car had passed me on campus. It was sporadic and random, keeping me in constant suspense and surprising me each time. I'd never seen a gun. A cell phone, binoculars, a camera, two men behind glass that distorted their features. Hell, maybe it was reporters. I laughed out loud. Next time, I thought, I'll simply walk up to the car and ask what the hell they're doing. Taking back my power, even if I knew I'd never act on that, made me feel stronger, and I suddenly missed Roger.

I had no sooner thought of him when my cell chirped inside my jacket pocket.

Connie Wesala

Chapter 12

I told a white lie that I'd slept all evening and never saw his calls.

"Well, I thought I'd go to Cambridge to check things out in person; want to ride along?"

"Sure," I said.

"Pick you up in a half hour."

The drive to Cambridge took us through lovely rolling hills of English countryside. We stopped a few times to take pictures of sheep—our inside joke now. I was mesmerized by the bucolic setting.

It took longer than I'd expected because of Sunday drivers, and we approached the town roughly three hours later. I wanted to see the university, sit in a pub or picnic in a park. Maybe another time. Roger was intent and focused on finding the truth.

He took a sharp left and pulled into the driveway of a small house on a road of other small houses. Nothing descriptive about the place except for the lovely stone that I found so pleasing. Moss grew on the left side of the house by the drive. The typical English garden flourished in the front yard— the haphazard blend of different plants like an artist's paint tray. Reds and yellows, blues and purples tossed together like a floral salad.

Roger went ahead of me and knocked on the door which was answered quickly. An older gentlemen, probably in his 70's, greeted Roger with a firm handshake and a strong pat on the shoulder. I stepped up, and Roger introduced me to his ex-father-in-law. Just inside, Melissa's mother, Evelyn, stood waiting to say hello, then raced off to prepare a spot of tea. I offered to help, but she waved me off. "Sit … sit, Roger, please."

He smiled at me, and his face said, "Bear with us." So I sat beside him on a softly cushioned floral sofa, and his father-in-law, Andrew, took his well-worn rocking chair. It was thread-bare in patches but fit him well. Small talk for a few moments before tea was poured and scones set on a blue and white patterned china plate.

Roger spoke first. "I know we talked yesterday, but I wanted to come in person, and I wanted Amy to meet you."

Andrew nodded. They spent a few moments discussing the weather, the older man's health, and Roger's final semester.

Tea was served on a large silver platter. Then Evelyn joined our circle.

Roger moved forward to the edge of the sofa and addressed them both. "You're convinced Melissa is doing well? You've seen no signs that upset you or any talk of anger toward me or possibly someone I might be seeing?"

Evelyn was the one to answer. "No, dear. As I told you, she's on a new medication that seems to be working perfectly well. She seems happier than I've seen her in years, Roger. No odd ideas or strange talk of any kind. No paranoia. In fact yesterday after you called, I went over and found her humming a tune as she gardened. She looks good. What is this all about, my dear; may I ask?"

Roger nodded, and I could tell he was carefully choosing his words. "I met Amy a couple weeks back … she's attending a seminar at Oxford … and we hit it off immediately. We've been seeing each other ever since. Someone seems to be following Amy, and it's pretty scary to be honest. Two men in a gray Ford … off and on for about a week."

He stopped to sip his tea and reached for a scone. "I'm not accusing Melissa, but to be honest we just have no other leads so I thought …"

"Sure, sure," Andrew said. "Understandable … considering …"

Evelyn turned to me. Her tone had a sharp edge about it. "I'm sorry you're having to deal with such an awful thing. But I can assure you it's not our daughter. Surely you must have someone else you suspect?"

I shook my head. I felt uncomfortable and wished I hadn't come along. It was one thing for an ex to question, but now it seemed that she was accusing me too. Instead of feeling like a victim which I most assuredly was, I now felt like the aggressor.

"I'd like to go by and see Melissa too. Should we ring her first, do you think?" Roger asked.

"Yes, yes, dear—I'll make a quick call and you can head right over."

I took a deep breath. I'd rather be doing just about anything except meeting my current lover's ex-wife. Perhaps I'd wait in the car. I thanked Melissa's mother for the lovely tea and stopped just short of saying I hoped to see them again. Good grief!

The drive was literally three minutes and just a few residential streets on into town. Roger pulled the car under the umbrella of a huge Linden tree, sighed deeply and took my hand. His eyes looked sad and lifeless. I felt sorry for him and also guilty that I was the one forcing this interaction.

"Come in with me," he said, his tone almost pleading.

I squeezed his hand. "Of course."

We walked up the front path, and Roger rang the bell. He fidgeted from one foot to the other, tapping his fingers against his pant legs, and then the door opened slowly. Her mother had warned her—it was obvious.

"Hello, Roger," she said, her tone somewhat formal.

"Hello, Melissa," he said and turned to me. "Amy Crawford from the states," he introduced me.

I offered my hand but regretted it immediately. She had already turned back inside leaving the door open behind her.

I raised my eyebrows to Roger. He motioned for me to go ahead of him and followed me closely. If her mother had seen her gardening the day before, it must be in the rear. Everything out front looked neglected and needed trimmed or tended. The inside of the house looked about the same—in need of a good straightening, though it seemed clean enough. Stuff was piled everywhere. Mail, magazines, items of clothing, dishes, several TV remotes and several pair of shoes lay scattered on the floor and furniture. I watched as she picked up a pile of what appeared to be clean clothes—at least they were folded—and she indicated for us to sit.

I began to watch Roger instead of Melissa. Wanted to gauge his mood-his demeanor. Was he just appeasing me? Or was he here to seriously investigate?

Melissa stood, her arms crossed in front of her, her stance somewhat defensive.

"Mother phoned that you were here," she said. "What brings you to Cambridge?"

I waited to hear Roger's response, wondering which tack he'd take. "Driving Amy around the countryside. She's in Oxford for a professional seminar this month, and we've been exploring."

Ah, ha, I thought. That route, huh? I took his cue. "Yes, it's all so lovely. Your country is beautiful, and I've fallen in love with Oxford."

She dropped her hands but stood leaning forward against the back of a chair. "Yes, I loved Oxford too, but Cambridge is home, right, Roger?"

He nodded.

"Could I use the loo, please?" I asked. "It was a long drive."

"Sure," and she pointed to the right where I spotted a hallway. "Two doors down."

"Thanks," I said as I left the room. I stood just out of sight. I'd move quickly if I heard a pause in the conversation. But I wanted to hear what Melissa had to say and give them space.

"You look good," Roger said. He sounded sincere.

"So do you," she responded. But she wasted no time. "You haven't been this way in two years, Roger; what's really going on?"

I could almost hear him squirm, but he handled it well. "No, Melissa, seriously. We were just driving through; I wanted to see how you were."

I thought I heard a chair scrape the floor. Maybe Melissa had finally sat down.

"I'm fine, Roger. Not that I believe you really care. So who's the woman, really? Don't tell me you're here to get my blessing?" She chuckled.

"I met Amy shortly after she arrived. We've been seeing each other. That's about all there is to tell." "A conference – she's a writer."

"I see," she said. "Can I get you anything?"

I raced on down the hall, shut the bathroom door and flushed the toilet quickly. A moment later I stepped into the hall and watched Melissa pour a glass of water from the tap in the kitchen. Her back was to me, and she seemed preoccupied. I heard her mutter something close to "asshole"; then "liar". But when she turned, there were tears on her cheeks and down her chin. I looked away, and when I turned back, she'd wiped them dry, smiled at me, and asked if I'd like something to drink.

Was I afraid of what she might put in my glass? I didn't think so, but I declined anyway.

Before she could walk away, I entered the kitchen and looked out the back. "You garden?" I asked. I could see tall vines of tomatoes and peppers and mounds that looked like lettuce or other greens.

She stopped and turned toward me. "Yes," she said. "It's soothing."

I nodded and waited for something more. But I was ill–prepared for what came next.

"Don't fall in love with Roger, my dear. You will sorely regret it in time. He drives women crazy and then leaves."

I wanted to ask the obvious. Did he drive her crazy literally? But I softened it. "Did he do that to you?" I ventured.

She smiled an insincere smile. "Oh, no, I was well on my way before Roger. He was just the tipping point."

She walked past me into the living room, and I heard her speak to Roger as she gave him the beverage. I followed and sat down next to him. I could test this since he wasn't doing so well on his own. I slid my arm through his and leaned against his shoulder, gave his shirt a quick peck like a kiss and gazed into his eyes.

OK, Missy, let's see your claws, I thought. Roger leaned down and planted a kiss on my nose. He knew where I was going with this.

I glanced at Melissa and caught the look on her face. Whatever feelings had caused the earlier tears had been replaced with anger. The proverbial daggers flew from her eyes directly at my heart.

"Sorry," I said, "What were you guys talking about before I so rudely interrupted?"

Roger patted me on my knee. "Melissa, have you been to Oxford recently? In touch with anyone we used to know?"

"I have no reason to go to Oxford, Roger; why would I?"

"Just wondered. I could have sworn I saw your car the other day."

I watched her glance at the floor and back up to him. "There are hundreds of cars like mine, Roger. No, I haven't been out of Cambridge in months. London is about as far as I venture."

I felt the claws now as she turned to me. Her face said, "see what I mean?"

"You keep in touch with anyone in Oxford?" Roger asked a second time. "A guy; maybe owns a gray Ford Focus?"

She shook her head but said nothing. If I had hoped to return to Oxford feeling a great sense of relief, that dream was gone. I elbowed Roger gently, hoping he'd take the hint. Instead he cleared his throat and stood but made no move toward the door.

"Melissa, are you taking your meds? Are you doing better? That's all I'm asking."

"I told you that when you asked the first time. Yes, I'm looking for a job. I'm gardening. I see old friends here. I am fine, or I was till you decided to stop by and check in."

The tension was thick, and we were making things worse the longer we stayed. I walked to the door and slipped out. "I'll wait in the car," I said just before I closed the door. But I waited on the top step and heard the final parlay.

"Don't bring your women to my house," she yelled. "Ever ... again!"

I thought I heard Roger's voice but couldn't make out the words.

"Trust me, Roger, if I wanted to hurt her, I'd have done it already. I think you'd better leave." Her tone was harsh and loud and clear.

I shivered for a moment and walked to the car. If I wanted to ... *Did she?* I wondered.

It was nearly five o'clock, and we had a three hour drive before us. Roger looked like a balloon that had been pricked—deflated. I almost felt sorry for him, but I was more concerned than ever about myself right about then. But I did suggest we needed food and not take-out. A nice place with a beer to relax and start fresh. He agreed.

The place he chose had probably been one of their spots as a couple, but I didn't care. The waitress seated us and asked, "Don't I know you?"

Roger looked quizzical. "Perhaps. Grew up here."

She took our order and dropped the conversation.

The meal was hot and good; the beer warm but refreshing and an hour later we were relaxed enough to head home. It would be 9:30 or 10:00 at least, but it was OK. My first seminar session was late the next day.

As he drove, Roger held my left hand until he had to shift; then took it again. He turned the radio to an old 70's music station. What was it with the Brits and American music? I sang along; he finally joined me; and we sang good ole music from the U. S. all the way back to Oxford.

Connie Wesala

Chapter 13

At 10:45 the following day, I backed out of the apartment and locked the door. We'd both been too exhausted to even mention staying over. I had slept off and on, occasionally waking from a dream about Melissa tearing my eyes out. After thinking it through, I saw no reason to connect her to the two men. Sure, she was a bitter ex, but something about her felt too fragile to plot such a plan or hire the guys.

If it wasn't Melissa, who was having me followed? And why? I felt my paranoia rising. As I slid into a seat in the farthest row of the conference room, I made eye contact with Shannon. She waved. But I saw her reach for her cell and quickly type a text. She glanced at me again, then to the professor at the lectern. It seemed a little too coincidental, plus we weren't allowed to touch electronic devices in class. And no one tested that rule. What was so important she'd risk the wrath of Dr. Montrose, and why the minute she saw me? I shook my head. I was totally paranoid and needed to stop this.

We had a twenty minute break at noon, so I stood in my row and waited for Shannon to reach the classroom door; then joined her. She looked startled for a moment, then smiled and greeted me.

As we walked on out to the court yard, I asked how she liked today's lecturer. She frowned and said, "A bit dry for me, I'm afraid. I'm just not a philosopher I guess."

I nodded in agreement. "The seminars are great, overall," I said, "and I love the required writing, but sometimes the lectures feel long."

I pulled a granola bar from my satchel and a bottled water. Shannon did the same—water and an apple. We floated among the twenty or so students till we reached the lawn and sat below a hundred-year-old Chestnut tree. She showed no sign of nervousness, and I realized I was over-reacting to every little thing now. We chatted about class, where I could find a decent black dress, and life in general.

As we returned to the classroom I said, "Would you like to meet for dinner this evening or tomorrow?" Her reaction once again made me wonder.

Shannon hesitated, and her eyes lost contact for a moment. "Sure, that'd be great," she said. "Tonight is fine."

"Are you far from Jericho? Or I can meet in town."

"I'm close to the train station," she said. "Why don't we meet along St. Giles?"

"Six-thirty, OK?" I asked.

We agreed to meet outside The Lamb and Frog. I returned to my seat as she crossed the room to hers.

As I touched up my make-up and put on a clean crisp shirt later that day, I wished I had a hidden camera or mic. Then I laughed at myself—Ridiculous! This young woman didn't even know me; there was no connection. I felt foolish as I locked the door and walked toward the #6 bus yet again. I glanced around. Hadn't seen the car since Friday. For all I knew, they'd give up soon or make a move ....

The closest bus stop to the pub was a block or so south, so I hopped off and headed that direction. From a distance, I saw Shannon approaching our designated meeting spot. She seemed to sway a bit as if to the beat of music. As she walked along, she spotted me, and we waved as she pulled ear buds from her ears and waited for me to catch up.

"I thought I was late," she said. "I'm glad you just got here." She seemed more open and friendly than at school. She smiled warmly, took my left arm and nearly pulled me inside the bar.

The pub smells rushed at us. Beer, oil, fish, grilled meats, hot ovens. Shannon spotted a table near the rear of the restaurant, just to the right of the bar in a corner. Dark, secluded ... *Don't go there*, I reminded myself. I unwrapped my scarf but left my leather jacket on as I scraped the heavy wood chair away from the table and sat down. The waiter approached us before Shannon could get her coat off; she folded it over the back of her chair.

"Two pints," she said quickly; then looked at me. "What brew do you want?" she asked.

"Oh, you order," I said, "but light—a pale ale—whatever you choose."

Shannon told the waiter two different brews, and as he walked off, she tapped her fingers on the top of our small square table. She was looking around the crowd as if she were expecting to see someone.

"Sorry," she said when she noticed I was watching her. "A bit fidgety tonight, I'm afraid."

Our beers arrived, and I took a sip of the warm, bitter ale. "Why's that?" I asked. I was suddenly aware that my back was to the door and whatever might be taking place behind me. How had I allowed her to place me where I couldn't see out?

Shannon focused on her glass for a moment and then responded. "Old boyfriend," she said. "An ex I'd rather not run into; if you know what I mean."

"Oh, I do …," I said. "Certainly do. We all have one or two of those, huh?"

She glanced at the door, and I felt a cool draft as it opened and closed. "Sorry," she said, "I'll focus."

And she did. We discussed how quickly the weeks were flying, how much we were enjoying each day, and what was ahead at the end of our stay. And then I heard a loud question in my head. "Shannon, if you live in France, how would you run into an ex here in Oxford?"

She looked surprised, and I wondered if I had caught her in a lie. But her answer was quick and sure. "Oh … yeah; Brian … met in Paris last summer at a similar two week workshop. One long weekend, he brought me here—to Oxford where he lives. He's a teacher. I've worried for the past two weeks I'd run into him somewhere."

"A bad break-up?" I said.

"Ugly," she said, and her face fell into sadness.

"Little rural English girl—gullible to a fault."

"I know how that feels," I said.

"Do you?" she asked.

I spent fifteen minutes describing my relationship with Luke—mostly the beginning and the end.

"A player, actually, though I didn't want to see that."

Our plates clanked onto the table, and the waiter asked if we needed anything else.

I picked up my fork; starving suddenly. Shannon looked so young and so fragile when she spoke about Brian. Certainly not an accomplice to my 'whatever it was going to be'. Murder? I shivered. Maybe they were robbing the apartment at this very moment. Maybe. But I knew Shannon was not part of it.

I glanced over to see tears streaming down her cheeks. I understood. I hadn't seen Luke in a year and a half, but occasionally the last two voice messages he'd left on my cell popped up to be saved or deleted. The minute I heard that Texas twang and him calling out my last name—which he always did—I felt the lump in my throat. Pressed 3 to re-save and knew I'd be hearing it again. I couldn't erase them. I just couldn't.

I handed her a tissue from inside my purse. She took it and grimaced and blew her nose and wiped her cheeks. "Sorry."

"No need; it gets better—just takes time."

After an hour, our conversation shifted to more personal things: hopes and fears, what's next in life? Would she return to the UK at some point? Would I like to stay on and never return? Maybe.

At 9:00 I knew I needed to head home, and I was frightened to walk to the bus, let alone ride it and then walk two blocks to the apartment. I had two choices. Call Roger yet again to come get me or ask Shannon to share a cab home and then get her clear back to her place. We split the tip and left the money on the table and walked out front.

The street was well lit though it was a dark overcast night. I could walk from one establishment to the next, watching carefully, wait till I saw the bus pull in and quickly board. But that two blocks to the apartment was the sticky point and what if one of them was on the bus? Unlikely, I thought. They have no idea what time I'd leave the pub. Course they could be watching from across the street.

Shannon was speaking, but I hadn't heard a word. "What? I'm sorry…"

"I was saying would you like to go to my place for a while, and we'll call you a cab?"

"Oh, well …" I hesitated. Two hours ago I had her as an accomplice and now? I felt foolish.

"It's only a ten minute walk from here—close," she said.

So I agreed. The night had cooled, and I was glad I'd brought a jacket. I pulled my scarf tighter and pulled it over my chin, breathing in the warmth of my breath.

We talked about the city and the shops as we walked along. Just before the rail station, we turned left, and she pointed to a two-story house that was now home to a dozen Oxford students.

I described my basement apartment. "No cell service at all, and I hear every flush and every verbal fight from upstairs."

She laughed. "I'm up." She pointed as she unlocked the front door and let us in. Her apartment was much smaller than mine. What we would call an efficiency in the states, but she had brought along a few personal items that made it feel cozy.

Shannon pulled two ales from the fridge, and I sat on the small sofa while she propped herself on the bed. I suddenly had the strong desire to talk about what was going on. 'Shannon, I'm glad you invited me over. A strange thing is happening."

After I gave her a brief run-down, she stared with mouth open. "You're kidding," she exclaimed. "Oh, my … I'd be scared to death, Amy. Oh, you poor thing. Do you have any ideas? Any at all?"

I told her about Roger's ex, left out my suspicions of her, and mentioned my ex.

"Tell me again about the car," she said.

"I think I've seen it a few times by campus," she said when I gave the description. "Yes, I'm sure of it. I wouldn't notice except for how slowly it was going. On that street people are speeding at all time. We need to follow them," she offered. "Find out where they live or hang or whatever."

She was onto something, but I had no car. Of course, I *could* have a car. I'd never considered a rental, but I could get one.

"I can't drive on the wrong side of the road," I said. "Well, not wrong … you know what I mean."

She laughed. "Well, *I* can."

"You can?" Well, of course—raised in England.

"Is there a pattern of days or times when you see them?" she asked.

"Mostly late afternoon, although there could be times I don't even know about I suppose." I was growing weary. For now, I just needed to call a cab—a very safe cab.

A half hour later, in the backseat of the taxi, I checked my phone. Two missed calls from Roger and one from my daughter. The time on the cell screen said 10:30—not too late for Roger. He wrote and researched all night when he wasn't with me. He picked up immediately.

"Amy, where have you been? Do you know how worried I've been all night?"

"I'm sorry," I said. "I told you I was meeting Shannon to check her out."

"And I think I told you that wasn't wise."

I smiled. "Yes, well … I'm pretty sure it isn't Shannon. She's even agreed to drive …" I stopped short. Roger would never agree to that. If anything he'd want to be the one to reverse the stalking and catch these guys.

"You been working all evening?" I quickly changed the subject.

"Yeah, except for a break to eat. I'm almost there, Amy. My thesis should be easy to defend."

"Fantastic," I said, remembering my own graduate paper and sitting in front of three PhD's—experts in their field—cross examining every statement; questioning every conclusion and every piece of research I used to support my thesis.

Suddenly Roger asked," Hey, where are you anyway? Your cell sounds too clear for the apartment."

"I'm in a cab, almost home." To the cabbie, I said, "Fourth house on the left."

"Roger, I need to pay this guy and get inside—I gotta run."

"No, no—no. Don't hang up. Just do what you need to do, but leave me on the phone, OK?"

"Sure." I put my cell in my purse, face up so it didn't disconnect, handed the cabbie a ten pound bill and climbed out of the rear. As I looked around, I turned back. "Can you wait till I reach that rear gate?" I asked the cabbie.

"Sure," he said. "I have to reset my GPS anyway."

"Thanks." I walked quickly through the wet leaves that glistened on the pavement, hopped onto the curb and approached the house. The exterior light sensed motion and came on, brightly illuminating me. I waved to the cabbie as I opened the back gate and began to descend the steps. I now had Roger at my ear again. "OK," I said. "No one on the steps. I'm going in so I'm going to lose you."

"Wait, Amy," he called. "I … uh … I miss you."

I'd laugh, but he sounded so sincere. We'd just been together all day yesterday, though he'd dropped me off when we got back from Cambridge and didn't stay over. "Me, too," I said and realized I meant it.

Chapter 14

The next two days were hectic with visiting speakers and several group discussions on top of our daily writing assignments. I spoke with Roger a few brief times each day, but I was much too busy to meet, and so was he. I could tell by the tension in his voice that the end was near for his thesis. He was excited, geared up, a nervous energy in his voice I'd not heard before. But he always sounded concerned when he asked if I'd seen the car, and surprisingly, I hadn't.

I met Shannon a time or two for coffee and a scone at the Java Co. café where I'd first met Roger, and we walked on to campus after. Most days we ate a quick lunch on the shaded lawn just outside the lecture hall. I was beginning to really like the girl. In some ways she reminded me of Sarah with her independent streak and assuredness. With the time difference, it was hard to Skype, but Sarah emailed daily, and so did I.

The visiting speakers were prestigious and well spoken. I hung on their every word, taking copious notes that my younger colleagues seemed to absorb and remember. I found myself watching faces more closely. One young man, William, smiled at me a few times and raised his arm to ask a question. At lunch, he joined Shannon and me under the tree. The next day Rebecca and Andrew did the same. I smiled broadly at Shannon as we sat under the umbrella of leaves and talked and shared. I missed Roger but not as much as before. I enjoyed the mother-figure role I was slipping into now.

One of the young men couldn't take his eyes off Shannon, and I mentioned it to her.

"No, I'm sure you're wrong," she said. But I noticed a sly smile when I said his name.

It was Friday night before Roger and I had time to meet. I stayed in town after seminar and browsed through downtown shops and department stores. I needed a few gifts for friends back home and something nice for the kids and Jennifer; cheaper gifts were easy—mementos from the visitor center like kitchen towels, book marks, pens or pencils. I'd picked up a few items in the gift shops, but I wanted something classier for the last three.

England ... tea, rain, the Royals..ah ha ..scarves. I found a lovely cashmere in an aqua blue that would set off Jennifer's eyes. It wasn't the traditional tartan plaid, but it was light weight and lovely to touch. $40.00 made me cringe. The exchange rate made it closer to $65 USD, but she was worth it. She stuck with me no matter what, and she'd been there through one break-up after another with Luke. Plus she never scolded me when I wound up letting him back in. I suddenly felt homesick and wanted to call her to go for coffee.

I smiled at the sales clerk as she ran my credit card and located a gift box and tissue.

"Thanks so much for your help," I said.

"My pleasure, Madam."

I turned to leave and glanced at my cell phone which was now showing the ugly face of a dead battery. Dang.

I turned back to the sales girl. "Miss ..." She looked up. "Do you have the time?"

She glanced at her watch. "6:03."

Dang. I picked up my pace trying not to look like a shop lifter on the run. How far? Five blocks? Hopefully Roger was running late too.

But of course, he wasn't. As I swung open the heavy oak door, I saw him standing near the bar; a pint in his hand. I took a moment to soak him in. He was solid. That's what I liked about him. Every inch of his 6'5" frame was compact and firm, neither too thin nor too heavy. Just a solid mass of muscle. Someone you could lean into; who could hold you up and keep you safe.

I watched his eyes fill with life as he spotted me across the room. I motioned for him to stay at the bar and pushed through a standing-room-only crowd. By the time I reached him, he held out a second pint of pale ale and said, "Cheers!"

"Thank you ... I'm sorry I'm late." I held up the three shopping bags.

"Ah ...." He smiled.

We slid over to a tall bar table that had just opened up. I placed my pilsner, purse and bags onto the table and turned to him with open arms.

"I need a hug," I said. I just wanted to feel him, and I held on a few seconds longer than normal. As I pulled back, he put his hands on each side of my face and bent to kiss me. He tasted of beer and lust. I suddenly wanted to say to hell with dinner, but I was famished.

We sat across from each other, and he held my hand while we both perused the menu.

"Shepherd's Pie here is good if you're in the mood," he said.

It sounded too heavy for my after-dinner desires, and I said so.

He laughed. "Well, in that case, two salads and a lot of beer or wine."

I did order a salad with chicken, and he, a burger and chips. I still called them fries. I was too American to change. And tomato sauce for ketchup? No way.

We discussed the past few days. Though we'd talked by phone each evening, there was a lot of catching up to do.

"I'm glad you've become friends with Shannon and the others."

"Seems funny that I once suspected she was part of this," I said.

"Foolish."

"No more foolish than me suspecting my ex," he said.

"I suppose."

"Any sightings?" he asked.

I shook my head. Sighed. It had been three days now since I'd last seen the car.

"We're sure about your ex, right?"

He scrunched his nose and twisted his mouth as he considered. "I just don't think so," he said. "Do you?"

"Well, I still think she's in love with you, and I am in the way." I shrugged. "But I don't know. I guess not." I remembered Melissa's remark about watching my back. "Still…" I dropped it.

"You know," he said, "We've never really discussed your ex-husband or your ex-lover, for that matter."

The mention of Luke startled me. "Well, the divorce was a hundred years ago. If Bruce wanted to off me, I'm pretty sure he'd have done it by now."

He grinned. "But?"

"Luke?" I said with shock in my tone. "No way."

"As I just said, you've not told me much about that relationship."

I reached for one of his fries and settled back into my chair. I let out an audible sigh. Luke. "OK … Luke was smart, funny, a high school principal, my boss at one time. Two kids. A pretty simple guy—at least that's what he always said. Oh, and Hispanic."

Roger listened intently. Then he stopped me. "Sounds pretty perfect—there must be more or you'd be with him." His eyes said, "Right?"

I nodded. "Yeah, OK … well … super private to a fault. Secretive actually. Never planned a thing which drove me nuts. I can be spontaneous to a degree, but it was always last minute, little thought, like I wasn't worth planning for." My voice trailed off. "I just felt like I was holding the relationship together with no energy from him." I hesitated, and the silence hung. "Just not a good fit," I said on an ending note.

"Who ended it?" he asked.

"I guess it was mutual, but I was the one who finally said 'enough'."

He nodded. "Ah …"

"Roger, I haven't seen Luke in over a year. He got over me three days after we split, I can assure you. There's no way he could be involved in this."

"Maybe," he said.

"No, seriously, you don't know Luke's pride and machismo—never would he keep tabs on me. Besides, he doesn't even know I'm over here."

"OK," he said, "I'll settle the bill ... be right back."

Roger had walked to the pub, as had I, so we set out for the bus stop. We held hands as we walked along. The night was perfect—unusual for Oxford even in June. Clear skies, a warm breeze, and a nearly full moon. We took our time, did some window shopping at the corner bookstore, and walked for the next two blocks to the bus stop. No sign of the #6, but we were a few minutes early. I leaned against the railing, and Roger put his arms around me in a gentle embrace. I leaned into his chest, my head just under his chin, and we stood like that for some time.

Suddenly I felt him tense, and I pulled back. "What?" But as he moved a few inches away I saw it—the damned gray Ford—windows up so we couldn't' see inside. Intentional, since it was warm enough to have them rolled down. It cruised by slowly, heading in the direction of the apartment.

"I'll be damned," Roger said. "No sooner said than …" He didn't finish.

We heard the bus shifting as it pulled to the curb. A half dozen people got off, and we lined up to board. After settling into our seats, we looked at each other, but neither of us had a plan—other than to get off at our usual spot and walk on home.

The bus pulled up at the stop prior to St. Margaret's, and as the driver pulled back into traffic, Roger said, "Let's stay on for another stop. It's only two streets down."

I agreed.

We hopped down into the cool damp evening. Instead of walking back south toward St. Margaret's, we decided to head east far enough to put us just past my apartment. Then we'd cruise south and take a left, putting us in front of the church and a few houses from the where they'd most likely be parked. We'd be approaching from the opposite end of the street and should surprise them if they were there.

We rounded the corner by the church; the apartment was now three doors down on our right. We had a good view of the street, but we saw no sign of any cars along the curb. Roger slowed the pace as we checked out both sides of the road. Two doors past the apartment and directly across the street, I spotted the parked car backed into a drive-way. Roger pointed at the same time. We pressed behind a tree which hid us from their view. The large thirty-foot tall oaks gave us good cover, and we whispered a few options. If we continued on this side of the street, we'd walk right up to the car. If we crossed the street, they'd see us in seconds. If we waited them out, we could be standing around for hours.

"If they're ever going to make a move, let's make it easy for them. They may just do nothing." As his feet hit the pavement, I took a deep breath and followed. Roger kept going—past the front of the house, onto the drive-way. Car lights popped on, and Roger sped up enough for the outside floods to illuminate the drive and sidewalk. I raced past him to the side door and rang the bell three times in less than a second, but the car lights turned right and were nearing the church on the corner. They shot a quick left and were gone.

I stood there regretting ringing the bell, but Mary quickly opened the door. Surprised to see us, she asked if we were OK.

"We are now," I said. I was trembling and couldn't stop. "Sorry to bother you," I stuttered.

Roger stepped forward and put his arm around me. "Just another scare," he told her.

She offered to call the cops but why? "I'll just get this one some tea and toast and tuck her in," he said. "Sorry, again …."

"No, no," she said. "Let me know if they show again."

We promised we would, and Roger made good on his promise to tuck me in. Only with wine instead of tea and sex instead of toast.

Chapter 15

Each day I tried to write. My second novel was slowly writing itself, though at this point I had no idea where the plot was leading. Friday was a bank holiday, and the morning was warm and sunny with no sign of rain clouds. I'd grown accustomed to the filtered sunlight and the almost daily morning showers. Today was an exception. I phoned Roger to check in, though I really needed alone time. I told him I needed the day to catch up on revisions.

"Where are you thinking of spending the day?" he asked.

"Campus feels safest," I said, "but I'm rather tired of the scenery, being there every day."

"Don't blame you," he said.

"Plus I want to be outside enjoying this beautiful weather."

"How about the meadow?" he offered. "They can't drive anywhere close to you there."

Port Meadow had become one of my favorite spots. I'd be out in the open, unprotected, but so far there'd been no sign that these guys were out to harm me. They'd had ample opportunity if that had been their intent. So I filled a canvas bag with my notebooks and pens, a small throw blanket, peanuts and a bottle of water. I took my wallet and cell phone from my purse and threw them in as well.

It was a ten minute walk from the apartment, down a residential street to the public park, left and over the railroad tracks, then through an unlocked gate and onto the worn dirt path into the expansive meadow. I headed toward the river bank where Roger and I had spent time last week. There were a few benches, but I walked on into the trees and placed the blanket on a grassy area under a large oak.

For the next three hours my pen moved swiftly forming word after word of what I hoped wasn't drivel. But you never knew. I stood to stretch a few times, glancing around. No one other than the usual hikers, photographers, and dog walkers. My editor had emailed, so I responded to her. Facebook postings drew my eye, and I answered a few, took a quick picture of the meadow and posted that to my page.

Chris had "liked" my recent photos of Cambridge. So I returned the favor and commented on his latest photography; then dropped my daughter a quick hello. I ate my peanuts with an apple I'd bought at the corner market, and grew sleepy. I must have dozed for a half hour and started awake, checking around quickly to make sure my belongings were intact. Not smart, I told myself. There were few people remaining in the meadow now, and I knew I needed to call it a day.

I counted. I had written nearly twenty pages, and it felt good. I had let Roger eat up my time the past few weeks, and that was fun, but I needed to get back to me for a while. The day had been good for me. I felt more grounded than I had in weeks. More myself, I admitted. Roger was a great guy—intelligent, interesting and fun to be with. The physical was whipping cream on top of my Frappuccino, and I loved it. I licked my lips without thinking. But I had come to England for two reasons: the intellectual stimulation of the seminar and the promise to my editor to complete the first draft of this damned book. I needed to focus on those two things.

When I saw Roger's text I grimaced; so hard to say no to him. But I did. "I hope you understand," I typed. Big smiley face and a thumbs up on my screen. I smiled.

I walked leisurely back to the apartment, once again relishing the front yard gardens and the green that surrounded me. The street was vacant as it had been that morning. None of it made sense. How many times had I gone over this?

Tomorrow was Sunday, and the thought of another 24 hours of alone time was just what I needed. After giving it some thought, I decided to go out to Blenheim Palace. I hated to go without Roger. We'd talked about taking a tour but hadn't found the time.

Perhaps I'd just enjoy the grounds. They looked lovely on the brochure I'd picked up. It was just an extra bus fare north of Summertown. I'd take one notebook and an extra pen or two. I'd grab lunch in the cafe and sit in the formal gardens and the rose gardens. It would be a real treat—all by myself.

Just before I reached the house, I dialed Shannon. "How's your day off?" I asked.

"Great and you?"

"Got some writing done. Felt wonderful."

"Good for you," she said. "Hey, you won't believe who called me."

I hesitated, but it didn't take long to figure out. "Jason?" I asked.

"How did you know that?"

"Well, it was a guess, but it's rather obvious there's an interest there," I said.

"Really?"

I smiled to myself. "Really," I assured her. "Did he ask you out?"

Her voice sounded younger to me—almost high school. Were we all the same when it came to attraction—to love? Yes.

"Yes," she said, "tomorrow … an afternoon movie and dinner after."

"Oh, Shannon, that's great."

"I guess." She sounded uncertain.

And I sounded too motherly when I answered. "Just enjoy it, Shannon; take it slow if you want, but go have fun."

"How about you?" Shannon said. "You seeing Roger?"

I told her my plans, and we hung up shortly after.

The trip to Woodstock the next morning took fifteen minutes. The bus dropped off in the center of town. The palace was another 15 to 20 minute walk. A small river ran through the 2000 acres of parkland that surround the stone walls of the castle. I paid at the ticket window, handed it to the young man at the gate, and walked through onto the cobblestone courtyard.

The brochure he'd handed me gave me some history. In 1704 the castle had been given to John Churchill, 1st Duke of Marlborough, by Queen Anne for the victory over the French in the Spanish Secession. Winston Churchill was born at the castle in 1789. The palace was under construction for thirty years.

There are many stories of lust and deception in the state rooms, but I was headed through the walkway by the stables out to the formal gardens that lay behind. It reminded me of a small Versailles, and I compared the dates of each. King Louis XIII of France had built the hunting lodge at Versailles in the late 1600's, but his son, Louis XIV transformed and expanded it into the palace it is today, and moved the court and government there in 1672. Roughly the same time period as Blenheim. Egos that needed to be fed no matter the cost.

As I stepped down the dozen or so steps and reached the statuary and baths, I took a turn to my left and followed the well-worn path that would eventually lead to the rose gardens. I stopped a few minutes later and sat on a stone bench facing the forested land. Squirrels scampered up the trunks of the ancient oaks and along the high branches, doing back flips and somersaults for my amusement.

I pulled out pen and notebook and laid my canvas bag beside me on the bench. I yawned and closed my eyes for a few seconds at most, and as I opened them I was stunned at the sight before me. A gorgeous peacock, open plume, looked directly at me and then turned away. No time for my camera— I simply enjoyed his preening before he disappeared into the woods. The stillness was palpable. Except for a few birds cooing or chirping I was totally alone. I began to write a description of the birds just to get started. But within a few minutes, the quiet brought a calm that made me drowsy, and I let my eyes close, and dreams creeped in.

I was walking in another shaded garden, and Luke held my hand tightly in his as we walked along a rocky path towards an unfamiliar body of water. He helped me up a steep incline by walking ahead of me and pulling me along. Then he stood on a large boulder above me and reached down to pull me up and onto the rock and into his arms. I felt the velvet of his lips. I would never forget the soft fullness that pulled my soul into his. His kisses always transported me to another plane where I felt safe and loved. I wanted to stay there forever, not knowing the other side of him—the fierce dominance that could replace that kindness and turn safety into fear.

As I stepped back from his embrace I began to fall, and I knew I couldn't stop or even slow my descent into the unknown. I fell backward for what seemed an eternity and felt myself collide with something hard and cold. I started awake as the back of my head met the back of the bench. I heard people along the path behind me and turned to see if they were watching. They were far off but headed my way. I gathered my wits and picked up the notebook that had fallen to the lawn. I hadn't dreamed of Luke in ages. And suddenly I wanted him to walk up so I could throw my arms around his thick neck and press against the length of him. A knot grew in my throat, and I felt tears begin to well; but I couldn't give in to those old feelings. "No," I cautioned myself sternly. "No … never again!"

I began to write gibberish just to regain my equilibrium and wrote for several hours, taking a short bathroom break and grabbing a bottled water back at the palace. At two o'clock, I was spent. I ate a late lunch in the café; then raced to town for the 3:15 bus to Oxford.

For some strange reason I had cell service on the return trip, and I wrote a long email to Jennifer telling her about the dream, my feelings, my lust and my fears.

She answered in minutes. "Strange," she wrote, "I ran into Luke yesterday at a conference, and he asked about you. Told him you were in the UK., and strangely he seemed to know.

"No way could he know," I wrote.

"Well, he mentioned Oxford, and I didn't," she answered.

I shook my head. No way could he know where I was. I hadn't talked to him in a year, and we had literally no mutual friends any longer.

"How did he look?" I wrote.

"Why are you asking? The same. A little grayer, maybe," came the reply.

Why *was* I asking? I dropped the subject. "Miss you," I typed.

"Me, too. Come home," she replied.

"Soon. Ten days, I think." It still amazed me that I could type and press send and get a response within a minute or two—clear across the ocean.

"Be safe. TTYL," she wrote back.

Thumbs-up emoticon . . . happy face blowing a kiss . . . back to her.

Now I not only missed Luke, I missed Jennifer. I missed my kids. I missed everything in my life. It was pure home sickness, and I had days to go.

Five minutes later I rummaged for the phone I'd thrown into my purse, found the last text from Roger and pressed reply. "You need a break from work? Meet me in town for a bite?"

And two minutes later ... "The White Rabbit in 20 min. C U there!"

I grabbed a table near the door and nearly attacked him with a hug when he arrived.

"I missed you too," he murmured in my ear before pulling away.

I knew I would not be going home alone tonight.

Chapter 16

The next morning I stretched awake and felt the still warm mattress beside me. From the kitchen I heard breakfast noises: the crackle of bacon, the tea kettle whistle, and the refrigerator door creaking shut, then the gurgle of orange juice or milk into an empty glass. I smiled broadly.

I dressed quickly, ate standing up, and suggested he walk me to campus. He held my hand as we walked along, swung it back and forth until I laughed at him. It was eight o'clock, and I should have been racing to class.

"I'm so happy you're here," he said.

I stood still and turned to him. "Ditto."

His look turned to hurt. "Oh, Roger, I didn't mean it that way ... really. I'm glad I'm here too, and I'm glad we met. You make me happy," I blurted out in one long breath. I pulled on his hand and ducked out of foot traffic, and under an awning of the unopened grocer, he let me take his face in my hands, and I stretched on my tiptoes to kiss him.

He looked down into my eyes, as if searching for confirmation. He seemed to find it. He kissed me again, and I lingered in his arms.

"I don't want to go to class," I said. I tried to persuade him with my look.

"I'll wait for you at the stop by campus," he said.

After a long day of lectures, I found him waiting with a duffel bag over his shoulder. That night, as we lay among crumpled sheets—his arm around me—my head on his shoulder, he asked first.

"Where is this headed?" he said quietly.

I would leave England very soon, and I had been wondering the same thing. But thoughts of my last hour with Luke kept showing up and fear set in, and I suddenly didn't want it to 'go' anywhere. I turned and ran a finger along his jaw line and then along his lips.

"Where do you want it to go?" I knew I sounded defensive and scared because I was.

I pushed onto my side, and he did the same. We were facing each other, a thin sheet separating us. In a week it would be thousands of miles between us instead.

I waited. I did not want to be the one who said it first—no matter what 'it' was. I love you or it's been fun or I'll miss you? What did I want it to be?

"You aren't helping me a whole lot, here," he said, but his eyes crinkled into a smile.

He was right. It was in my court. I cleared my throat and took a breath. "I know what I don't want," I said. His eyes questioned me. "I don't want to lose you."

He nodded. "And I don't want to lose you either, so I guess we have some decisions to make in the next week."

"Yes," I said. It would be easy to walk away—call it a summer fling—a good time and wave good-bye. That wasn't what I wanted. But I also had no idea how to make it work. I was in no position to stay in the UK, and he wasn't going to move to the states. We were both being silly and unrealistic. But when Roger reached for me, I forgot about classes, about my lunch with Shannon the following day, and my return plane ticket, and my body welcomed his.

The next few days mirrored each other. Long busy days on campus for both of us, holding hands on the bus ride home, swinging arms like school kids along St. Margaret's Road, long leisurely showers, bottles of wine, take-out from our favorite places and hours and hours of touching.

We relished Tuesday morning, and I made a late brunch.

"I have to meet with the committee at 3:00, but I'll be back for dinner if you want me to bring something."

"Since I'm being bad and skipping school today, I can cook," I said. My face felt all smiles. I reached for a notepad and started a grocery list. "But you could grab a bottle of wine," I said.

"OK, dear," he said his voice full of humor.

I laughed. We walked out of the apartment together at 2:30. He turned right to the bus stop, and I went left to the corner store.

Chapter 17

I couldn't miss one more day of the conference, so we left the house at the same time.

Wednesday morning. No car—no stalkers—of course.

Shannon was waiting for me. "You OK?" she asked. "We were worried."

"I just needed a day."

Shannon accepted my lack of info, and I asked about her Sunday date with Brian.

Just then someone chimed a bell, and we all raced into the lecture hall.

"I'll tell you at lunch," she whispered as we took our seats.

That afternoon I had an appointment with Dean Montrose. She had offered to read my manuscript, and I knew her critique was exactly what I needed to get back on track. I had to focus on writing this final week. I knew deep down Roger and I were going nowhere. I liked him a lot; enjoyed him in every way, but there was no future for us.

"I loved your opening ten pages," she said. She handed a file folder to me with my manuscript inside. "I made some margin notes and wrote a quick summary for you with possible changes. But over-all, I loved it. Your writing is genuine; your voice is unique; it has all the makings of a great book."

I couldn't stop smiling, but I wanted some serious criticism. "You said you like the first ten pages. Was there a point where it stopped working?"

"Not really, Amy," she said. "I think my margin entries will be clear. You need about a half dozen more paragraphs to set up the initial scene. A bit more description, a little more back story—whatever you decide."

"So over-all the story is believable?"

"Oh, yes, I wouldn't change a thing with the plot points or the ending. Just some padding here and there."

I nodded and thanked her profusely for her time.

"My pleasure," she said. "We don't get many Americans in the summer program. We've enjoyed having you so much. Your maturity and experience helped the group immensely."

"Well, thank you," I said. "I started off feeling pretty old and possibly stuffy."

"Not at all; a great addition." She hesitated; then made direct eye contact. "I wonder, have you ever considered teaching again? Perhaps, even here?"

Her questioned startled me to a point where I was tongue-tied. I couldn't think of a response to save my life. I finally stuttered, "Here? ... You mean at Oxford?"

"Well, yes, certainly. You know your craft; you've been a teacher before. We could use someone in our Creative Writing department with your background."

"I have to admit; I'm somewhat dumbfounded, Dr. Montrose."

"Well, give it some thought, why don't you? And get back to me in a few days. Our time is coming to a close so quickly."

"I agree," I said. "I can't believe we're down to less than a week. I'm going to miss the city and the university."

"Well, then, perhaps that will help you make the decision to stay."

I smiled.

"And Oxford is quite beautiful in the snow. Those gorgeous pine trees that stand fifty feet in the air—covered with white—absolutely spectacular."

I couldn't wait to call Jennifer. I dialed as soon as I left the dean's office.

"Jenn," I said. She sounded groggy. "Oh, shit, I'm sorry ..." I realized the time.

"No, no, it's OK," she said. I could hear her rustling as if she were getting out of bed.

"I can call you back ..." I began.

"No, absolutely not," she said. "You'd never call if it weren't important. Talk to me, girl."

I spent the next few minutes telling her about my conversation with Dr. Montrose and about her offer.

She squealed with delight. "Amy ... are you considering it? I mean, would you like to stay?"

"I love it here," I said. "I really do. I don't think I've ever been anywhere so absolutely beautiful, at least in the summer. I'm sure its damp and very cold come winter though."

"Would you enjoy the teaching?"

I knew this had to be hard for her. I would be upset if she mentioned leaving Phoenix and just moved away suddenly. I would miss her terribly; already was.

"That I don't know," I admitted. "I really don't know much about the students. They may be total elite British snobs, you know?"

"Well, I doubt that. Probably a mix like every other college."

"I wonder," I said, "I mean, it is Oxford for heaven sake. Bill Clinton was here, you know."

"Well, that doesn't speak so highly," she said and laughed out loud.

"Yeah, OK, point taken."

"You need to think about it, my dear. It sounds like an opportunity too good to pass up. And how about this new guy, Roger?"

I groaned. "Oh, Jenn, you know!"

"I do?" she said.

"Well, it's nice. He's intelligent, funny, good looking, sexy. Nothing not to like really. But ..."

"What's the 'but'? I don't hear any 'but.' If you stayed, it's something you might want to pursue."

"Maybe," I sighed as I said the word. "Maybe."

"Any more weird guys hanging around?"

"Not this week, but honestly, Jenn; each time I think it's over, I spot them again. Still has me spooked."

"I imagine it does."

"I have to let you get back to sleep. You can kill me when I get back for waking you."

"No way." she yawned. "But I think I will climb back into bed."

We said good-night and good-bye, and I headed back to the apartment.

Chapter 18

I hadn't seen the car in days, although it was possible they were simply hiding better than before. Sure enough, as I left campus, the gray Ford rounded the corner and sped away quickly.

When I got home I told Roger, and he raged. As I prepared dinner in the next room, he said, "It's time we do something, Amy."

I took the baked potatoes out of the oven; the chicken could bake another fifteen.

"I don't disagree," I said. "But what can we really do? They haven't actually done anything they could be arrested for. We don't know if they intend to harm me or just scare the hell out of me. It's still bizarre."

Roger nodded. "I know. But the police can never show up at the right time. They've had a description for weeks and every opportunity to find them. They're worthless." He was growing more agitated.

"I know, Roger, but in all fairness, they do have bigger fish to fry; robbers, murderers …."

He laughed. "My girlfriend's mental health."

"Well …" I let it go. "So do we just walk up to the car with a finger stuck under a jacket like a gun and ask what the hell they're doing?"

"Crap," he spit out. "I don't know! Let's eat."

I appreciated Roger's concern—I did. But I had dealt with every aspect of life independent of a man, for nearly fifteen years. All the daily ins and outs, the hassles, crises, unexpected challenges. If I were honest, I'd probably done it my entire life—even when I was married, I was in control. Was it a positive or a flaw? I wasn't sure.

I had one more day of classes for the week; Roger was going to be tied up day and night, so he packed his belongings and returned to his own apartment. I had a few days on my own. When he first left, I felt lonely, but then it felt like a relief. What could I do this weekend, I wondered? Well, for one thing, I needed to work on revisions. I had put my editor off as long as I could. She knew I'd be back in the states soon, and she wanted a final revision by that time.

On the way back from Cambridge, Roger had mentioned the town of Bath—home of Jane Austen and a hundred other famous people. He had offered to plan a day trip if I couldn't spare time for an overnight. But we'd both gotten busy, and now his thesis was due in two days. The more I read about the city, the more it called to me. Seeing a piece of art with someone else, or even a movie, brought another viewpoint that often added to it. But experiencing a "place", especially a place like Bath—a Roman city built in A.D. 43, sounded like a one-person excursion. The guidebook said it was called the Golden City due to its amber-toned stone. The famous Roman baths still there, if you wanted to partake.

I thought about strolling cobbled streets where Jane Austen and Charles Dickens had walked, sipping a coffee at Colonna and Small's where Mary Shelley or Henry Fielding possibly sat. I envisioned retracing Jane's steps from her house to the wrought iron, gated Queen Park. I wanted to stand high above the Avon River and envision Thomas Paine and Horatio Nelson walking along the river bank discussing war and naval strategy. Sit in the abbey and feel the worn indentations where Sally Lunn or Richard Nash might have sat and prayed. Maybe just sit and figure out the ending of my novel. I wanted to feel it on my own.

I didn't want to hurt Roger's feelings by going alone though. To make up for it, I would mention the new play at Oxford Theater and ask if he'd like to join me; then surreptitiously plan my excursion to Bath. Perhaps I'd tell him once I got the rail ticket and an itinerary for my day. Or perhaps it would be later, once I returned. I told myself he wouldn't care—one less thing on his full plate.

A scene from the past flitted into my mind and back out ... fast ... almost too fast to register—Luke looking at photos of the clouds above Sedona after a long weekend up north where I had holed up in a small cabin and wrote nonstop for three days. How do eyes all by themselves look hurt? But his did for a brief moment before they shifted to acceptance and excitement, and he said, "Nice!", and we moved on.

And just as quickly, I moved on as well and asked about his kids, his weekend, his plans for the upcoming week. Only now did that look of 'not knowing', 'not being invited', 'not understanding' registered for me. Of course, he'd been hurt.

But he never wanted to travel anywhere. He never wanted to get away together—to take time from work to go with me. How could he have been hurt at my going? Did my eyes have that same look when I asked, and he refused? Or when he told me about the baseball game he'd taken the kids to on Saturday? Did that tiny disappointment gnawing in my gut register in my eyes? He never saw it or pretended not to. Although his response of "what?" may have been because of that very recognition. "Nothing," I would say.

After our last group meeting for the week, I walked to the train depot and checked the daily schedule to Bath. It was an hour and fifteen minutes from Oxford with one required change of train in Didcot Parkway—wherever that was. In order to do a round trip in one day I needed to leave no later than 8:00 a.m. and could return at 8:00 that evening. I spoke with a woman at the information desk who assured me that the train depot in Bath was only a few blocks from city center, and I'd have no problem walking the entire city on foot. I bought tickets at the window, and the agent said to be at the station fifteen minutes early in case the platform changed.

Connie Wesala

Chapter 19

At 7:30 Saturday morning I grabbed my backpack, double checked my RT ticket, passport, phone and cash and headed to the #6. After five minutes, I re-read the daily bus schedule. "Oh, no!" I cried out. What? It was Saturday. I had misread the schedule yesterday. No bus to Glouster Green for another half hour, and I'd miss my train.

I checked the time on my cell and suddenly remembered that my smart phone could access a cab company. I fumbled with the tiny keyboard. Come on, I raged. I re-typed Oxford ca_ or should I put in taxi? Shit! As I turned back toward the street, I spotted it—a green cab going the correct direction on the opposite side of the street. I waved my arms in the air and yelled loudly, "TAXI!" TAXI!"

I jumped into oncoming traffic that luckily had stopped at a light. I yelled again, racing across the street as I saw him slow and pull to the curb. Damned wrong-side-of-the-road English driving.

I jumped into the back seat. "Train station—I have an eight o'clock departure."

His expression asked if I was nuts, and I waited for him to tell me it was impossible. But I knew, from the many times I'd been there, we were five to ten minutes away with good traffic.

"OK," he said, and he slammed the gas pedal down and lurched forward. When he spotted a red light ahead, he pulled a quick right-hand turn; then a left to access the same road we'd been on. He screeched to a halt seven minutes later, and I threw a ten-pound note at him and raced up the stairs and into the lobby.

On the departure board, I found the train to Bath—Platform 4. I took a deep breath and walked to the turnstile, spoke to the authority, and he checked my ticket and pointed outside and to the right. Platform 2 – Platform 3 – then 4. The engine pulled in just as I got there and would leave in six minutes. I was winded from racing down the tracks, and my backpack suddenly felt a hundred pounds. I pulled it onto one shoulder and climbed aboard. A woman just ahead of me entered the third car, and I followed.

"Do I have an assigned seat?" I showed her my ticket.

"No," she said, "You can sit anywhere you like." She had a kind smile.

"Thank you," I said. "And could you tell me how many stops before Bath?"

She nodded. "Sure, there will be four stops, and you'll change trains in Didcot; then Bath. You'll be fine. Just watch as the train begins to enter the station; the signs are huge. And they announce in advance."

I knew I looked as nervous as I felt, and I was craving coffee and a donut to raise my blood sugar and my caffeine levels. Half-way through the car, I deliberately settled into a window seat facing forward. One thing I couldn't handle was sitting backward on buses and trains. I hadn't thought to bring an iPod or even a magazine or book, so I focused on the maze of rail tracks running parallel and then crisscrossing. The system was not a good as in France, but I'd heard there were fewer strikes.

At exactly eight o'clock the train began to move, picking up speed quickly as we left the city limits of Oxford. A harrowing way to start a morning, but I was here. Would it have gone smoother with Roger? I had no doubt. For one thing, he'd have known the limited bus schedule on weekends and would most likely have scheduled a pick-up with the taxi service the night before. But he was also a native which gave him a huge advantage.

I'd managed—if by the skin of my teeth—and I'd made it work. And, I added to make myself feel better, *"I'd have simply taken the next train."* Even though I wasn't sure when that would be. I spent the next hour watching the country side race by, dozed a couple of times and woke each time scared that I'd missed my stop. Had she said 3 stops or 4 before Didcot? I nervously bit my lip. I checked my watch. Only 9:15—we weren't due in Bath until 10:00. But just in case I turned toward the man across the aisle from me.

"Excuse me."

He looked up from his paper. "Yes?"

"Do you know how many more stops before Didcot?"

I saw him assessing my ... my what? Hair, clothing, back-pack? I bristled just a little.

"Next stop." His tone was a bit sharp, I thought. Stupid Americans? Stupid woman? *Who cares?*

I was less than polite when I said, "Thank you" in a formal British tone.

Inside I laughed. I was gathering funny stories to share back home. When Didcot was announced, I gathered my belongings, clambered down the train steps and found the nearest porter who directed me to the Bath Spa train—Platform 2 in five minutes. I walked quickly and made the change with no problem.

The train rumbled into Bath station, and the wheels squealed to a stop. Most of us stood to exit, and I stepped into the aisle just as the curt gentleman from the previous train appeared from the row behind me. His hand gestured for me to go before him, and I did.

I followed the departing passengers into the terminal and through to the other side; then realized I was starving. Back inside, I found a coffee kiosk that had some pastries left in a glass case. "Chocolate croissant, please, and a short coffee."

"Cream and sugar?"

"Just black." I paid the five pound, then walked down the outside steps of the building and onto the sidewalk where I located a bench. The sugar energy kicked in, and I watched a maze of people wind down the street toward what I assumed was the city center. It seemed like just as many walked toward the terminal. Bath was a busy city. I wiped the crumbs from my lips with a napkin, took my coffee cup and joined the masses.

Chapter 20

Bath had a totally different feel than any of the places Roger had taken me the past month. The Roman influence was distinct. The Georgian buildings had a strength to them that I didn't feel in Oxford. The creamy gold stone that the tour book had described shone brightly, but underneath the shine was a feeling of something undefined. Power, perhaps.

I walked past the Roman Pump House and peered down twenty feet into the ancient baths which had been dedicated to the Roman goddess Sulis after their invasion. A temple built between 60 and 70 AD stood just beyond. The dates still astonished me, even though I'd been in England for some time now.

Bath Abbey's flying buttresses, parapets and honey-colored classical façade rose in front of me at the end of the street. I quickly toured its interior of fan vaulted ceilings and took note of the fifty stained glass windows that lit the interior. Twenty minutes later, I exited at the rear of the abbey, and within a few blocks I found myself high above the River Avon. It wound its way through the city, tamed by the weirs that forced it into a single channel. Below me I saw a mile or more of formal flower gardens, unlike the haphazard array of color one found in Oxfordshire.

I wandered back toward the abbey on a narrow cobble stone street and spotted a place described in the tour books as the best ice cream in England. I wasn't sure I believed that, but how could I pass it up? George and Danver, in Oxford, made the same claim.

At Sally Lunn, I ordered a double-dip of pistachio and ate it as I walked along residential streets. Ornamental stone signs adorned many of the three-story lodging houses: Here Dwelt Sir Walter Scott 1775. Fielding, Shelley, Dickens, Nelson, Pitt. I began clicking photos with my camera until it started to feel redundant. I'd never seen so many famous names within a short few blocks.

Around 11:00 I followed my city map and located Gay Street; then headed uphill to the Jane Austen museum. I passed the iron-fenced Queen's Square and within a few steps spotted the life-size wax image of the famous author in full-length blue dress and bonnet. I stood beside Jane on the outside steps and asked someone coming out if he'd take my photo. I handed him my phone and smiled broadly. "Thanks."

"Sure ... enjoy!"

I stepped into the tiny foyer. One small room adjoined the entrance, and it had been turned into a gift shop. I bought a ticket from the sales woman and climbed the steep wooden stairs. There were several rooms of exhibits, and I tried on a typical bonnet from that period. Several women were laughing together as they dressed up in full attire. I declined that option.

On the third floor was a formal tea room. "Will you be joining us?" a maître d' asked. The pricing on the menu astonished me, and I politely declined. If I'd been with Roger, he'd have insisted. "How can you not have a formal English tea with Jane Austen?" he'd have said. He'd have insisted on paying as well. But Roger wasn't here, and my good judgement won out.

At that point I felt I'd seen the city, so as I emerged into the sunshine, I double backed to the park and just beyond. A coffee house seemed to call to me, and I was hungry. I ordered a latte and a small cheese sandwich and sat outside at a picnic table. Taking my pen and paper from my backpack, I sat back and let Jane serve as a muse. I lost track of time and startled when someone said, "Excuse me, may I sit at your table?"

"Of course," I answered and glanced at my watch. 4:00 p.m. already. I gathered my belongings, wished the couple a good afternoon, and walked in a large square several blocks each direction just to get the feel of the town. What to do in the next four hours? I had not a clue. Perhaps I should have waited for Roger to bring me, but we were running out of days. I grew angry with myself for not planning better. I knew there were a dozen more sites on the tourist list, but I suddenly didn't have the desire or the energy to find them. So I meandered back to the river, walked down a long flight of steps into the garden and sat quietly on the expanse of green grass.

I leaned back against the broad base of an ancient Oak and imagined the Romans building this city with slave labor. Imagined the wealthy kings and lords enjoying the hot springs of the baths, then slipping into their long robes to return home where a feast awaited them and perhaps a wife or concubine to complete their day. Were there war ships that came up the river to invade them? Or did they set out to conquer the rest of Britain? Hard to image these buildings standing in 43 A.D. It must have looked much the same except for the roads of automobiles and tour buses.

At 6:30 I walked back into town, found a restaurant and ordered a heavy meal including red wine. I was back at the station at 7:45 feeling a little lonely and a little disappointed. Not with Bath, per se, but with myself. I'd never needed a man to complete my adventures or make my day, but today, after having Roger so close for so many weeks, I felt very alone and found myself wanting him to appear. My Mr. Darcy.

Chapter 21

At 10:00 p.m., I arrived in Oxford and walked the few blocks to the bus station. It was dark, and I was tired from the long day in Bath, but I found myself humming on the way back to the apartment. I watched carefully out the bus windows. Even at night, I could make out the ancient stone buildings, could see in my mind the parks in bloom and the lush landscape everywhere. I tried to envision it in snow and ice. Pretty, yes; but also miserably cold and slushy; coats, hats and gloves; a dank basement apartment with heat that most likely didn't even work. I'd probably have to find a cheaper place to room, and who knew where I'd find that. I might have to share like Shannon did … a room with access to the kitchen and living areas. Suddenly my excitement settled into question marks. I hopped off the bus and headed on home.

As I reached the drive-way, I noticed someone standing just off the sidewalk but out of sight from the house itself. He was far enough from the flood lights to prevent them from turning on. I slowed and readjusted my backpack. The man was tall and lanky; skinny if he'd been a pound or two lighter. He was smoking a cigarette and took a long drag just as I stepped forward. Then he threw it down and ground it into the dirt. He wore a brown plaid driving cap which covered his forehead, and his face was tipped downward so I couldn't see his eyes. What to do? Just as I was considering retracing my steps back toward the bus stop, he looked up and met my gaze.

His accent was a thick brogue—more Irish than British, I thought. He spoke my name, though I'd have been hard-pressed to understand it if it weren't my own.

I answered, but stood perfectly still about half-way across the drive from him—perhaps six feet away. "Yes," I said, "And you are?"

"Tom's my name," he said. It sounded like Tome to my ear. "Can we have a moment?" he said, and I spotted the second man crossing the street toward us. He walked quickly and was beside me before I could answer. I stepped forward, and the flood light sensed my motion and lit up the entire drive. I could see the men clearly, and neither looked particularly menacing.

"Why have you been following me?" I asked pointedly. Might as well get to the meat of it. "I want to know why you are following me. Did someone hire you?"

Tom laughed. "Pretty astute, lady. You must be smart, going to Oxford and all."

"What are you after?" I said sharply.

"We ain't after nothin'," he said. "Just keepin' an eye on things is all."

"What do you mean keeping an eye on things? On me? Is that it?"

"We're just part of your protection plan," the second man said. He moved closer to my side, and I moved back a step.

"We ain't out to hurt you, lady," he said. "Figured it was time to let you know that, since you keep calling the damned gendarmes."

He hocked a wad of spit to his right and onto the grass.

"Well, that's very nice," I said. "But who the hell has you watching me?"

"We can't rightly tell you that, ma'am," the first man said, "Can we, Fred?"

I wasn't sure if he was asking an actual question of Fred or if he was making fun of me.

The man in the cap tipped it forward and off his head. "Good-day to ya'," he said, and both men walked down the street. I could now see the car several houses down, and I watched as they wandered toward it, got in and sped off.

Once they passed me, I began to shake and realized how scared I'd been for the past few minutes. "Well, that was odd," I said out loud. Were they really just telling me they were protecting me? From what? And who hired them? I shook my head and walked toward the open gate and down the steps to my apartment. I should feel better, I thought. I had made contact, talked to them, been assured they weren't out to harm me. But there were still too many questions, and I wanted answers.

Now, on top of a job offer, I was faced with a mystery to solve. It was exhausting, and I was starving. I let myself into the apartment, rummaged through the refrigerator and came up with some left-over Chinese.

I blamed the soy sauce for my lack of sleep. I tossed and turned all night; ruminating on who would possibly have me watched and why. And I had drawn up list after list of pros and cons as far as the job was concerned.

Weather, salary, job description, student demographics, Roger, where to live, would I need a visa? How long was the semester? Did they want me permanently; a semester; two? I had a lot of questions that needed answered before I could even consider staying. And would I be able to go back to the states to get my stuff? To say good-bye to my kids for a year? To see friends and figure out what to do with the cat and the house? It was all too much.

I woke still feeling like I was in a fog. My eyes looked swollen from lack of sleep, but I applied as much founda-tion and eye cream as I could, threw on an over-sized blue sweater and jeans and headed to campus to work on my final paper at the library. It was Sunday, but I knew I could use my swipe card to get in.

Just as I reached the top of the steps, Roger startled me. He'd been standing near the side door of Mary's house, and when he heard me, he walk-ed over and gave me a hug.

"What are you doing here?" I said.

"Glad to see you too," he said, but he laughed.

"I *am* glad to see you," I said. "Honestly I am, but I'm just surprised is all."

"Thought we'd grab a coffee unless you don't have time."

"I do have time for a quick one; but it will have to be quick. I'm headed to the library on campus for the day. This paper will never write itself."

We took the bus into town and bought drinks and split a muffin at our café. He took my hand across the table. "I'd like to spend as much time as possible before you leave," he said. "I hope you want that too."

I nodded. "Of course, I do." I thought about the job offer and decided to keep it to myself until I had more answers and until I made a decision on my own. I didn't want Roger to be a factor in that decision; as hard as that might be. This had to be all about me, and I knew it. I had made decisions based on one man after another most of my life and given Luke my all. I wasn't going to make that mistake again.

I also decided not to bring up my trip to Bath or my visitors the previous night. After a half hour, I left Roger to finish his breakfast and read the paper.

Five hours later, I dragged myself back to the apartment and opened a bottle of wine. The past 24 hours had been too much for me. I couldn't get a handle on why these men were protecting me. Who had hired them? It was mind boggling, and I couldn't think fast enough to figure any of it out. I was exhausted. I slipped into a semi-conscious dream-state as I sipped one glass after another. My thoughts turned to the past.

Chapter 22

Looking back, I now take total responsibility for my divorce from Bruce. I blamed him, of course, when we split. Blamed him for working 24/7; for leaving me alone with two kids even on vacations when he promised to join us and never did. Blamed him for building two houses that I wound up overseeing and moving into alone. I was full of blame for so many years, it ate me up and spit me out. It also blinded me to my part in the death of our marriage.

Had I ever really loved him? I still wasn't certain. But within the past year, as I muddled through my breakup with Luke, I had given serious consideration to those years as well. Maybe I was simply incapable of having a relationship.

There was something about giving myself to another person that felt like losing my own identity, and I didn't want that, ever again.

Boundaries are what set us apart from others; that make clear, "this is who I am and this is what I am willing to do to be with another person." I seemed to lack boundaries. I melded into the other person until I couldn't see my reflection or feel my separateness. If I were looking in a mirror, I might have seen myself becoming gelatinous, soaking into the skin of the man I was with, until only a small bit of me--just the edges of my form--could be seen. And in order to return to myself, I had to literally suck myself back into my body as quickly as I could so I wasn't totally absorbed.

That pulling back must have felt to Bruce as it felt to me—a sharp pain of the vacuum that sucked me away from him. Once severed, I could breathe— and talk and laugh and cry and make dinner, and plan parties and mother the children. But once I tried to reconnect, the vicious cycle would begin again. A melding into and a pulling apart. Over and over. Bruce drank well into the night; he required little sleep, worked long hours and often came home after the kids and I had eaten. And I would crawl into bed hours before him while he sat in the den and downed Scotch, watched TV or did more paperwork.

Just thinking about it exhausted me even now. The divorce severed us to the bone, and there was no way to mend it. Not even enough for friendship or co-parenting. It was simply over.

When he moved out, I felt whole for the first time in years, and it felt good. Good to be alone, to feel my own feelings, think my own thoughts and go my own way. I swore I'd never try again. Love. Marriage. Relationship. I was better off alone.

And then, three years later, I walked into a new job and met a pair of deep umber eyes that sucked my soul right into his in an instant. I knew better. When I thought about it now, a year and a half after the break-up, I had known. It was too intense—too sudden—to be good for either of us. There I was—melding right into another man, having learned nothing from the past.

Luke was a good guy. I blamed him for everything because blame is so much easier for us humans. Another self-absorbed man. Another emotionally unavailable man. Another headstrong man who had to have his way at all times. I had cast the role and chosen him for the part. Perhaps because this time I really did love the man, I fought hard to make it work. I gave in. I was always available. I was thoughtful, kind, helpful—overbearing.

Once again, when I sorted it out, I knew I was the one to blame. Blame does nothing good for us. So instead I had decided to call it accepting my part and understanding that I cannot be in a relationship without losing myself and resenting it the entire time. Wanting it and fighting it. Leaving and coming back. Yelling with anger and crying with regret. Such passion. Such push and pull. Such an unhealthy way to live.

It is a coin toss as to who ended it that morning. It simply ended itself I suppose. Luke said something; I reacted; I walked across the room and sat looking at the floor; he waited and waited and then walked out saying "Take care." And I responded, "You too." No screaming match. No tears of sadness. Simply over, and I felt dead more than sad. Dead.

And I had been dead for the past year and a half. And now here was Roger—obviously an intelligent, good-looking, kind man. A good lover. Someone who could be a good friend. Someone I could care for. But I knew it wouldn't work, and I needed to end this now before either of us got hurt. I am incapable of this one thing – this thing that comes so naturally to almost everyone on the planet. It should be easy to fall in love and live as two separate people—a couple. I wasn't capable of coupling.

How sad, I thought. And yet ... truthful and self-aware ... to realize that no matter who he was or how much he cared and loved, I would be my own undoing—and the undoing of the relationship.

I knew what I had to do. If I took the job, it would mean the possibility of something going further—something that I would inevitably kill. If I returned home, we would slowly pull away from each other. That would be the easiest solution.

As I sat there acknowledging my fault-line, I sobbed. Tears ran until there should have been no more. And yet they continued to run down my cheeks, drop from my chin and soak my shirt. I silently wept. It was simply my body grieving quietly and wetly. I knew my decision, and I would meet with Dr. Montrose the next day.

I must have fallen asleep with my head in my hands for that is how I awoke some hours later. The apartment was dark as I hadn't turned on lights. It was quiet and black and casket like. I stood, and every muscle ached. As if my body itself was injured as well as my psyche and my soul.

I walked slowly to the kitchen and poured myself a glass of water and sipped it as I walked into the bedroom and lay down fully clothed on top of the bedcovers and fell into a deep empty sleep.

I woke around 3:00 a.m. with a headache. I wanted to talk this decision through with someone. And I had no one here who could be objective. Was I just wanting someone to reconfirm my decision? Did I want someone to talk me out of the job? If so, I was going the right route. I waited for Jennifer to pick up.

"Miss you!" she literally chirped into the phone.

I laughed. "I miss you too," I said. "What's new there?"

She knew from my tone that I was not truly asking.

"Not much; what's up?"

I hesitated and gulped back sudden tears. "Oh, Jenn, something has come up, and I really need to talk this through with someone who can think straight."

"Wow, that's asking a lot," her voice teased, "but I'll try."

"You know I've told you about Professor Montrose, the woman who heads up this workshop?"

"I do."

"Well, I met with her last week, and ..."

"Yes?" Her tone changed.

"How do I say this?" I said. I released an audible sigh. "She's asked me to join the faculty for a year, possibly longer."

A heavy silence followed. Neither of us knew what to say next. Finally, Jenn spoke up.

"Oh, Amy," she said. "I ... I ... well, I don't know what to say. I mean; it is a great opportunity, right?"

I agreed that it was.

"And you are loving it there. You talk nonstop about how this experience is making you grow. I mean ..."

I nodded. She was right. I had grown as a writer and as a thinker. The workshops and critiques and the group discussions made me feel totally alive.

"That's very true," I said, "but a year is a very long time without you and my kids—I mean, my God, leaving my kids?"

"Well, they are adults, Amy." She said the obvious, and I knew she was right.

Kids move away from parents all the time— most of the time in fact. I had simply been lucky they had hung around these past ten years. They would want this for me, and I knew they would encourage me to stay. If I thought someone was going to talk me out of this job, I was gravely mistaken. I would have to make the decision alone.

"It sounds like a wonderful opportunity, Amy. But only if it's something you want to do—teach that is, and I'm sure England winters aren't easy. When would you start?"

Good question. "I have to find out specifics; fall semester so I'd come home for a while and pack up for a lengthy stay."

"What about this Roger dude?"

"I'm not considering him in this decision; I can't. I mean – yes, it would allow me to get to know him better but honestly, he may not even stay in Oxford. He will defend his dissertation next month and get his degree. I can't let him play a part in this, Jenn."

"Well, you'll make the right decision," she said. I could see those intense blue eyes and the way she holds her head cocked to the right when she's listening intently.

"You're the best, you know it?" I said. "So I guess I'm back to making lists of pros and cons, huh?"

"Think so ..."

"Well, you are no help," I said, teasing her. "But of course, you are ... always. Thanks."

Just as I was about to say good-bye and start my list making, Jennifer interrupted. "Oh, Amy ... shit, I almost forgot this. I saw Luke again the other day, and I am convinced he knows you are in England. In fact, he mentioned how he hoped you were enjoying Oxford and hoped you were safe."

"What? No way," I said. There was no way he could know I was over here.

"I'm telling you ... he knows where you are. And ... he said to tell you "hi" when we spoke. So ... hi."

I shook my head. "Jennifer, how could ...? I mean; it's been over a year; we have no friends in common any longer."

"Just passing it along," she said. And we said our good-byes and hung up.

Chapter 23

I stood in the kitchen, and even though I needed sleep, I turned on the kettle to boil water for tea. As the hot water steamed onto my face and I placed the tea bag into the cup, I felt tears adding to the moisture on my cheeks. Luke. Every time ... tears. Did I honestly miss him or just the idea of him? The job situation left my mind as I took my tea cup and went to the back patio to sit in the early morning sun. It had been unseasonably warm for days now.

Luke had probably been the first man I had ever truly loved. There's a song I've liked for years from a movie with Jeff Bridges—"Timing's Everything."

I found myself humming the words, "That's when love ... just in time. I remember that day when our ... It can happen so fast . . . or a little bit ... timing's everything."

When our eyes first met; how many times had I relived that moment? If he'd have just been a minute later; if he'd gone a different route, none of it would have happened. But in less than a minute, I walked out of my office, and he stood eight feet away with those dark chocolate eyes that I melted into. We stood and talked, and I would never be the same. Timing's everything.

There is a thin black line that runs through love and hate; a hair's breadth between them. And Luke and I always found ourselves skipping it like a jump rope. Sometimes we landed in the love zone and just as often we found ourselves in the chaos we created to balance out the love.

The thing about Luke was ... he enjoyed the chaos. He enjoyed the tightrope and would laugh when I got angry as if he had planned it all along. He liked keeping people on the edge of their seats. He liked to keep you waiting and wondering and asking. For a short while it was intriguing and sexy and soon became infuriating and irritating. I handled the chaos for a few years, but the exhaustion it created became too much for me. I left on numerous occasions, but the magnetism drew me back each time. It had been a year and a half this time. Had we been separated that long in the past and gravitated back to each other? Close. Very close. *Oh, God; I cannot do this again.*

I fell asleep close to four and had nonvisual dreams until morning. Clouds of feelings that washed over me as I tossed and turned. Sensual, warm, giddy, breezy before it was all swept away by a tornado of fear.

I woke up feeling unrefreshed and moody. I brushed my teeth and stared directly into my own eyes. *This is what happens when you allow him in, just the least bit. This is what happens. Take the damned job. You need another year.* Was that true or melodrama? I was exhausted from flip-flopping an important decision around these two men.

I had an eight o'clock group meeting, so I moved quickly to dress, slap on make-up and brush my hair. As I locked the door and said good morning to Spidey a thought emerged. Luke would never run into Jennifer. That was no coincidence. The two men following me said they were just protecting me. That was no coincidence. I stood on the top step, dumbfounded at where my thoughts were leading me. Luckily, I was late, and the race to the bus and the sprint to campus took my mind elsewhere.

Roger called as I was leaving class to ask me to meet for a drink. I knew I needed it so I accepted, and twenty minutes later we sat in yet another pub, ordering yet one more ale.

"Cheers," he said.

I lifted my glass. "Cheers."

"How was your day?" he asked.

When Roger asked you a question, you knew he really wanted to know. Luke's questions had always been a double-edged sword and sometimes they were sincere, and other times they dug till they brought blood. You never knew which side of the blade you were getting. Part of the crazy-making. The uncertainty of the outcome.

I smiled. I was ready to talk about the chance to stay on.

"What's going on?" he asked. His eyes were bright with interest.

"I'm trying to decide on something," I said. "Maybe you can help."

"Sure," he took a gulp of beer and sat back to listen.

"Well, I've been offered a job teaching at the American school for at least a year, possibly longer." I watched for his nonverbal response. It would tell me more than his words.

His mouth opened to speak. Across his face washed surprise, genuine pleasure and then something I hadn't expected—concern.

"Wow, didn't see that one coming. My gosh, Amy; that's fantastic."

Was it? I heard hesitation.

"Well, yes and no," I replied. "I mean, it is a fantastic opportunity and a real honor. I was so surprised when the director spoke with me about it; shocked actually. Me?"

"Well, why not you?" he said. "Hell, I'd say they are the fortunate ones … that is, if you're going to accept the position." His eyes formed question marks.

"I haven't decided. I told her I'd let her know in a week. … which is actually in two days I guess. Whew!"

I could not make this about Roger—not at all, and yet … I guess I had expected more joy or excitement … something.

"What are your plans after graduation?" I asked. Might as well hit this head on.

He nodded. "Good question," he said, "I've been pretty unclear about that. Thought about Cambridge, of course." He hesitated while that sank in. "Or London if I really want to use this degree."

I leaned forward with my chin tucked into my open palm and my elbow on the bar table and listened as he listed the possibilities. I pushed back and took a sip of beer. "And?"

"And …well …" He hesitated for a moment; then smiled. "I've been offered a teaching position here as well."

I was stunned. "What? Really? … You're serious?"

"Dead serious." He smiled at me and reached for my hand. "How about them apples?"

I shook my head. "I know … right? Oh, my gosh."

"Well, I'm like you … have to let them know soon, but hesitating to make the decision. It's a big move. I mean, it sounds like you'd be committing to one year or possibly two, is that right?"

I nodded yes.

"For me, I'm thinking it could become permanent, and I wonder if that's what I really want to do for the rest of my life; you know? I mean I got this second master's degree for a reason, and it wasn't to teach. Part of me feels like I have the choice between being an adult and going to London to pursue a real career, or continue being a campus hanger-on and teaching for the rest of my life."

I understood his concerns. I wasn't sure I'd want to teach for the rest of my life either, as much as I had enjoyed being around students in my past life. I wanted to write. That's what had brought me here; not to teach. "Hmm," I said and licked my lips. I gulped down the rest of my beer. "I think I need another."

Roger stood and walked to the bar to order. I sat in stunned silence. Wow; not what I'd thought we'd be discussing. Not that we should be discussing "us". There were much larger issues on the table. We weren't twenty-five; we were adults with lives and children and friends and family. Much different than thinking only of one's self as you do in your twenties.

I rearranged my face as Roger placed the beer mug in front of me. "Well, let's talk it through with each other and see if we can make sense of it," I suggested.

For the next two hours, we bandied about the advantages of teaching, weighing those against our desires for larger careers … writing for me, a large think tank in London for him. College life was tempting. We both enjoyed young people with their energy and excitement for learning. Oxford itself was a huge plus; the prestige and world acclaim for the university. How many U.S. presidents had attended Oxford as a Rhodes Scholar? Several.

Academia kept you on your toes with constant new research studies, advancements in every field, students challenging your ideas and your life's work. It would keep us both young. It would be fun and interesting, and the city was an incredible place to live, though expensive. We found ourselves debating with each other, playing devil's advocate to get the other one to think carefully. Trying to catch him up when he almost made the final decision. But what if? But what really?

After three beers, I was feeling their effect. But it didn't concern me as it usually did. If I got drunk, we'd manage a way home and probably something remarkably enjoyable after. I laughed out loud.

Roger grinned from ear to ear. "You're getting tipsy," he said.

"Most definitely," I said and equaled his smile. "But this is good; this is really good."

"Have we made a decision?" he asked. "Did I miss something?"

I laughed. "I think one more beer will be the turning point. Why don't you order hamburgers with the next round, and I'll go to the lady's room?"

"You got it," he said. He was asking for a menu as I walked toward the loo.

When I returned to the table, I was feeling almost giddy. With french fries in my mouth, I mumbled, "Let's not tell each other our decision till tomorrow even if we decide, OK?"

"I like that," he said. He took a potato off my plate and dipped it in tomato sauce. "You Americans and your french fries. They're called chips, you know?"

"Oh, I know," I said. "And you also drive on the wrong side of the road."

"Let's get out of here," he said.

"Is the #6 still running?" I asked.

"Always."

We held hands on the way to the stop and queued up in line. Sitting closely on the bench seat, Roger put his arm around me and pulled me close. The Brits rarely engage in public displays of affection. But just before my corner, he tipped my chin up and kissed me gently and softly. I was quite close to a decision if he planned to stay.

That night was slow and sensual and intense. In place of the heat of passion was a deeper more meaningful pleasure for each of us. I slept soundly and woke first. I tiptoed to the bathroom, then to the kitchen to make coffee. In my satin robe, I sat cross legged on the sofa with my journal and pen. Outside clouds had gathered over night, and the sky looked gloomy. Could I live with that for the next nine months? That constant cloudy grayness, snow, ice, boots, wool scarves, and a cold damp apartment? We hadn't determined salary so I had no idea what I could possibly afford on my own. But it might be possible for Roger and I to share a place. It wasn't too early for that, was it?

We'd both be better off financially if we did. And if we were going to continue this relationship, we needed to really know one another. By the last drop in my cup, I knew what I was going to do. Now I just wanted to hear him say he was staying on.

"You look like the cat that swallowed the mouse," he said over breakfast. "I take it you've made a decision?"

"I think so."

"Well, don't you have to tell the director today?" he said.

I nodded. I swore I'd make no decision based on a man, but I was. No, I corrected myself, if he doesn't stay it will still be a fun year with all the perks of putting Luke and my old life behind. It will look good on my resume, and I could spend time on the novel as I huddled indoors till spring.

I decided not to even ask him what he was going to do. I needed to dress and walk to the director's office. I didn't have an appointment, but it wouldn't take long to discuss the calendar and the salary ... and possibly lodging.

"Hey," he said as he pulled me to him before I left the apartment. "You really aren't going to tell me what you've decided?"

I shook my head. "We said we'd make independent decisions, right?" I was teasing but ....

"If you're staying, I'm staying," he said.

"That's not fair, Roger." I tipped my head and pretended to glare at him in anger.

"I'll be here when you get back," he said. "Why don't you grab some cold cuts for lunch?"

I agreed, put my arms around his neck and kissed him. "I'll be back soon."

Connie Wesala

Chapter 24

Director Montrose was in her office--her secretary's desk vacant and her door open. She saw me as I entered the reception area. "Amy," she called. "I was hoping to see you this morning."

I smiled and shook her hand. I placed my purse on the floor and sat up straight in the chair across from her. "I have just a few more questions," I said.

"Of course," she said.

"Salary, calendar and lodging." I listed them quickly.

She smiled and walked around the desk and sat beside me in an adjoining chair. The school year began in late August; I'd have three weeks off at Christmas if I wanted to go back to the states for the holidays; and the salary was not high, but on top of my current retirement, it would suffice.

"So?" she said.

I looked at her carefully. The next words out of my mouth were going to change my life as I knew it. And I hadn't even discussed this with my own children. Geez. But why put them in the middle of a decision they wouldn't want to make for me? It made no sense to postpone this.

"If I can have a couple of afternoons for my writing, I'll accept." The minute the words escaped my lips, I panicked. Jennifer, my other friends, Arizona, my two kids, my home. What was I doing? I was taking a risk—not something I did very often, but it was time.

It took a half hour to negotiate terms and begin the paper trail of application, contract, and all the rest. I'd be covered medically while in the UK and part of the university system. That was a bonus. Four classes each week and plenty of time for writing, even with all the meetings and faculty responsibilities. I would need to meet with the head of HR. but that was a formality, and she would rush it through so I could head back on my return ticket next week.

I texted Roger as soon as I left the appointment. All I wrote was: "News!"

"A beer news or a Scotch news?" he wrote back.

I laughed. Scotch, I assumed, meant I had declined the offer and would be leaving soon.

"You'll see. White Rabbit at 5:00?"

"Make it 4:30. I can't wait."

I glanced at my watch and responded "Yes", then headed over to the lecture hall to catch up with the day's lecture notes and assignments if any. Shannon was sitting in her usual spot. I slipped in quietly and took the seat next to her, hoping the speaker wouldn't notice.

Twenty minutes later, we had our usual afternoon break. "I was worried," Shannon said. "You're never late."

"I know, but I had an appointment with Dr. Montrose. You won't believe what I've done?"

We both pulled out our water bottles and began to walk the perimeter of the courtyard. Shadows through the trees cast odd images. Soon those leaves would be turning umber and crimson and would cover the ground. And after that, the brittle grass would be hidden under a layer of white. And I would be here. I still couldn't comprehend it.

"I'm staying on," I said, "as an instructor."

Shannon's mouth dropped and then turned upward into a huge smile. "Oh, my God, that's fantastic. Oh, Amy, how fun!"

"I hope so," I said. "I haven't told my kids yet. I was offered the position last Friday, but I just can't talk to them until I get back. Is that selfish?"

Shannon shook her head. "No, I understand. Much easier talking face to face."

She gave me a big hug, and we headed back into the building. For the next hour I listened as intently as I could and took copious notes. But my thoughts swirled. Is that the lectern I would be using? Would I be in a small classroom? How many students would I be responsible for? I didn't even have a firm curriculum. For someone who didn't like change; I seemed to be making a lot of it.

Roger was waiting curbside when I reached the pub, gave me a peck on the cheek and put his right arm around my shoulder, leading me inside and to the nearest table. He yelled across the room, "Two Guinnies."

I shrugged off my sweater and wrapped it around the chair back.

"You're staying," Roger said with a grin. "I can tell."

"And how on earth can you tell?" I teased.

"Because you'd be looking very sad if you weren't. I mean … how could you leave me?"

I shook my head, and he headed to the bar to retrieve our drinks and pay the tab.

"Thanks," I said as he pushed the warm ale toward me. "Roger, seriously though, we do need to talk about this. I mean, you graduate within weeks now and are you headed back to Cambridge? To London? What have you decided?"

"I haven't made up my mind, or I hadn't anyway," he said. "I guess I was waiting to see what decision you made." He grew quiet and reflective. "And now you have." He didn't say more.

"We agreed not to do that," I said. "Not to let each other play a part in these decisions."

"I know," he said. "And yet, now that you've made your decision, it does somehow play a part in what I do. Maybe it shouldn't, but it does."

I no sooner opened my mouth to speak, than he whispered, "Hush. We've had this conversation; let's not have it again, please."

He was right; there was no reason to talk it through again; we had had the discussion; we had agreed to make our own separate decisions and, somehow knowing Roger, I thought I was probably just one piece of his puzzle. He was practical and thoughtful, and he was male I reminded myself. I was suddenly glad I had made my decision first. Now I didn't have to weigh the factor of him going or staying, although I also knew that I would be deeply affected by what he chose to do.

"You know," I said finally. "No matter what you decide, we'll be in the same country, and it's a small country at that." I grinned and placed my hand over his. He felt warm and smooth and he smelled of cologne, and I suddenly wanted to leave the pub. He took my cue and handed me my sweater as he stood up to leave. "Unless you've decided on something I know nothing about—like moving to the states." I was teasing, and he knew it.

"I'm free for the rest of the evening, if you are," he said as we walked toward the bus stop.

"Oh, I'm so glad you are," I leaned toward him, bent my head onto his left shoulder, and hooked my arm through his. The only word to describe how I felt was content.

I turned the key, said hello to Spidey; then noticed a note attached to the door with scotch tape. It was from my landlady. I had a guest who would return around six o'clock. I glanced at my watch—already 5:45. It had to be Shannon. "Hmm," I mumbled.

"Everything OK?" Roger asked. He walked into the living room and plopped down on the sofa while I stood in the kitchen still looking quizzically at the message.

"Yeah, I guess. Someone is stopping by in a short while."

"Well, that timing is bad," Roger said with a smile.

"Yeah, huh?" I stood in the doorway, unable to stop guessing who had dropped by. Dr. Montrose wouldn't come by the house; she'd call me into her office. I knew so few people here. It had to be Shannon, but I had told her I was meeting Roger for a drink so even that seemed unlikely.

"You have any wine?" He turned to me as I stood in the doorway, and I shook my head.

"No," I said in a distracted tone. "Uh, huh."

He stood and straightened the legs of his khaki slacks. "Well, the little store is closed. I can walk further up to the liquor store. I'll only be gone a half hour or so. And that way, your guest can stop by and you can get rid of her ... or him ..." He poked a finger into my side trying to get me to smile which I finally gave him the satisfaction of doing. That was a good idea actually, and I was glad he'd thought of it so it didn't look like I was trying to get rid of him.

As soon as he shut the door, I raced to the bathroom and straightened my clothes, ran a comb through my hair and swiped some pink gloss across my lips. I had no idea why. It was Shannon for heaven's sake. Probably something about tonight's assignment. Maybe she wasn't clear on it and needed me to help her get started. I put water on to heat and pulled out two tea cups. I'd have it ready for her, and we could sit at the kitchen table and work through it together. Unless it wasn't Shannon ....

Chapter 25

Within ten minutes, the doorbell rang. "Just a minute," I called. I placed the tea bags into the cups and set them on the table. The kettle was whistling with steam.

I climbed the three short steps to the tiny landing, unlatched the deadbolt, opened the door and gasped.

If I were a fainter, I'd have fainted on the spot and fallen down the steps onto the floor below me. Instead, I simply felt the blood rush to my face in a hot flush and my hands begin to shake uncontrollably. And stupidly, the tears began to flow.

"Oh, my God, Luke," I whispered. "What are you ...?" I stepped sideways down the steps allowing him to stand on the landing before following me further into the apartment. I stood by the stove where the kettle was still screeching, and he walked into the kitchen and stood beside me.

"I'm sorry for the surprise," he said softly. "I ... I ... was afraid you wouldn't see me if I called to let you know."

I shook my head in a mix of astonishment, joy and anger.

Luke's dark brown eyes washed over my face and downward; he put out his hands and took both of mine. His broad shoulders pulled the knit of his shirt tautly. He stood barely three inches taller than I was in my bare feet.

As his hands released mine, his arms went around me, and he quickly pulled me into his arms, and his wet lips took mine into his mouth, and he sucked and bit slightly as I responded without wanting to.

When he lifted his head, I pulled back roughly. "Luke, you can't just do this," I yelled. "You can't just walk in here. And why are you here?"

My voice was harsh and my shoulders tensed as I walked around him and into the living room. My back was ramrod straight with fury. And inside my guts had turned to mush. My breathing ... labored, at best.

He followed me and stood for a moment before taking a seat across the room in the one large lounge chair. He pushed aside the ottoman and sat comfortably, never taking his eyes off me.

"My God, you're a vision for sore eyes," he said. "Pardon the cliché, English major." He grinned. His thick hands settled into his lap, and he sat back. "Amy, please let me explain." He was suddenly serious and looked full of doubt and regret.

I sat on the sofa facing him head on. I placed my shaking hands between my legs to calm them. I took in a deep breath that ended with a sound I didn't like. A slight whimper, like a puppy, escaped my lips. "Oh, Luke," I said finally. "This cannot be happening. Why? How? I mean, how did you even know where I was?"

"I have my ways," he said and smiled slightly. "I've known where you were for some time. And then two days ago, I simply booked a flight and said to hell with it. And here I am."

"And that's supposed to be explanation enough?" I asked. "Luke, I have a friend here … I mean, he'll be back in a few minutes; he's not here right now, but … you really need to leave."

"I've flown a hell of a long way to talk to you, Amy. I'm not leaving until we've had a chance to do that at least."

He waited for my response. I looked at the floor, then to the patio doors, and back again before allowing my eyes to meet his. That was my downfall—always had been. His eyes.

"This cannot be happening," I said. I shook my head. "Luke … please … don't do this. Why did you do this?" My assuredness softened to something less; something I didn't want to feel.

He took out a pen and note card from his shirt pocket and wrote something down. He stood and walked toward me. I couldn't look up at him; I stared at the ground. "Amy," he knelt down in front of me and placed the card into my hand. "Call me later, and we'll make a plan to meet. I'm staying right in town."

"Luke, I can't …."

He interrupted me. "I'll see you in the morning. If you don't call me, I'll just show up, but I need you to hear me out."

I stood and faced him, my hands in fists. "You can't just walk in and make demands."

"I'm not demanding, Amy … far from it. I'm begging." And his face did plead.

Someone knocked at the door, and I turned quickly.

Connie Wesala

"Luke, you have to leave, right now," I hissed. "Shi ..." I cursed. It had to be Roger. How was I going to explain this? Introduce them? There was no other exit. It had to be handled. I blew a long breath into the air and shook my head vehemently. "God da...."

I pushed Luke aside and walked to the door; it was unlocked, but Roger had no way of knowing that. I always followed his direction to lock it the minute I came inside.

I pulled the door open and let out a heavy breath. "Mary," I said.

"Did your friend find you OK?" my land lady said.

I smiled. "Yes, yes, he did. Thanks for directing him."

"No problem," she said. Her eyes glanced furtively around the door. I was not going to introduce her. I stood and smiled politely. "See you later?" I asked as a hint.

"Oh, yes, absolutely; have fun," she turned and walked up the steps to her house.

"Get out," I said to Luke immediately after she turned the corner. "Please leave now."

Luke nodded his acceptance, but as he squeezed past me in the tiny narrow kitchen, he reached for me again, and I felt my head on his chest. He smelled of sandalwood and musk. He felt soft like velvet and strong like oak. I was sinking, melting into memories.

He pulled back and kissed me again. "I'll see you tomorrow. Shall I meet you here?"

"Absolutely not. I'll call you."

He walked through the door, and it closed behind him.

I had always thought the phrase rocked my world an exaggeration of the grandest proportions. It suddenly made sense. The ground below me had shifted along a fault line, and I was falling down a deep crevasse. I put my face into my hands and sobbed.

By the time I heard Roger's voice calling as he entered the apartment, I had slumped onto the living room sofa trying to get my bearings.

"Sorry that took so long," he said loud enough for me to hear. "Everyone and their brother must be having a party tonight." I heard his steps as he walked through the kitchen area and through the doorway. "You alright, Amy?" he said. "You look almost gray. Are you sick? Can I get you something?"

In fact, he just had. He had given me an explanation for what I was about to do next. "Roger, you walked all that way, and here I am feeling like crap. I wonder if it was the beer we had earlier?" I made my voice end with a question mark and felt like the devil incarnate.

"I'm so sorry. I think I'm going to have to pass on tonight. And I don't want to give it to you if it is a bug of some kind."

I sounded reasonable and sane—and felt neither. I stood and walked toward the kitchen.

"Of course," he said. He put the two bottles of wine on the countertop and pushed them back under the cabinets out of the way. "We'll drink this tomorrow night … to celebrate both our decisions. I think I've made mine, actually." He smiled warmly. "Oh, come here," he said, "let me give you a hug. Go get undressed and into bed. Shall I make you some tea or something before I leave?"

"The water is still hot in the kettle." I pointed to the two tea cups on the kitchen table. "I can pour it myself. Thanks."

He pointed at the cups. "Oh, what did Shannon want?" he asked.

"Ahh," I said, "I turned her away. Felt so awful—didn't want her to get it. I explained the assignment, and she's OK going home to do it."

I gave him a brief hug. "Get out of here, before you get sick," I said.

He tipped my chin upward and looked into my eyes. "OK, I won't kiss you, but my eyes are undressing you as we speak," he teased.

"I'll see you tomorrow." I pushed him toward the door.

"I'll call you later." He turned before he shut the door. "Oh, damn, I just remembered. I have to meet with my committee from ten to noon; how about we take a drive in the afternoon and eat outside of town?"

"Sounds great," I said. I locked the door after Roger said good-bye to Spidey. I smiled. Such a great guy! I was not going to let Luke screw this up. What was he thinking, just coming here? My anger returned, and my fake stomach flu mended.

I did pour some tea as well as a glass of burgundy from one of the bottles Roger had bought. As I rummaged through the refrigerator with one hand, while drinking from the other, I found some brie, some grapes and an apple—enough for a meal. I had an evening of hard thinking to get through. I might go through an entire bottle.

I poked at my iPod and turned the wheel slightly. You're kidding me? You have to be kidding me! Of all the dozens of songs on that damned iPod, there it was. "God bless the broken road that led me straight to you."

I never listened to that song without crying—when I was with him and when I wasn't. My song for Luke. I set the food and wine on the table, walked to the bedroom and threw myself onto the bed face down, sobbing loudly. This was not over, and I knew it.

Chapter 26

The next morning I picked up my toothbrush and glanced into the mirror. A sleepless night was etched on my face. All I wanted to do was get dressed, put sunglasses on and head to my morning lecture. It would take my mind off my stupid life at least for a few hours. On the way out the door, I grabbed a bagel and my bag and rushed to the #6.

"Wow, you look …" Shannon began.

"Don't say it," I said more curtly than I wanted. "And don't ask."

Shannon put both hands in the air, palms toward me indicating an obvious "OK."

I focused intently on the speaker of the day. He was extremely well known in the art history community, and it wasn't difficult to concentrate as I took notes. In fact, by lunch break, I had almost forgotten the previous evening. We had heard the rain pattering on the roof of the lecture hall most of the morning, so I had my umbrella in hand as Shannon and I pushed through the doors and onto the lawn of the quad. Too wet to eat outdoors.

"Let's run across the street and grab a quick sandwich at the deli counter inside Java & Co.," I suggested. "I'll treat."

Once we were settled with our pre-made sandwiches, chips and drinks, Shannon tried once again to ask how I was.

"Sorry to be so rude this morning," I said. "I got no sleep last night and was really on edge."

She nodded as she took another bite of her tuna salad.

"I had a surprise guest show up last night, and it has me pretty shaken."

Her eyes widened in surprise. "Really," she said as she wiped her mouth with her napkin. "Can you tell me about it? I mean, I don't want to pry …."

Could a twenty-something come close to understanding the situation? I wasn't sure it was wise to tell anyone. I probably just needed to call Jenn back in the states as soon as the time difference allowed.

"I'd like to, Shannon," I said. "It's not that I don't trust you or anything. It's just a lot, and I need to process it myself."

Connie Wesala

She nodded her understanding, and we sat in silence for a few moments. "Can you believe … two more days? It's gone so fast." She did a good job of changing the subject, and I appreciated it.

"I know," I said. "I can't believe we'll be heading home soon."

"Yes, but you'll be coming right back, right?"

I knew she was referring to my new position. Would I be coming back? I had no idea what I was doing—in the future or even today. I'd get through the remainder of today's seminars and our group session and go from there. We walked back to campus, and as we walked into the lecture hall, we both twisted our mouths downward into a sad clown face. Then we smiled. "No good-byes today," I exclaimed.

"Oh, Amy. It's been such a fun month with you. Hey, Paris isn't far, you know? A chunnel away." I agreed to come visit during a school break, and we exchanged phone numbers and email addresses one more time.

Just then I spotted Dean Montrose walking toward me. "Did you get your flights arranged?" she asked.

I told her I had and would send my itinerary, and she promised to keep searching for a cheaper apartment for me to rent.

Tom Brady walked past and shook my hand. "I can't thank you enough for your help this summer," he said. "I felt like I was in over my head so many times."

"Well, you weren't," I assured him, "but thanks. It was great meeting you."

Stay in touch seemed to be making its rounds, and everyone within hearing distance was saying it over and over. "Stay in touch," I called to another student. Word had gotten out about my job offer, and several people stopped to wish me well and congratulate me. I felt pleased and even impressed with myself. Me, a teacher at Oxford. My head was still in the clouds.

When I checked my phone at our afternoon break, I had several texts from Roger and one missed call from Luke. I decided to ignore both till end of day. I would hide as long as possible, but I couldn't put it off much longer. I had to have a conversation with Luke. Not that I owed him anything! I did not. But the piece of me that was curious had reared its ugly head. At 4:00 I texted Roger about my day and said I was going to be tied up on campus for a few more hours. Then I dialed the local UK phone number Luke had given me. He answered on the second ring.

"Hi," he said. His gravelly voice sounded uncertain.

"Hi," I said. "I guess we should meet, huh?" Before he could answer, I added, "Where did you say you were staying?"

"A guest house sort of in the center of town, I guess. I'm kind of lost, to be honest."

"Are you next to Gloucester Green? The bus terminal," I explained.

"Not far from there, no. That's where I got off the bus from London, right?"

"I would assume so. Just walk toward town along George Street, turn right on Cornmarket and go up a block or so—it's a pedestrian street. There's a Café Nero on the left side. You'll see it—big sign."

"OK," was all he said, and we hung up.

I found a near-by bathroom and brushed through my hair, applied a little mascara and lipstick and called it good. I still looked like hell from not sleeping, but at this point who cared?

I got to the restaurant first, stood in line and ordered a tea and scone, and took a seat around the corner from the cashier where I could watch for him. The scone stuck in my throat as I took a bite, and I knew I needed water, and probably a Xanax or two. I hadn't talked to him in so long. Was he the same person I once knew? Was I? I had to tell him to get back on the bus to London, take the first flight back to Phoenix and never contact me again. I was livid at his audacity.

I spotted him first and called his name as I waved. He walked toward me and released butterflies into my heart. How could he still do that?

"If you want something, you order at the counter," I offered.

"Maybe in a few minutes," he said. "Right now I just want to sit across from you and look at you."

"Oh, Luke, please …."

"No, I mean it. You look great. It's been a long time."

I wanted to say not long enough, but I waited to see where this was going.

"I'm listening," I said. "Explain what's going on. And are you the one who hired the two guys that scared the hell out of me for a month?"

He looked sheepish; I knew the look all too well.

"I was worried about you, to be honest."

My head shook vehemently.

"No, seriously, Amy; I heard you were in England for a month-long seminar all alone; not even with your kids. I just wanted to make sure you were safe."

"Safe?" I said. "Well, I would have felt safe if I hadn't had stalkers following me day and night. You had no right, Luke. None."

"I know. I knew you'd say that. But I love you and I was worried about you, OK?"

"Love?" My neck would never be the same; I shook it wildly once again. "Love, Luke? That was ages ago. What are you talking about?" My voice had risen, and I became aware of people turning slightly in their seats to glance over.

I lowered my tone. "What are you talking about?" I said again. "Luke, we've been over for a very long time. Tell me why you're here … honestly!" I hissed the last word.

Luke hesitated, then stood and walked to the counter without saying a word. I sat there fuming; feeling my curiosity growing by the minute. He had a way of pulling you in.

I drank my tea and looked around. The place was nearly vacant; just a few tourist types having coffee, gawking at street maps or staring at cell phones on the Wi fi.

As he sat down I noticed how thin he was. Luke had always been stocky. He was short with thick shoulders and neck, and he had always had a slight paunch which seemed to be gone.

He smiled as he stirred sugar and cream into his coffee. When Luke smiles, his eyes look like stars in a midnight sky. The sunlight glints off his iris, and his dark chocolate eyes look like hot cocoa you want to dive into.

Stop! I told myself. *Right now.* I waited for him to speak first.

He took a sip. "Good coffee," he said. "I thought the Brits only drank tea." He loved to joke, especially at the expense of others. One of his less likeable qualities.

He placed his cup on the table and reached for my left hand. I pulled it away quickly.

He sat back in his chair and looked directly into my eyes. "I'm sorry."

That was it? I'm sorry? I stood and reached for my bag which hung on the back of my chair. "Luke, I can't do this."

He stood quickly and took my elbow. "No, please. I've come all this way; it cost a fortune at the last minute. Amy, you have to hear me out, please."

His face was lined, and his eyes saddened.

I sat down and pushed my chair toward the table. I could sit silently and listen. He was right; it was the least I could do under the circumstances.

"My mother is dying," he said with big tears in his eyes.

"Oh, Luke, I'm so sorry." Luke and his mother were the closest mother-son I'd ever known, and since his father died many years ago, as the eldest male in a Hispanic family, Luke had taken care of her every need. I'd never met her, but I felt I knew her. According to him, she had buffered the abusive relationship with his alcoholic father. There was no love lost when he died, though he had tried to make amends before the man's death. How many times had he called me from his childhood bedroom in the house his father had built with his own two hands? He drove back to eastern Texas any time he had a few days off work.

"But that's not why I'm here, really," he said. "Amy, a year ago we were both stubborn enough to let our relationship go. Neither of us truly ended things. We just both walked away in opposite directions. I've regretted that ever since."

I nodded.

"I spent the past year and a half year trying to forget you; well, trying to forget how much I loved you. But the honest truth is I've loved you since I met you, and I still do. I can't just walk away from this another time. I felt like I had to find you and try to get you back into my life."

I remained silent, letting him spew it all out. Maybe I wouldn't have to go through this again if I just let him say it all now.

"I ran into Charlotte Becker, you remember her? She had heard through the grapevine that you were summering in Oxford. At first I didn't think much about it, but every morning I woke up wondering where you were, how you were; wondering if you were safe. I called a local place just outside Oxford that does investigative type stuff and hired them to keep an eye on you. It wasn't supposed to scare you. They were supposed to be under the radar. Guess they weren't so good at that, huh? Maybe they should get out of the investigative business." He laughed.

As much as I hated to; I smiled. *Too true*, I thought.

"I didn't mean to frighten you. I really didn't. When I heard they'd made actual contact with you last week, I was pissed. And you know me when I get pissed." He waited for me respond, but I only shrugged and nodded.

"I decided I had to just fly over here and make amends. Oh, and fire them, obviously!" His smile was warm and full of humor. He could be so charming.

Luke sat back and tipped his chair on its back legs for a few seconds. When he pushed forward again, his face scrunched into a soulful, tearful demeanor. "Oh, my God, Amy. Why did we meet in the first place? I've asked myself that so many times."

"I know, Luke," I finally spoke. "I've asked myself that a million times too. Not sure there's an answer, except we did."

"I still believe we're supposed to be together, Amy. We've been apart several times for almost this long, and we always managed to put it back together. Why can't we do that now?" His eyes pleaded with me to agree.

"But that's the problem, Luke. We've done it too many times. It doesn't work. Surely we've learned that by now. It just won't work." I hoped I sounded more certain than I felt.

"I disagree." He shook his head adamantly. "I've grown up this past year. We're both older and wiser; at least I am. I want to make this work, and I will make changes—any changes you need to take me back. I love you, Amy Crawford, and I'm not taking no for an answer."

His words were tiring me out. I was already exhausted from not sleeping and from putting in a full day of seminars and discussions. Now he was sending me over the edge of fatigue into a chasm of exhaustion.

"Oh, Luke," I said. "I've got to get some sleep. I didn't sleep all night. Walk me to the bus stop just past George, and we can talk later or meet again tomorrow. I'm here for a few more days."

"OK, I can live with that," he said. I gathered my belongings, and we walked past the other diners and out the side door. Luke put his hands into both pockets. I walked briskly, but he kept pace with me.

"I like the place where you're staying," he said.

I thanked him. "It has its problems, but it's been a good location."

At least we could still make small talk, I thought.

At the stop, I told him good-bye and reached for his hand as if to shake it. Instead, he pulled me by my hand and into a non-passionate embrace. His long-sleeved cotton t-shirt gave off a sweet smell of maleness, and I felt his heart pounding against my ear. He released me as quickly as he had pulled me in; smiled warmly and said, "Tomorrow."

I nodded and entered the bus as it pulled to a stop. If I waited one more minute … I quickly tapped my card against the reader and raced to the rear of the bus.

As soon as I walked into the apartment, I realized I hadn't called Roger. I'd take a quick shower, a short nap and call to see if he wanted to meet for dinner.

Next thing I heard was the door-bell. I picked up my cell phone to check the time. 6:30. My God. I had slipped on a robe after my shower and apparently slept for over an hour. It had to be Roger.

"I'll be right there," I called loudly. I pulled a white cotton T-shirt over my head and zipped into a pair of jeans lying on a chair by the bed.

I fingered my hair into some curls as I raced through the kitchen to the door.

"Amy," Roger said. He looked frantic and worried. "Where the hell have you been? I've called and called." He closed the door behind him.

"Oh, Roger," I said. I put my arms around his neck and unexpectedly sobbed.

He held me tightly, stroking my hair, then my back, then whispering against my neck and into my ear, "It's OK; it's OK."

As I calmed myself, I wondered how I'd tell him. We walked into the living room, sat beside each other on the sofa, and I began.

"So he flew all the way over here to see you without even calling first?" His voice sounded accusative, and I bristled a little at his tone.

"Well, people *do* do those things, you know," I said, anger seeping into my words.

"I guess," he said. "I don't know. Seems a bit rash to me, but whatever …."

"I guess it was; I agree," I said. "I didn't appreciate that either."

"So what now?" he said.

"Well, I'm going to meet with him one more time tomorrow just to hear him out. I leave in three days for the states. I assume he's leaving earlier than that."

"That's not quite what I meant," he said.

"Oh … you mean 'us'?"

"Yeah, I meant 'us'. Does this change anything—his coming here?"

"Does it have to change anything?" I asked.

He shook his head and gave an exasperated sigh. "Amy, look; if he still means something to you, I understand. We can take some time apart. When you come back ... if you come back ... we can see where things stand. I'm OK with that."

"You're OK with that?" I said. "You're OK with just saying good-bye and letting me go off with some other guy?" I regretted the words as the last one flew out of my mouth. Shit! That would put any guy on edge, even a good guy like Roger.

"I didn't mean it like that," I said.

"Yes, you did," Roger said. And then he laughed. "What you mean is— am I not going to get out my suit of armor and my sword and fight for you? Admit it."

"I did not mean that," I said. "I just meant are you giving up so easily? Do you not want me to come back? Do you not want us to explore this relationship?"

"I do want you to come back, and I do want to explore this further, but I also know that past relationships rekindle sometimes, and I won't stand in your way. I want you to be certain about Luke, before we become certain about us."

I hated it when men made perfect sense. It was so damned rare. But he was right; of course he was right.

I sat back against the sofa cushions and put my feet up on the ottoman. "Can we have some wine and just sit here?" I said.

He gave a half laugh. That's what I liked—maybe loved—about Roger. He was so damned easy going and amenable. Everything, literally everything, Luke was not!

After two glasses of wine, Roger put his arms around me and kissed me. "I care about you, Amy Crawford; you know that, don't you? I may even love you. But I also have to make sure you are truly done with this guy before I can commit to moving any faster than friendship."

Friendship? I nearly gagged. And then I said it, "Friendship? I think we're well past friendship, aren't we?"

He smiled and put his right hand on my thigh. "Well, yes, I guess we are. But we can back off into friendship for a while and give you the time you need."

"I don't want to be given permission to get back with my ex." Even I was surprised at my honesty, and Roger looked downright dumbfounded.

"Well, I'm sorry, my dear; it isn't that I don't give a damn," He laughed at his take on Rhett Butler's quote. "But I'm trying to be realistic and sensible. Two of my best qualities, I think," he teased.

"Yes, they definitely are," I agreed.

I held my wine glass to his and clinked. "To us."

"He held his glass higher and repeated, "To us. To a future us."

It was late, and neither of us was going to initiate anything physical, so at 10:00 I walked him to the door and kissed him good-night.

"Can we have dinner tomorrow night?" I asked. "I feel like it's been days since I've seen you."

"Sure," he said. "Pick you up at seven, and we'll get out of Oxford. I'll choose a place that I know you'll like."

I smiled and hugged him one more time. "You're the best," I said.

"I know," he said softly, "I am. Remember that, will you?"

I fell into bed shortly after Roger left and was comatose for the next nine hours.

Connie Wesala

Chapter 27

Just as I regained consciousness, I remembered I had to see Luke again today. When was I going to do that with classes? I suddenly resented his intrusion into my life. I mean, my God, could he not have waited till I got back home? I felt like killing him.

I dragged myself out of bed, dressed carefully and made sure my make-up was perfect. After yesterday, I felt I owed it to myself and everyone else. A crisp white cotton shirt and blue jeans, black heels, and a new cardigan I'd treated myself to at Debenham's department store last week. I chose my diamond stud earrings and a silver necklace the kids had given me last Mother's Day. "J'dore," it said in script lettering. I loved it. We had been to France together on two separate trips, and I looked forward to doing it again. My life was so damned full. Why did I need either of these men? To reconfirm that, I dialed Jennifer's number as I walked toward the bus stop. She answered on the third ring.

"Amy," she squealed. "How good to hear from you. When will you be home? In two days?" I couldn't stop her mid-sentence, so I waited till she took a breath.

"Jenn, I'm sort of racing to class, but I had to talk to you. You won't believe who just showed up here out of the blue … unannounced? Luke." No reason to play the guessing game. "I mean, isn't that just unbelievable? I'm so mad at him for ruining my last few days here. How dare he just show up without calling? Oh, and he had hired the two stalkers—well, the P.I.'s that is."

Now she was the one letting me take a breath.

"Oh, my God," she finally said. "Amy, that's sort of romantic, right? I mean … don't you think?"

"Romantic? Please!" I said. "Audacious maybe; thoughtless maybe, but romantic?"

"Yes, romantic. Come on, Amy; you are still hetero aren't you?" she teased. "What woman wouldn't want a man flying across the ocean to reclaim the woman he loves?"

"Seriously?" I said. "You're taking that approach? I can't believe you, Jennifer. You hate the man. Oh, my God. I can't believe what I'm hearing. He's totally messing things up with me and Roger. I don't need this, Jenn." Anger seeded into my words, and I hated that. Jennifer wasn't the one I was mad at.

"I'm sorry," I said. "I'm just on edge, and honestly it is awkward and horrible timing."

"I get it," she said. "That part I do get. But Luke must really love you, Amy. He is not a man who would do that sort of thing. You have to admit *that*. Luke's the type to force you to come running to him; not the other way around. He has to be serious."

"My bus is here," I said. "I have to go. But I'll call you tonight, OK? I still need to talk this through."

"I'll be here," she said. "Take it slow and relax. Nothing has to be decided today except enjoying your last couple of days in jolly old England."

I laughed. "I love you, Jennifer; thanks for that."

I saw Shannon as she headed into the lecture hall and called to her. "Shannon, wait up."

"Hi! You look better this morning. Rest or romance?" she teased.

"Rest," I said, "And boy did I need it."

She laughed, then glanced at her watch. "We'd better move."

As I sat through the morning session, I felt myself glowing. Here I was sitting in a lecture hall with Oxford scholars: thinking, discussing, and debating. Me, a little girl from small town America, at one of the world's more prestigious universities. Working on my second novel which was coming along really well at the moment. Hired to teach classes in the fall while I completed it. My God, could any woman want more? Travel with my kids. My friends, especially Jennifer. I loved my life at this very moment. I needed nothing more and no one else. I was suddenly certain of my future. I was staring it in the face.

"Dean Montrose," I said as I approached her in the breezeway between buildings.

"Amy, how good to see you," she said. "Haven't changed your mind, have you? Please tell me you haven't."

"No, I haven't; not at all." I smiled warmly, and I wanted to give her a hug but Oxford scholars didn't do that sort of thing. Instead I put my hand out to shake hers. "I'll probably see you once more before I leave, but I just wanted to say thank you again, and I can't wait to see you in a couple of months."

She started to leave but turned back. "Can't tell you how pleased I am; we'll have some swimmingly good times this year."

Swimmingly. I had to laugh. Yes, I thought. That describes it. Life is just swimmingly wonderful. And neither Luke nor Roger was going to change that one bit.

I had two emails when I left campus that afternoon. Both of my children had offered to pick me up at the airport when I arrived at midnight on Saturday. I wrote each of them and said, "Come together. Can't wait to see you both. Have news." That would temper it a little; they'd be expecting something.

I called Luke right after that and said I would meet him at a pub where Roger and I had drinks so often. It might be fun to see him in the same environment and do a compare and contrast. I was feeling so lighthearted, I thought I might fly away like an untethered kite.

I ordered two light ales and took a seat close to the window to watch for him. It wasn't far from where he was staying. It wouldn't take him long. I knew what I needed to say and would make it short and sweet.

When he walked in, a memory floated in with him. Crisp white cotton long-sleeved dress shirt, sleeves rolled up; expensive watch on his left arm; silver cross on a chain peeking from the V. Jeans with a wide leather belt and cowboy boots. If he'd had a Stetson, he'd have been a British cowboy. I loved him in that outfit. And damn him, he knew it. He wasn't going to make this easy.

He pecked me on the cheek and slipped something out of his left pocket. A tiny something wrapped in tissue and tied with a string. "Fancy wrapping," he joked.

"Oh, Luke, you didn't have to do that." The butterflies flew from his eyes into my heart once again. Damn fluttering insects.

He sat across from me after placing it on the table. "Thanks for the beer … open it." He pointed to the small package.

I picked it up; light, almost weightless. I glared at him, but he knew it wasn't sincere. I untied the string and carefully laid it aside, taking my time to pull back the first layer of tissue. I gasped. And then tears filled my eyes as a lump the size of a golf ball settled in my throat. "Oh, Luke, you remembered."

Four years ago at Christmas, I had seen a necklace that I wanted. It was unusual. Made of glass with the colors melting into each other producing geometric shapes. It was curved like a flower petal with one end coming to a tip. A tulip—that's what it reminded me of. Each necklace was individual, and I had admired one with purples and reds. He had stopped by my house on his way home to Texas to spend Christmas with his mama. And just like today, he had simply wrapped a Kleenex around it and tied a piece of yarn as a bow. "Don't make too much of this," he had said.

"You remembered," I had said gently that day. "Thank you so much." And I had put it on and swore I'd never take it off. That year we broke up in February. In April as I swiped a bit of lipstick on my lips in the college bathroom, preparing for the very first reading of my fiction, I felt the clasp give as if it hadn't caught clear through the silver hoop. I grasped for it as it slid out of my hands and shattered on the tile floor.

When we got back together later that spring, I told him what had happened and how bad I felt. His remark, off-handed as usual, had been, "An omen obviously." An omen that we weren't meant to be? An omen that nothing lasts? I was never sure what he had meant.

In front of me now, glistening in the midst of the Kleenex tissue, was one almost identical. The coloration was just a little different—more purples and blues, less red, but individual and beautiful in its own way. How had he remembered that? Five, maybe six years ago?

It was hung on a black velvet cord with a silver clasp, and I didn't dare pick it up. My hands were shaking too bad to trust not dropping it to the floor, and I didn't want to see it shatter again. I couldn't breathe as I looked into his deep velvet eyes. "Oh, Luke, how did you remember that?"

He picked it up and walked behind me, placing the lovely amulet at my neck and attaching the clasp underneath my hairline. He sort of patted my neck and slid his hands down my back as he finished. I felt the warmth from his hands, and I suddenly wanted them all over me. His smell overpowered the ale. His large hands felt firm and sure. His lips called for mine. As he slid onto the wooden bar stool and asked if I wanted to eat something, I saw his lips moving but I heard nothing.

I blinked. "What?" I asked.

"Do you want to share some fish and chips?"

I knew I was supposed to be having dinner with Roger, but it was nearly five o'clock. "Sure," I said. The world had shifted slightly in the last two minutes. I was on a fault line, straddled with one foot on each side as it split between me.

"Ketchup?" he asked.

"Even in England," I said. "Well, they call it tomato sauce, but ..."

He laughed. "I like fish and chips. I think I've had them like five times already, and I've been here three days."

"You exaggerate, but I know what you mean. And cheap." I added.

"My kind of food, as you'll recall. Hamburgers, pizza, calzones and now fish and chips."

"You were always a simple man," I said.

"I've always told you that; in more ways than one, too."

I laughed out loud. "Well, I won't debate that one." We had somehow slipped into a level of comfort that I hadn't thought possible.

"Remember Papa's Pizzaria?"

"How could I forget? You took me there every danged Friday night."

"Not true ... but close."

"Do you also remember the day we had that huge fight over the damned pizza?" I said.

"Remind me."

"Oh, Luke, come on. We agreed to meet; you got there way earlier and called to say you were ordering even though I was nowhere close to the place. The only thing I said was, 'order half without meat for me.'"

He was grinning from ear to ear. "Oops, I remember," he said. "I was already eating when you got there, and I was watching a football game behind your head."

"Yes, and more importantly, you had ordered a three meat pizza and didn't bother to have them half it for me. I was so damned furious with you; I think I ordered something else like a salad for myself. I don't recall."

His face turned serious. "I was an A-hole back then," he said.

I nodded but didn't verbally agree. He had been difficult, that's for sure.

"The chaos you always created is what did us in, Luke," I said. My tone had turned serious as well. "You enjoyed doing that so much, and I could never understand it. Why would you want to make people so angry at you?"

"I think I've figured some of that out," he said. He took my hand across the table. "It's a good way to create distance, isn't it?"

"Look, Luke," I said. "I don't see any way to get past the past—excuse the pun. I really don't."

"I do. I can see a way past it, but you have to give me some time to prove that," he said.

"I don't have that kind of time, Luke. I'm sorry. I haven't told you this yet, but I'm coming back to Oxford in the fall to spend a year teaching. I'm not going to be in Arizona to work anything out."

Disappointment settled firmly on his face. "I see," he managed, but his voice sounded choked. He took a moment to compose himself; took a deep breath, and I saw his shoulders rise and fall as he did so.

"I'm sorry, Luke."

"Me, too."

Then he grinned again. "Are you kidding me, you believed that bullshit? Honestly, Crawford! You think I won't win you back by then? Hell. That gives me two or three months. When are you coming home?"

"I leave for Phoenix day after tomorrow. I'll be home until end of August, but I have to be back here a week before the session begins. I don't think that leaves you nearly enough time to convince me we can make it work, Luke."

"I'm leaving tomorrow," he said.

I was surprised. "So quickly?"

"No reason to hang around here; plus that's when my return flight was scheduled."

"You spent thousands of dollars to come here for four days?" I was astonished. "You can't afford the fish and chips."

"See … you're worth it. I told you. I love you, Amy. I'd do anything for you; spend any amount of money on you. We are going to make this work. And if you're here for a year; I'll come visit, and you'll come visit your kids and me. And a year will fly by."

"Oh, my lord, Luke. You are impossible." I fingered the velvet around my neck and then touched the lovely glass medallion one more time.

"I have to be somewhere at seven," I said. "I need to get back to the apartment to change."

He stood and helped me down from the high bar stool. He took me in his arms right in the middle of the pub and kissed me softly and deeply. "I'll

Connie Wesala

see you back home," he whispered in my ear.

Tears formed in my eyes, and I found myself wishing we had another week here, alone, in England. We could go to London together—maybe Stratford. We could have so much fun. Part of me wanted to say, "Let's stay." But I knew better. And Roger would be waiting outside my apartment if I didn't leave now. I slid from Luke's arms and kissed him on the cheek. "I'll see you back home," I said. And suddenly I knew I meant it. Luke's eyes told me he knew it too.

Chapter 28

On the bus back to the apartment, I texted Roger that I was running about ten minutes late. He texted back, "c u then! can't wait!"

I shook my head. Shit!

I jumped into the shower, toweled off quickly and pulled on jean capris and my white tank and a royal blue loose-knit sweater. I wished my hair was long enough to pull into a pony tail, but I simply wet it and pulled it behind my ears. I heard the doorbell, grabbed my purse and raced to the door. Roger stood there smelling of soap and water and a lovely scent I'd noticed several times in the past month. He needed a haircut, but the extra length made him even sexier.

In his left hand was a paper-wrapped bundle of gerbera daisies—my favorite. When had I told him about that, I wondered?

"Oh, they're beautiful," I said as he handed the bouquet to me. "I'll put them in water, and then we can head out."

Roger glanced around the apartment. I noticed his eyes taking in every inch. "So ... how did your meeting go with whatshisname?"

"How about we talk about it over dinner?" I said.

He pursed his lips, and I thought he was going to confront me; instead he just muttered, "Humph."

I placed the glass water pitcher on the dining table. I hadn't found a vase. "They are so beautiful," I said again. "Thank you so much." I reached up and put my arms around him and kissed his nose. "Oh, Roger," I whispered into his ear. "I care so much about you."

He pulled back with a questioning look. After a moment, he said, "Me too. Let's forget dinner." He grinned impishly.

I punched him in the gut. "No way, buster; you have to feed me first." After eating with Luke less than an hour ago, I wasn't sure if I could eat a bite, but I'd try.

Roger eased the car into traffic, veered sharply left at the corner and headed out of the city limits. I recognized the road from our many excursions.

"Where are we going?" I asked.

"It's a surprise," he said as he took my left hand and squeezed.

I sat back and closed my eyes, letting the wind through the open window sweep over me. It was relaxing, and I began to unwind from the stress of Luke's arrival. If I pretended, I could imagine him back in the states instead of here in Oxford, and I could slip into my current life with Roger with no complications.

But life was always complicated. It was messy and stinky and uncomfortable. I wasn't going to get through mine without difficult decisions.

When I opened my eyes, I watched Roger focus on the road, shift through the round-abouts and hum along to the radio. So easy, I thought. He is so uncomplicated and easy. Why would I ever let Luke mess this up with his chaos and confusion? I couldn't.

I slid my left arm over his shoulder and touched the back of his neck where his hair curled at the nape. I ran my fingers along his temple, and then I touched his ear sensuously.

"Hey," he said, but it was a teasing tone. "I'm trying to drive here." He laughed. "You keep doing that, and we'll be finding an inn instead of a restaurant."

I pretended to like that idea by raising my eyebrows and blowing him a kiss. "OK, I'll stop."

Within twenty minutes I knew where we were headed. We were just a few minutes away from Lower Slaughter and the ice cream place where we'd stopped on one of our first drives through the Cotswolds. At the only stop sign on the one street into town, he pulled the car into a parallel parking spot and pointed to a pub just beyond. "Great fish and chips," he said. "And it *is* Friday!"

Fish and chips. As if I hadn't eaten a basketful with Luke just two hours ago. My stomach churned. I'd definitely need to wash it down with more ale. But I smiled. "Sounds great!"

When we walked into the pub, an aproned bartender yelled out, "Roger Dodger, how the hell are you?" He came from behind the high intricately carved wood bar and threw his arms around Roger. The two men pounded each other's backs and cursed profusely. I'd never heard Roger curse in the month I'd known him. I couldn't help but grin at the two men.

"Amy." Roger turned to me and pulled me toward him. "Bobby Flannery. Bobby … Amy Crawford."

"Nice to meetcha', ma'am," Bobby said, and he reached out to shake my extended hand. He quickly said, "Hey, I'll grab you a couple of pints, mate. Find a table; dinner on me," he said.

Roger started to argue, but Bobby shoved him hard. "I said, it's on me, damn it. Can't a bloke buy a friend dinner once every year or two? It's the only benefit of owning this dump." He walked back behind the bar, and Roger pointed to a table off to our right that looked out onto the street.

I climbed up onto the tall bar stool while Roger met Bobby half-way and brought our beers to the table. "Old friend?" I offered.

"How'd you guess?" he teased. "Yeah, old friend of ours. Melissa and me, that is."

I nodded. Well, sure—of course.

"Actually Bobby and I go way back to primary school. He used to live in Cambridge till his parents moved away in about seventh or eighth grade. But we kept in touch, and in high school we started to go out bar hopping together. We'd meet half-way which is pretty near here actually."

His eyes look sad. "Bobby had to drop out of school after junior year. His dad suddenly died of a heart attack, and being the eldest, Bobby had to provide for the family. He worked here for years until he saved up enough to buy the pub."

"Hard worker," I said. "Admirable."

Roger looked like he'd withdrawn; I almost felt him fade from me and from the present. He sat silently for some time. I sipped my beer and people watched, allowing him time to think or grieve or whatever he was feeling.

I thought about the few friends I still kept in contact with—very few. One really. A friend since we were five years old. She still lived in my home state, so we rarely saw each other. I needed to change that, I thought.

I felt Roger touch my hand and turned back to find him smiling into my eyes. "What?"

He leaned forward and kissed me on the lips. Not sensual. Just a wonderful happy friendly kiss. "What's that for?" I asked. "Not that I didn't enjoy it."

"Life passes so quickly," he said. "So damned fast."

I knew that seeing Bobby had brought back memories—both good and bad and also the realization that time marches on. Both of the men looked their age. Roger had aged well with money and status to help him. Bobby was hardened and weathered with ragged edges.

I touched Roger's cheek and let my fingers run along his lips. He looked into my eyes without saying a word. The words between us didn't need a voice. Was I in love with this man?

Bobby sent one of the waiters over with our baskets of fish and chips and a second pint of ale for each of us. He waved from the bar. Roger nodded our appreciation.

Roger was kind enough to keep his questions unspoken for some time. We were almost finished with our meal when he licked the fingers of his right hand; then wiped them with his napkin. He held his finger up and caught Bobby's eye. Another round of beers. We were staying awhile longer.

I didn't wait for him to ask again. I pushed my plate forward out of the way and placed my mug in front of me. "It's complicated," I said. I didn't bother with prefacing my remarks.

He nodded and drank the last drops of his pint. He wasn't going to make this easy. He sat stone still and waited. Not even a "yes, it is." Anything would make me less tense.

Tears welled in my eyes before I could stop them. I would not cry. I took a deep breath and wiped my mouth with my napkin one more time.

"Roger, I didn't ask him to come here. I haven't seen him in over a year. I did not cause this."

"And why is that important, Amy? Why would I think you caused this? But now that you've brought it up, did you? Did you invite him?"

"No," I insisted. "No, of course not. I told you; it was a total shock. Roger, let me finish this, OK?"

He threw up his hands. "Fine."

I looked down for a moment to collect my thoughts. "I heard him out, like I agreed. He wants to get back together, but I told him it wouldn't work. He's headed home tomorrow. Look, Roger, this changes nothing between you and me—nothing." As schizoid as that sounded, I believed it.

"I believe you," he said. "So what now?" I could tell from his tone that he wasn't sure he wanted me to answer.

"Now? Nothing. I told him to go home, and he's leaving."

"Just like that?" he said. "Seriously? Are you that naïve?"

"What do you mean?"

"A man doesn't fly across the ocean to see someone; doesn't pay to have someone followed if he doesn't love her. Amy, really?"

"Whether or not he loves me doesn't matter. It's how I feel about him that matters. And I've told him to go home."

"So what's complicated?" he asked. "Just wondering ... since you used that word."

Yeah, Amy, I thought, *what's complicated?* I bit my upper lip and considered.

"I just meant. His showing up and my feelings for you and this job offer and not having told my kids about leaving them for a year. It's all freaking complicated, Roger. It's complicated!" I looked around to see if I was drawing attention with my volume. No one seemed to be aware.

I put my elbows on the table and formed a church steeple with my two hands, blew out a deep breath onto my fingers and felt the tears wash down my cheeks.

Roger reached for my hands, unfolded them and kept one in his grip. He sighed. "I'm sorry. I'm not making this easy, am I? But I need to know if you're considering taking him back, Amy. Don't lead me on, OK?"

I shook my head. "I'd never do that. If I knew I wanted to be with Luke, I would tell you immediately. But I don't, Roger. I do not want Luke back in my life. He's ... well, he's just too much."

Roger looked thoughtful for a few seconds. "Amy, I told you recently that I think I'm falling in love with you. I was excited when you said you were coming back to teach in the fall. The one thing I haven't told you is that I've decided to take the teaching position here too. The offer was a good one, and I love to teach. And having you here was just going to be icing on the cake. And then ... this."

"You've decided to stay in Oxford?" I said. "Really?" I felt the lightness of joy in my gut. "Oh, Roger, that's great! I'm so glad."

I leaned forward and tempted him to do the same. He finally gave in and met me half way and kissed me gently. "Let's get out of here," he said. "I'll say good-bye to Bobby. Be back in a sec."

"I need to use the ladies room anyway," I said.

I walked toward the hallway that led to the bathrooms. He was staying. Was I part of that decision? I wondered. We had said we wouldn't allow that, but could I honestly say he hadn't been a factor in my own decision to stay? Complicated didn't begin to cover what I was feeling. *Luke, God damn you!* I thought.

Bobby was shaking Roger's hand as I walked up to the men. I smiled and shook Bobby's hand again. "Thank you so much; it was delicious—best I've had so far." I smiled as warmly as I could. Some small piece of me felt it was important for Bobby to like me. *How well did he know Melissa? After all those years?* Probably quite well. I wondered if he was thinking I seemed very normal after Melissa. I wondered if he'd be happy for Roger. I wondered why I was wondering.

We drove home in silence all the way back to Oxford. The radio played softly in the background; Roger had rolled all the windows down, and the cool moist air hit me in the face and made my hair straight from the dampness. It felt so good. No Arizona heat. It would be 95 degrees at ten o'clock at night with no break until end of October.

The sky was beginning to darken and sliding into night. Stars were popping out in the deep navy expanse. We were miles from civilization on a two-lane road winding through some of the country's most beautiful scenery. I felt like someone had picked me up and dropped me into an English novel—Jane Austen perhaps. Or maybe Thomas Hardy. I could definitely be compared to Bathsheba Everdene who had three men in love with her but wanted to remain single and independent until she fell for the bad boy.

As we entered the last round-about and took the main highway back to the city, I turned up the radio and twisted the dial. I found one of the many stations playing '70's American music and began to let my arms and hands dance to the beat. Roger laughed out loud. He turned it even higher and joined me by singing loudly. We swayed our shoulders and pretended to rock out all the way back to the apartment. As he approached the house, he turned the radio down and patted my leg. I knew he was staying the night. I wasn't going to ask; I wasn't going to comment. No need to talk about this.

I slipped into the bedroom while Roger turned on the TV. When I came out, I turned off the light and joined him on the sofa. I had on my pink and white striped satin robe with nothing beneath. I pressed myself into an embrace, and his hands went directly underneath the fabric as he gripped my behind and pulled me to him. I eagerly responded to his touch and unbuttoned his jeans and slid them off his hips.

Tomorrow was Friday—no classes; just a half day of final review and good-bye's. On Sunday I'd be on a plane back to the states; back to family and friends and a life I barely remembered. But I was here now, and I didn't want to be anywhere else.

Chapter 29

Around seven o'clock the next morning we climbed out of bed and showered together; soaping each other from head to toe. Before I could argue, he took me and I exploded into stars. He tipped my head up to his eyes. "I love you, Amy Crawford." It was like he was claiming me, I realized. And inside, I was saying "I am yours."

He took the car to get orange juice and bread while I brewed coffee. Just after he left, I looked at my cell. Two emails from the kids; one text from Luke that read, "On my way to airport. Will see you in a few days. I love you." I bent forward and shook my head no. "No," I cried out.

I was on campus at 8:30 and caught up with Shannon as she entered the lecture hall where we'd spent so many days together. It seemed much longer than five weeks. Dean Montrose collected our evaluations and put in a plug for next summer's seminar.

I waved to Miriam across the crowded room. It seemed like yesterday that I'd felt so old and out of touch with the young people and so concerned that I would never fit in. We rushed around after dismissal gathering last minute information from each other. Jason and several of the younger students came up to wish me well next year. And I said good-bye to Tom one last time before heading back to the apartment.

Roger had spent the morning leisurely reading the London Times and was busy doing the cross word puzzle when I arrived. We sat together on the sofa, sipping tea and tearing apart each layer of our croissants which we fed each other. Heaven had slipped into my life. When Roger figured out an eight letter word for "phylum of animals with pores" without thinking twice, I realized how smart and kind and perfect he was. "I could see myself doing this for a very long time." I said it aloud without thinking first. When I gasped, he looked up and laughed. "It's OK; I'm thinking the same thing."

It rained off and on; then cleared by 4:00. Roger pulled out the old charcoal grill half hidden in the bushes behind the patio. "I'll bring the meal and be back around 6:30." He kissed me on the tip of the nose and headed out.

As soon as he left, I began to pack. I pulled my suitcase from the closet and assessed the pile of clothes on the bed. I had bought a few souvenirs and gifts along the way, but I had no idea it would add up to what I saw before me. *Eeeks*, I thought. Here I go again, and I didn't have Jennifer to sit on the suitcase. I was already transitioning back into my old life. "Can't wait to see you," I texted her. I was going home, and it felt good.

Around six-thirty, Roger called and said he'd be over in ten. I couldn't wait to see him. He'd been gone a few hours, and I missed him already. When he walked through the door loaded with grocery bags, I hugged him and wouldn't let go.

"Amy," he said, "I'm going to drop everything." He was laughing as he said it.

"I know, but I can't help it." I hugged him one more time and then took one of the bags.

We made dinner together; moving to and fro from counter to fridge to stove.

"We make a pretty good dance team," he said. "Maybe we should go on that show you Americans have."

"Dancing with the Stars?" I said.

"Yeah, that one, what do you think?"

"I think we'd better practice some more." I moved backward and purposely bumped him. He nearly dropped the salad bowl but caught it just in time.

"Oh, yeah? Well ..." He took two steps forward and shoved my right hand away from the spatula I was reaching for. I grabbed it and hit him hard on the butt. Before we knew it we were playing swordplay with a spatula and a pair of tongs. We laughed till we cried.

Roger stepped out to the turn the steaks, and I tried to stop laughing. I had never had fun like this with a man before. With Luke it was always so serious. Once in a great while I could get him to laugh with my kitchen antics, but it was rare. He preferred drama over comedy. I liked both in movies and television; in life, not so much. I needed more laughter at my age. Had it only been a day since Luke had given me the necklace and I had wanted him back? I couldn't even keep up with my roller coaster emotions.

That night, Roger sat on my large suitcase while I zipped it closed.

"I hope it doesn't spring open half-way there," he teased.

"Well, if it does; I'll just throw half of it out."

"Yeah, right." He scrunched his nose and smiled. Then I saw sadness draw across his eyes like a curtain.

"You OK?" I asked.

"Just missing you already," he said.

We sat on the couch quietly with my head on his shoulder but no other physical contact. We were sated from the weekend plus we didn't need another reminder that it would be awhile.

"I love you," he said. He looked at his watch. "I'd better let you get some sleep. Tomorrow will be hectic. I'll pick you up at eleven. Your bus is at 11:30, right?"

I nodded.

"Plenty of time. It's five minutes from here."

I didn't need to be reminded. How many times had I raced to Gloucester Green or to the train station in the past month?

We said good-night, and I went to bed early only to lay there awake for another hour. I had stopped in earlier to finalize my payment with Mary Madden. I had even walked to the corner to say good-bye to the owner of the little market. Nothing much left to do except turn in the keys as we left in the morning. I turned on my side and watched the time on my cell phone roll forward. It finally put me to sleep.

Roger was right on time and took my suitcase and carry-on to the car while I gave Mary the key and told her thanks and good-bye. "If you decide you want the apartment for fall, let me know," she said. "Not rented yet."

I agreed to let her know and hopped into the passenger seat and waved a final good-bye. The trees along the street appeared to be changing to their fall colors. It seemed too early, but I wondered how soon they did turn and drop? So much I still did not know about England. But I'd be here to watch it happen, I reminded myself.

I spent the drive rummaging through my bag, patting my tickets and finding my passport. I looked at Roger, and found him watching me. "I'm not good at good-bye," I said. "Sorry."

He took my hand. "Me either, so let's just say, see you in a few weeks."

"Good idea," I said. And so ten minutes later, that's what we did.

"See you in a few weeks," he said, and he kissed me softly and pulled me closer to him.

Connie Wesala

"Mmm, maybe I should just stay," I said and then laughed.

"No argument here," he said. "You know that."

"I'll call you when I get there. In about 20 hours. Ugh."

I sighed and pulled out of his arms. If I didn't board the bus now, I wasn't sure I could. I turned and climbed the stairs, turned one last time to throw him a kiss, and found a seat half-way to the rear. I purposely sat on the side opposite from where he was standing. Tears welled and then rolled over the edge and onto my cheeks. I couldn't look at him; not one more time or I'd lose it. An hour later, I was on my way through customs and onto a plane back to Arizona.

Chapter 30

After a seventeen hour flight across the ocean, my plane was fifteen minutes early, but both of my kids were waiting at the gate. I had told them to pick me up outside baggage, but I should have known. "You guys," I said.

"Well, we figured you'd be so damned tired you wouldn't be able to even find your luggage," Sarah said and hugged me.

Chris put his arm around me and walked me toward the escalator and down to baggage claim. He found my suitcase some minutes later, and we were at my house in another half hour. "We'll let you get some rest," Sarah said, "but tomorrow I want to hear every single thing. I'll fix brunch."

The next day was July 4th. I didn't think I'd have the energy for fire-works so we planned a simple mid-day meal. I'd go home to bed, and they could celebrate if they wished.

"You got it," I said and hugged them both good-night. I went to the bedroom, petted the cat, found a clean nightgown in my dresser drawer and pulled back the covers. Nothing in these bags needed to come out tonight.

The next morning I pulled clothes out and threw them in piles by color on the bedroom floor. Everything would need to be washed. I found the kids' presents and tucked them into tissue and gift bags. I texted several friends that I was back but not back among the living just yet. They would understand jet lag.

I arrived at Sarah's house at the agreed-upon time and was met with champagne, flowers and more hugs. As usual, she had prepared a feast. Quiche, croissants, fresh fruit, mimosas and coffee. I groaned as I took the last bite. "I may not need to eat for a week," I said.

She laughed. "Well, or until dinner at least."

After she poured orange juice over my champagne, I held up my goblet to toast.

Chris clinked my glass; then all three together. It was now or never.

"Guys," I said, "I have some news."

I felt the air leave the room. "I'm not dying," I teased.

After I told them about the job offer, my acceptance and my plans to return in seven weeks, they remained silent. I felt like maybe I *was* dying after all. "Look ..." I began.

Sarah was the first to speak. "Wow, mom; you don't mess around when you tell news."

Chris looked sullen at best. "You didn't want to discuss this?" he said.

I knew I looked sheepish; I certainly felt that way. "Guys, I had to make a quick decision. It didn't seem right to ask you to jump into the middle of it when I'd have to make the final decision, you know?" I hoped I sounded logical.

"Wow," Sarah said again. She looked at her brother. "Hey, Bro ... this is a great opportunity for mom, you know?"

He nodded. She always had a way with him. Within a few minutes, they were planning our Christmas vacation. They would come to England instead of me coming home. I was thrilled.

Luke came to mind. Then Roger. I couldn't do that to them on top of the quick return to England. When could I tell them? I wasn't sure. And *I* thought disclosing the job would be the worst part. I knew better.

It took a week before I casually mentioned Roger and only because Sarah had asked about him. "So tell us about this guy you met," she said. There was no way to not answer, although I downplayed the relationship like a good mother of adult children.

It *had not* taken a week for Luke to show up, however. I had no sooner walked into the house after my brunch with the kids, than the doorbell rang. I was still jet-lagged and had no fight in me. I opened the door and stared him down.

He must have seen the glare in my eyes as he stepped backward slightly and sheepishly said, "May I come in?"

I opened the screen door and stepped aside to let him in. He hadn't seen the house I'd moved to after our break up. He looked around before walking further into the foyer.

"Nice," he said. "Very nice."

"Thanks," I said politely.

"It looks like you," he said as he looked closely at the framed pictures of Italy that lined the wall.

I stepped past him and led the way into the open living, breakfast, kitchen area. I pointed to the sofa. "Have a seat," I said. "Can I get you anything to drink?"

"No, no …" he said. "I won't stay but a minute. But I wanted to welcome you home and also ask if we could set a time to really talk. I know you're too tired so soon after the trip."

"You haven't been home much longer than I have."

He smiled. "Well, a few days and that's a lot of recovery time. You'll be fine in another day or so I'm sure."

I sighed. "Hope so; I'm still exhausted."

"How are the kids?" he asked.

We sounded so formal I wanted to throw up.

"Luke, look, I told you in Oxford and I'll tell you once more … this is not going to start up again. No way."

"Well, you did agree to hear me out, and I haven't really gotten that opportunity. Couldn't you reserve judgement just awhile longer before making that edict?" He seemed to tense up; he was used to getting his way.

At the moment, all I wanted was to climb into my pj's and into bed and die for another twelve or fifteen hours. I had to get back on U.S. time. So I gave in to get rid of him.

"OK," I said," I stood and indicated that he should do the same. "I'll meet you for dinner Thursday night. I will listen. But nothing is going to change, Luke, so don't get your hopes up at all."

He stood and followed me to the front door. I could tell him I'd had a change of heart later; right now, I just wanted him gone.

He opened the door for himself, started out the doorway and then turned back. He leaned forward and gave me a peck on the cheek. "Glad you're home," he whispered. "See you Thursday. I'll call with a time and place unless you want me to pick you up."

"No," I said quickly, "No; I'll meet you somewhere—just let me know where."

I turned the deadbolt, leaned my back against the door, and closed my eyes. The scent of him lingered and brushed my cheeks as I breathed him in. I groaned out loud and headed to the bedroom for what I hoped would be half the next day.

However, that was not to be. I had barely fluffed the pillow to fit my neck when my cell phone rang. I groaned and reached across the nightstand to retrieve it. As I glanced at the screen, I bolted upright and pressed the speaker button. "Roger," I said. I was suddenly wide awake. "Why are you calling instead of emailing?"

"Can't talk long but I wanted to hear your voice, not read a damned message."

I smiled and felt my heart flutter a beat. "That's very nice," I murmured. "Thanks."

"Miss you," he said.

"Me, too," I replied. "Are you at your apartment?" I wanted to picture him in a specific spot to make it more real.

"The apartment, but I'm headed over to campus in a few."

"I thought you were all finished," I said.

"Oh, yeah, everything is done. I'll walk graduation next week. No, I'm going over to meet the Dean about the job I was offered."

"Anything wrong?"

"No, I'm just going to clarify that I'm taking the position for one year. Don't want to commit beyond that."

"I see ....Does this have anything to do with us?" I wished I hadn't asked.

"Absolutely not. You are, as you said yourself, just icing on the cake. You haven't changed your mind about coming back, have you?"

"No, no ... I made a promise and I intend to keep it. Wow," I said, not able to think beyond that word. Wow.

"How was your flight back? You must be exhausted."

"The flight was fine; just long ... and yes, I am tired. In fact, just going back to bed for maybe the next twelve hours." I laughed.

Roger laughed also. "Well, I'll let you get to sleep then. I can't pay these international rates anyway. I'll email you after we hang up with some details."

"Please do, and I'll do the same when I'm back in the world. Oh, and Roger ..."

"Yes?"

"Maybe we can Skype this week if we can arrange a time. Wow," I repeated. "This will be a fun year, won't it?"

"Yes, it will," he said. "I'm looking forward to it."

"Me, too ... wow." I was suddenly aware of how many times I'd repeated the word, but it was how I felt. What an exciting adventure and someone to share it with. I was more than excited. It felt like karma; maybe even déjà vu.

"Get some sleep," he said. "Bye for now."

"Bye." I put the phone on mute and crawled under the covers. As tired as my body was, my mind was now wide awake with thoughts of a snowy night in Oxford, of standing in front of my classes that first day, of Christmas with my kids in England. It was magical. *How lucky can one person be?* I asked myself again.

When I woke at midnight, I read Roger's email and typed out a brief reply. It was already the next day in Oxford. "Let's Skype on Fri.—name a time."

Connie Wesala

Chapter 31

Thursday afternoon after my shower, I applied make-up and took time blow drying my hair. I put in my diamond stud earrings and fastened a silver necklace around my throat. Standing in the closet in bra and panties, I surveyed my racks of clothes. Nothing. How can I have a closet full of clothes and nothing to wear? I wondered. I finally settled on a pair of black capris and a designer pink and black crepe top I had gotten on sale a year ago. It was a soft look and made me feel feminine. Probably the very thing I should *not* be feeling while alone with Luke. But once I slipped it over my head and pulled my necklace onto the blouse, I liked what I saw.

He had texted me the name of a restaurant I knew by name, though as far as I could recall, we had never been there together. I walked into the restaurant at five o'clock on the dot. He was already seated in a booth. Always early; always the one to wait. He didn't believe in being on time. He raised his hand and slid out of the booth to greet me. I allowed a brief hug, then scooted across the leather seat, placed my purse by the wall and took a moment to settle in. When I glanced up, he was watching me intently. "What?" I said. I sounded like one of my kids when they found me observing them.

"Nothing," he said. Just then the waitress reached our table with a bottle of white wine and two glasses. She placed one in front of me and the other, along with the wine bottle, in front of Luke.

"I hope this is OK," he said. "I recall you prefer white wine."

"One glass would have been plenty, Luke; unless you plan on drinking a lot."

He smiled warmly. "Well, I may have to, huh?" He reached for the menu. "Shall we order?"

I quickly settled on chicken parmesan with bread sticks and a small salad; Luke ordered his usual. He had always teased me that Texas men only ate red meat. He ordered the small filet, and the waitress left us alone.

"OK if we talk now, or do you prefer to make small talk till after the meal?" he asked.

I tilted my head and gave him a look that said I could care less. Although inside, I did care more than I wanted to. Ever since he'd dropped by, I'd wondered what he would have to stay about our last break-up. Would he take ownership? Or would he blame me?

I leaned back against the cushion of the bench and lifted my wine, took a sip, and sat silently; giving him the cue to go on.

He took a big gulp of wine and refilled his glass. "Amy, I'm an A-hole; we both know that. Always have been I guess. I've spent a lot of time going over that last day, trying to dissect it to see how we got to that point so quickly. One minute we were sitting at the kitchen counter bar reading the paper and having coffee, and then you were on the sofa, and I was walking out the door." He shook his head. "I remember standing there waiting for you to speak, to yell, to do anything but what you did."

I nodded. The scene in my mind was clear. It was true. It had taken me less than a few seconds to push off the bar stool, cross the room and plop down on the sofa. And the silence between us seemed to last for ten or fifteen minutes though it was probably only a few. And then I had silently let him leave. But the words that rang in my head were his words, and I would never forget them as long as I lived. They were sharp-edged and honest. I wondered if he remembered.

So I asked. "Do you recall what you said just before I walked away?"

He looked down at his lap, picked up his wine glass and drank it half-way down. We would need the entire bottle if this continued, I thought.

He sighed as he looked up and into my eyes. He nodded. He couldn't say them, and I knew why. If he said them out loud; it would be like reliving the moment I stopped loving him. And he didn't want that. I didn't either. I'd rather not ever hear those words again.

Instead, he continued with the specifics of that day. "I sat there waiting for you to say something because I felt like an ass and because you always called me on the carpet in the past, and suddenly here you were silent as stone. You looked like stone as well," he said.

I had felt like stone as I recalled. When he had said, "I don't love you, Amy," my heart had turned to stone, and my body simply took the cue. There was nothing to say after that. I wasn't going to beg or plead or even acknowledge his words. I simply wanted to sit until he left, and I did.

"Amy," he said in a quiet voice, "I'm so sorry. What a horrible thing to say to a woman you love. What was wrong with me?" He stared into my eyes; his brown eyes piercing me once again.

"I don't know, Luke," I said. "What *is* wrong with you?" It was not an empty question, and I hoped he might shed some light; not that it would matter.

Just then the waitress arrived with our meals, and we waited until she had left before speaking again.

Luke reached across the table and took my right hand. He entwined our fingers and the warmth reached my gut. I didn't pull back as I thought I would. I waited until he let go on his own.

"I don't want to rehash all our previous discussions, Amy. You know me very well; you've seen me on my knees crying in your lap; you've listened to me talk about how I treat everyone around me – not just you. I guess I thought you'd always forgive me."

"Just because you were honest with me, Luke? You thought I'd always forgive you just because of that?"

It was true. Luke had always been honest. But he also could not change who he was, and that was the reason I finally left. Not because of who or what he was; not because of his faults. It was because he acknowledged it all and then never tried to change— not for me, not for his family, not for himself. He did not have the capacity to change and that's why that day, I sat silently until he left me one last time. I hadn't wanted to rage or cry or talk. I had simply wanted him gone. Just as I wanted him gone now.

I had averted my gaze after posing the question. Now I looked up and saw wetness muddying his deep brown eyes. Some men softened and felt emotions; Luke did not. So I spoke from the heart. "I can see this is as painful for you as it is for me, Luke. We don't have to do this."

He shook his head. "No, no, I do. I need to talk about this."

I picked up my fork and pushed my salad around, avoiding his eyes. I couldn't help but wonder what was to be gained by going over the most painful moments in our eight-year relationship. How could he possibly think that the words "I don't love you" could ever be made right?

I cut into my chicken breast and took a bite, taking a moment to compose myself. It seemed to help. I heard Luke's silverware clink against his plate and heard the scrape of his steak knife. When I looked back up, he had taken a bite and was looking past me at a spot above my head. It felt too familiar.

How often had I cursed myself for not taking the opposite seat? He just did it so naturally. It pissed me off then, and even now I felt an anger build. There was no television behind me this time; his habit was simply to zone out which was what he was doing now. I ate in silence.

Suddenly I heard the sharpness of metal as it fell onto the table, and I looked up to see that he had forcefully slammed his knife and fork onto the table top. "I love you, Amy. I want you back. I don't know what else to say. I was an idiot. I did everything wrong. I abused you. I was unkind. But I *have* changed. I have no idea how I will prove to you that I've changed, but I have."

Then he went quiet and wiped his mouth with his napkin. He made no move to pick up his silverware and begin to eat. He simply sat and stared at me, tears in his eyes, mouth quivering—obvious pain. And shame, I thought. He was truly feeling ashamed. I had never seen that in all our years together.

Sure, as he said, he would occasionally break down and cry on my bosom about his behavior and how badly he wanted to change. I had finally believed him when he said he could not. Was I to believe him now?

I was the one to reach out. I rubbed the back of his hand at first; then pulled my fingers through his and held tight. "Oh, Luke," I sobbed.

The noisy room seemed to have fallen silent. Later I would realize I had simply slipped into another dimension. I wanted nothing more than to believe him and to trust, but I didn't.

"I love you, too," I said. "I've loved you since we first met. I will always love you. But loving someone and being with them are two totally different things."

I let go of his hand and pulled back. I was not hungry, and when the waitress returned to ask how we were doing, I asked for a take-out container and so did Luke.

"May I interest you in some dessert?" she asked. I almost laughed. Neither of us had taken more than two bites of our meals.

"No, but I'll have coffee," I said and wiped my lips. As she walked away, I excused myself to go the bathroom. We both needed some space.

When I returned, two cups of steaming coffee sat on the table, and our take-out boxes were pushed to the side. He stood as I reached the table and waited for me to be seated. Always the gentleman. He knew how to behave, and then suddenly a monster would emerge like Jekyll … or was it Hyde?

I took a sip of my coffee, and so did he. He licked his lips; added more cream and stirred it. "I haven't done such a good job tonight, huh?"

"I wouldn't say that," I replied. "I don't know exactly what either of us expected, I guess."

"I don't know what to say except to ask you to give me another chance. If you love me; and you say you do, isn't it worth trying again? Isn't it worth at least allowing me to prove myself one way or the other? I'll either be able to be a better person or I won't."

"Tell me one thing," I said. "What have you done in order to make this change, Luke? Therapy?" I had hoped at one time that he would get counseling; had begged him to, but he would never consider it.

He nodded. "Yes, for the past year. Weekly. Then lots of practice with my family and my kids. I've gotten quite good at recognizing triggers and that sort of thing." He smiled at the incongruity of using a word like triggers.

I even had to laugh out loud. "Oh, my God; seriously? You recognize your triggers?" I covered my mouth with my napkin. "I'm sorry," I said through bursts of gulped back laughter. "I don't mean to laugh. It just seems so …."

"Unbelieveable?" he offered.

"Yes, and unlikely." I leaned my chin onto my fist, elbow on table and watched him.

"Tell me more," I said.

"OK … well … I now know what sets me off, and I've learned coping skills and what to do when those feelings come up. I've learned that my angry outbursts were only because I felt out of control. I raged when I was sad or embarrassed or ashamed. Now I try to just feel those things and not act on them. Once they diminish, I can decide what to do with them."

I couldn't believe what I was hearing. Eight years with me and a previous twenty with his ex-wife, his sisters, even his mom. And now he was telling me he had figured this out? I tightened inside and put a lock on my heart. I was not letting him in again. He could find another guinea pig.

I sat quietly for several seconds, letting this information wash over me. I knew my triggers as well, and one of them was someone asking for forgiveness. It was almost impossible for me to deny them. Which is why I continued to get hurt time after time; because I wanted so badly to trust. Roger popped into my mind then. He was the first man I'd met who was so totally truthful and dependable from the very beginning. Granted, we hadn't known each other long, but he'd had several opportunities to walk away from me; I had been a mess during this past month.

"Well, I'm glad for all that," I said. "I really am. I'm proud of you for wanting to change and for all the work you've probably put in."

"But?" he said.

"Luke, I just don't know that I have it in me to believe you one more time. I'm so sorry." And I was. I was so sorry I wanted to cry. I wanted to put my arms around him and hold him and kiss him and make love to him and believe that he would never hurt me again. God, how I wanted that.

"Will you at least think about what I've said and consider giving me another chance? Please?" he said. His voice was pleading—another change I never thought I'd witness.

I would be heartless if I didn't at least say I would do that much. So I nodded. "Yeah," I said, "I will think about it."

He placed his cup in the saucer and indicated he was paying the tab and would be right back to collect me. I watched him place the bill on the counter and pull out a credit card.

He returned to the table and took my arm as we walked out. At my car, he pushed me gently against the driver's door and leaned against me. I could feel the Luke I had always loved to feel. He kissed me deeply, and I caught myself starting to respond. At the same time I screamed at myself to stop.

"I'll call you tomorrow," he said. "Drive safely."

"You too," I replied as I unlocked the door and slid in. As I drove home, his words began to sink in, and tears rolled down my cheeks and wet my lovely crepe blouse all down the front. "Damn it!" I pounded the steering wheel once at a stoplight. I cried all the way home and fell into an exhausted sleep before ten o'clock.

Connie Wesala

Chapter 32

Friday morning I called Jennifer. We had spoken briefly the day after my return and texted a few times the past few days. I needed coffee and conversation, and I was glad when she said she was free to meet.

"9:30 at P.B.?" she said.

I hugged her as we walked into the bakery. We ordered coffee and muffins and took a table near the windows. Once we were settled, I handed her a Debenhams's bag; the gift-wrapped box peeking from its edges.

"Oh, you shouldn't have," she said.

"Of course, I should have. I just hope you like it."

When she pushed aside the tissue paper, her face lit up. I knew I had made the right decision. Even though it was still in the box, I could see it was exactly the right shade for her blue eyes.

"I love it," she exclaimed as she fingered the soft scarf. "It's pure cashmere. You shouldn't have."

"Yeah, you already said that," I teased. "Not sure how much good you'll get out of it living in Phoenix, but maybe in January, huh?"

"Hell, I may just wear it tomorrow. It's beautiful. Thanks so much."

"You're welcome."

"Now tell me everything from the beginning, including Roger," she said.

We sat for well over two hours. Luckily the place was nearly vacant.

"Sounds like you loved the classes," she said. "Did you work on your novel?"

I told her about Dean Montrose's critiques, and that it was ready for a final edit.

"Good," she said. "I figured that was the case. You're always so hard on yourself."

"As for Roger, he's going to take a teaching position at the university as well, so I guess we'll just see where this goes."

"But you really do like him, right?"

I nodded. "Yes, I do; more than I've liked any man for a very long time."

She looked surprised. "Even Luke?" she asked.

"I loved Luke; I didn't like him so much," I said.

"I get it," she said. "Liking is important. Speaking of Luke-boy. Have you seen him?"

I spent the next fifteen minutes going over recent events; him showing up at my house the day after I returned and our dinner the night before.

"You mean he thinks he can just waltz back in?" she said. "Seriously?"

I didn't like the fact that I felt defensive. "No, not really. I mean, he really did want me to know how much he's changed … or thinks he has. He wants a chance to prove that, and I guess I understand that. I mean …"

Jennifer interrupted me. "Wait a minute! You aren't seriously thinking about giving him another chance, are you?" She looked almost angry.

I sighed deeply. "Jennifer, I told him 'no'. I don't want to get involved again, and I explained that to him. But on the other hand, I guess I can understand how it might feel if you really had changed and wanted someone to give you the chance to prove it, you know?"

"Your counseling background is not healthy," she said.

I smiled slightly. "I didn't say I was going to do it. I said I can understand; that's all. Besides, aren't you the one who insisted his visit was romantic just a week or so ago?"

Jennifer looked down for several seconds before making eye contact again. "I did say it was romantic, and it was I suppose. Doesn't mean I want you to be with him."

I sat back and relaxed my posture.

"I love you; you know that. And I'll always be here for you, Amy. But honestly, I just don't think I can take any more Luke drama, my friend."

"I understand that as well," I said. "I'm not going to see him again, Jenn; I promise." I reached for her hand and squeezed. "You were always there for me; I'll always appreciate that."

She smiled. "Mutual," she said.

I pulled my hand back and sat for a moment without breaking the silence. We were both content with our silences after all these years. I thought about her cancer scare last year and remembered sitting quietly with her at the oncologist. She was a strong woman; stronger than me. Because even though I had no intention of seeing Luke again, I truly did understand his need to be understood and believed. I couldn't tell her if I did choose to meet him again. That was asking too much of our friendship.

We finally left the bakery at noon, and I headed out to buy groceries and cat food. I was beginning to function again. I had exactly twenty-eight days before I returned to the UK. Being there for a month was one thing, but for a full year, I'd need to ship a great deal of stuff ahead of time. And I had to get busy immediately if I was going to find an apartment to lease.

When I Skyped Roger that afternoon, I asked him to help me find a one bedroom or even an efficiency. Dean Montrose was watching for one as well. I couldn't afford much on the salary they were paying me. Even though I had my monthly income, I still had all the expenses of the house in Phoenix. And I had to have a place that would take my cat, Hermione. That would require quarantine on both ends of the trip. I felt overwhelmed on top of my fatigue from the trip home. I kept telling myself it would all work out.

I hid out over the weekend except for phone calls to Sarah and Chris. My other friends just had to understand that I needed a few more days before resurfacing. But I made some phone calls to them as well. I slept ten hours each night and slowly felt myself recuperating.

Luke had left the proverbial ball in my court, and he hadn't phoned or shown up—so far. I was glad. I wasn't certain what might happen should he push me again. I wanted to believe that I'd be strong, but when it came to Luke, I was never strong, and I knew it.

When he called after work Monday evening, I was polite and casual. He asked how I was doing, and I asked about work.

"It's hard to believe the school year started this early," I said.

"Yep, I know," he said in that nasal Texas accent. "Earlier every single year."

"Well, I hope you have a good year," I said. That sounded pretty final in my mind. Sort of like: I wish you well in life.

He didn't let it lie. "Wondered if we could have a beer Friday evening," he said.

I closed my eyes and clutched the phone tighter. *Don't do this*, I silently told him.

"Just a beer," he said again before I could respond.

"Luke ..."

His voice grew quiet, and I wasn't sure if I heard him correctly. "Please?"

I felt my heart pounding; could almost hear it pulsing in my ears. I opened my mouth to speak. "No, I can't" was what I thought. But what came out was, "Just a beer, Luke—one beer."

What???

I would have backed out immediately except he was saying, "Thanks. I've got to hang up; parents waiting."

Before I could respond, he had hung up the phone. It was Monday; I had the entire week to call and cancel. Hell, maybe I'd even stand him up. He'd certainly done that more than once. Only because of commitments, I reminded myself. He wasn't that thoughtless. I shook my head at my naiveté. Jenn would kill me. But I knew Jenn would not know.

The days filled with phone calls, arrangements, flights, and packing boxes to ship. I met with two good friends for lunch on Wednesday, gave them their small gifts and talked over wine and crostini for several hours. I had dinner with the kids Thursday evening. I talked with Jennifer daily.

On Friday, I realized I hadn't called to cancel on Luke. Shit! By three o'clock, when I still hadn't made that phone call, I knew I was going to give in. So at 5:30, I walked into a brewery we both liked in Tempe. Four Peaks had been around for years and was packed on Friday evenings. It took me some time to just find a parking spot, and several minutes of searching the bar before I spotted him off in the corner. He didn't see me. So I watched him closely as I approached. Blue shirt; tie knotted perfectly; khaki slacks—his uniform. And damn, he looked good. He smiled when he saw me and waved me over. He stood, pulled out the bar stool and helped me push forward to the table. "I ordered nachos," he said. "Hope that's OK."

I nodded. "Sounds good," I said.

"I'll get you a beer," he said, and he quickly turned toward the bar to order.

As he walked away, his scent lingered, and I took it in and closed my eyes as memories flooded my mind. This was not a good idea, and I knew it. Had known it all week I reminded myself. He returned to the table and placed the glass of beer onto a napkin and pushed it toward me.

"Thanks," I murmured. It hit me with full force now. This was where we'd had our first unofficial date nine years ago. How could I forget? I felt the sting. Not only did the memory sting; but the fact that he had planned this did as well. I had walked right into his bee hive.

I glanced at my watch, and he saw me do it. "I have to get home early, too," he said. "You can relax."

I smiled, but I figured it looked more like a grimace. "Luke ..."

He looked innocent and wide-eyed. "Yes?"

"Never mind." I didn't want him to know I even remembered that first afternoon. Didn't want to give him the satisfaction of knowing how uncomfortable I was. So I made small talk. The move, my hectic week, my search for an apartment. And asked about his first week of school.

"Pretty good start to the year," he said. "Remember how that first week was?"

He didn't have to remind me; I remembered it well. I nodded. "Oh, yeah; long days of changing schedules, registering kids and meeting with teachers. Seems like a hundred years ago."

"Somehow I doubt that," he said and smiled at me.

"Well, yeah, and it feels like yesterday." I smiled back. "Good years," I added.

"I hired you three times," he said, as if he had to remind me. It was a long-standing joke of how I'd turned down his first two offers.

I looked down; then took a gulp of my beer. I twisted the cheese on the nachos till it gave way and took a bite.

"So how are your kids?" I asked.

"Ah ..." He hesitated, and I knew he was registering my refusal to talk about the past. "Good," he finally said. "They're both really good." He talked for a few minutes about the two young people I used to know so well.

I lost track of what he was saying about Sammie, and a vision of her covered in powdered sugar as we baked Christmas cookies settled itself in front of me. I felt the tears before I realized I was crying.

Luke reached for my hand. "I'm sorry," he said. "Was it something I said?" He sounded genuinely concerned. He handed me his napkin, and I used it to soak up the tears from my cheeks and chin. "I'm so sorry," he said again, although I couldn't figure out what he was apologizing for, and I was certain he had no idea either.

"Luke, it's alright," I finally said. "It's just that ..."

He nodded. I bit my upper lip and swiped at my eyelashes one more time. I lowered my gaze to my beer and gathered my feelings. When I looked up, I saw that his eyes were full of unshed tears too.

"Luke, I think we'd better call it a night," I said, my voice tight with tension. "Don't you?"

The plate of nachos was quickly congealing, and our beers were growing warm, but we sat without speaking. Both of us apparently considering what would happen if we left and what might happen if we stayed. It was a line neither of us was ready to cross. And so we sat at the bar table and people-watched around us.

It was a good five minutes before he broke the silence. "I miss you so damned much, Amy." He took my left hand in his and wound his fingers through mine and squeezed. "I was such a fool."

When I met his eyes they were like magnets, and I couldn't look away. I floated inside his black eyes and began to feel the chill inside of me grow warm with memories, with love and with hope. It was not unlike the first day we'd met. His eyes had caught mine across the room, and I had melted into them and drowned for the next eight years. How was I going to avoid that now?

Luke finally downed the last of his beer and wiped his mouth with his napkin. "Let's get out of here," he said.

I had no idea where we were going or why, but I let myself be led out into the harsh sunshine of a hot day refusing to give way to evening. He walked me to my car, and I dug in my purse for my keys. "I'm sorry I upset you, Amy. But I love you; you have to know that."

He opened my door for me and waited until I clicked my seatbelt into place. Through the open window, he bent forward and kissed me softly on the lips. He didn't say another word; just stepped back and let me start the car and ease into a turn and toward home. I concentrated on driving the freeway, and it wasn't until I pulled into my garage and parked the car, that I let myself go, and I sat in the car, put my head on the steering wheel and wept tears of grief. The tears I hadn't let myself shed when I'd let him walk out. They were spilling forth from a deep well where I'd held them for so long.

At seven-thirty, I finally grabbed my purse from the passenger seat and walked through the rear door and into the house. I threw my purse onto a bar stool in the kitchen and flung myself onto my wide red over-stuffed chair, slipped out of my shoes, and placed my feet onto the ottoman. Hermione leaped onto the back of the chair and purred into my ear, and I felt myself dozing off.

I slept for a half hour and woke when I heard the doorbell. I assumed it was my next door neighbor who regularly stopped by after her evening walk. I didn't bother looking through the peep-hole. I gasped as I gazed through the screen door. My hands didn't seem to be shaking, but the rest of me was. It was like shivering from the cold; my entire body seemed in motion.

"Luke?"

Sheepish didn't begin to describe his demeanor. His chin was tucked and his shoulders stooped, but his big brown eyes looked up at me. I could tell he was trying to gauge my reaction. "Hi," he said quietly. "Sorry to just show up. You got a minute or two?"

I sighed deeply and considered my options. My mouth had clinched shut before I realized it. I was trying not to say "go away" even though that was how I felt. I shook my head side to side in frustration. Sighed again.

I unlocked the deadbolt on the screen door with the key that always remained in the lock; then pushed it open for him to enter. Hermione appeared in the doorway between the kitchen and the foyer. She ran toward him and rubbed against his pant leg, leaving white cat hair along the hemline of his khaki slacks. She had never been crazy about Luke when we were seeing each other, so it surprised me to see her so welcoming.

I motioned for him to go on back and followed him through the kitchen and into the living room where I took a chair, and he collapsed onto the chaise lounge portion of the sectional. He smiled warmly and settled into the deep cushions. The old sofa I'd replaced had an indentation that matched his butt, and I'd had the chair recovered with new foam seat cushions where he'd nearly destroyed it after years of use. If I were honest, Luke's presence was everywhere, even though I had moved to a new house. The first book he ever bought me was still on the shelf above the TV, several pieces of furniture that he'd hauled home for me still in the bedroom, CD's we'd once listened to together sat by the stereo.

"Gotta a beer?" He smiled warmly, but his voice sounded hesitant.

I thought for a second. "Probably a couple of Bud Lights." I stood and walked to the refrigerator. I felt his gaze on my back, so I continued talking to break the ice. "So why are you here? Not exactly on your way home."

"Yeah, no … not on the way. I just wanted to make sure you were OK. You were so upset when we left the bar."

"I'm fine," I said as I popped the top off the bottle and held up a glass for him to choose.

"Bottle is fine," he said.

I crossed the room and handed him the cold beer and placed a coaster on the small table in front of him; then plopped down in the chair and curled my feet up and under me, trying to relax. The silence grew uncomfortably long as he downed about a quarter of the bottle before setting it down.

"Amy," he began.

I waited.

"Shit, this is hard, isn't it?" He puckered his lips in frustration. "So when do you leave for England?"

"In three weeks," I reminded him.

"And you'll continue seeing this Roger guy?"

"I don't know, Luke." My voice sounded harsh, even to me. I softened it a little. "I mean, really; I don't know what the future holds. Maybe? Sure, probably."

He picked up the beer and drank the remainder of it in just a few gulps, stood and moved toward the end of the couch just across from where I sat. I tensed.

"Amy, I love you. I don't want you to go, but I know it's a great opportunity. But I'm going to tell you this …" He hesitated before continuing. "I am not giving up on us. I'd like to see you a few more times before you leave. I'd like to arrange a time I can come visit this fall. I want to keep trying with the hope we can get back to where we were."

I shook my head and felt the anger rise. "Where we were? Really, you want to be back where we were? That was not a great place, if I may remind you!"

He lifted both hands up as if to fend off my words. "I know. I didn't meant it like that. Not how we were at the end. How we were at the beginning."

Of course, I knew what he had meant. My reaction was just a way to keep him at a distance, and I knew it. I sighed again and shrugged my shoulders.

"Luke, this is not going to work." I felt like a sound bite playing in a loop. "How can we go back? No one can go back, Luke. That's impossible. There's too much water under the bridge. Would you go back to Caroline?" The sound of his ex-wife's name took him by surprise.

"That's totally different," he said.

"Really? What's so different about it? I'm an ex. She's an ex. Why would you want to start up again knowing that we will end at the very same spot where we left off over a year ago?"

Luke sat forward off the edge of the cushion and took my right hand. "Amy," he said. "Why can't you believe that I've changed? Is that really so hard? I mean, for God's sake, you were a counselor. Your whole career was helping people change. But you think I'm not capable of the same thing you helped dozens of people do?"

His voice sounded angry now, but he didn't release my hand. "Shit, that makes me angry, Amy. Do you honestly think I have no feelings? No ability to become a better person?" The anger suddenly turned into sadness, and I saw it wash across his face. He looked as if I'd slapped him hard.

I felt like a heel all of a sudden. I had built this wall for over a year. It had protected me from this very situation; not only with Luke, but with any man I met. I didn't like the possibility of tearing it down and caring again.

He gripped my hand tighter, took my left one as well, and pulled me so I was looking directly at him. His black eyes were so intense, I felt myself leaning into them. I knew the next step could mean falling and drowning one more time. I pulled my hands from his and put them back in my lap. But I remained where I was—directly in front of him. I looked at the floor for a few seconds, then back at his face. The flood of feelings made tears well in my eyes. "Oh, Luke," I whispered. "We can't …."

He rose quickly and stepped forward, pulled me into his arms, and kissed me long and hard. It was not wet and sensuous; his lips were not their usual softness. He kissed me with force and ownership, and I responded.

As he pulled his mouth off mine, he continued to hold me, but not close enough to feel his desire. He stared into my eyes and didn't say a word. My breath was shallow from the kiss and from wanting more, but I would not move into him. I waited.

And then he released me and said he'd better get going, and within seconds, he was walking toward the front door with me close behind. He leaned in one last time, gave me a peck on my cheek, winked and said "I'll call you tomorrow."

My heart pounded loudly in my chest, and I was just beginning to catch my breath. I simply nodded and closed the door after him. After I turned the lock, I leaned backward against the door and felt all the old feelings of love and lust wash over me.

I spent the next two days creating piles of items I'd need for a year in Oxford. Because of the expense of shipping internationally, I had to carefully consider what I truly needed and what I could buy cheaper over there. Having lived in Arizona for years, my winter clothes would not fit that description in England. It might make more sense to simply buy a new wardrobe once I settled in.

During my month in Oxford, I hadn't ventured out to the suburbs. I knew there was a large outlet mall somewhere not too far from the city. I'd seen it advertised, but it hadn't been on my things to see in jolly England. I hadn't taught in several year, so my business wardrobe had been weeded down to nothing. Would I need suits? Dresses? I had no idea.

Tuesday afternoon I emailed Dean Montrose to ask a few of those questions. She was very kind and even offered to loan me a heavy wool coat and a trench. Absolutely no suits needed. Pants and sweaters, a few jackets and low heeled shoes would be fine. I felt better after hearing back from her. I had a lot of slacks; perhaps not warm enough for England, but they'd get me by, at least until the dead of winter.

Chapter 33

On Wednesday I caught up with Jennifer. We talked almost daily, but I hadn't seen much of her since my return. She seemed quite depressed. I parsed my words and managed not to ask what was wrong. It would come out piece meal as it always did with Jenn. When she was ready, she would share. I just prayed it wasn't medical after the past year.

"So," she said. "Packing once again, huh, girl?" She grinned.

"This is so hard. I finally decided I had to ship a box or two or I'd have so much luggage it would cost me a fortune just to take it on the plane."

"Yeah, with baggage fees these days," she agreed.

"So … I guess I'm doing OK. Taking what I can; shipping as little as possible; and hoping to just buy some stuff once I see what I need."

"Have you found an apartment?"

"Not yet. Roger has found nothing and Dean Montrose is looking for an option for me. She thinks she can locate something through university housing if nothing else."

"I thought you didn't want to be in a cramped room on campus?"

"I don't, but I also don't want to be sleeping at the bus station." I laughed. "It's possible I can do a month-to-month at first if I really have to and get moved to something more permanent once I find it."

Jennifer nodded. "And how's Roger?" she teased.

I grinned from ear to ear. I had Skyped with Roger five times since I got back and each time felt more familiar and more comfortable. I told Jennifer about our talks. "I really like this man," I said. "I hate to admit it, but I do."

"Well, now you'll have time to just let it happen naturally," she said.

"I agree."

I knew what was coming next but I wasn't going to offer it up.

"And Luke?"

It had been five days since Luke's last visit and the kiss, but he'd phoned almost every evening on his way home from work. He shared his day at school, and I shared my packing details. It felt casual, like it had in the past.

And it also felt warmly familiar. I dabbed at my lips with my napkin, knowing full well I had eaten nothing to produce crumbs. I knew Jennifer noticed. She didn't miss much. "Well …." I hesitated.

She tilted her head and waited, her eyes squinted a little like she knew what was coming next. "You saw him?" she said. Her tone was not accusatory, and I was glad. Just a simple question.

I nodded again. "Yes, a few times," I admitted. I knew my tone was conciliatory, begging her not to judge me. "Drinks one evening, dinner another, and we met for a beer last Friday."

"How did that go?" she asked.

I told her the specifics of each encounter, leaving out the fact that he'd kissed me.

"I've told him I won't go back into the same relationship we had, and I won't."

Jennifer shook her head. "What the hell does that mean? That's pretty open ended. 'The same relationship you had?' as in … a different relationship? Are you seriously considering this?"

"Jenn," I said. I straightened my back trying my best not to sound defensive. "I'm going to be in England; Luke will be here. We are not going to pursue anything, I promise."

"You don't need to promise me," she said. "Just promise yourself you won't fall for his lines again."

"I know," I said. I sipped my coffee and stared ahead as my memory went to the kitchen kiss. Those feelings refused to leave. I had loved this man for so long. I'd have given him my life and every penny I had. It went way beyond love in the present. We were like star-crossed lovers from a different physical plane; had known each other over several life times. I had been convinced of that then, and I was still pretty sure of it now. As awful as it could be, the good was fantastic, and I remembered it so well. All the good was back inside my body, and my mind would not let me remember the bad. I could not admit that to my best friend. I was too ashamed.

"How about you?" I finally asked. "You look a little under the weather." I let it go at that.

"Just tired," she said. "Oh, I'm fine." She waved her hand to brush it away.

I met her eyes directly.

Connie Wesala

"No, really," she said and laughed. "Seriously, I'm fine."

"I hate the F word, and you know it." I glared at her. "You'd tell me?" I didn't finish the sentence. *You'd tell me if the cancer was back, right?* I thought. *You'd tell me if Paul had contacted you, right? You'd tell me ...*"

"Hey," she said. "You know I would tell you anything. I have an appointment next week for a blood draw, but I don't feel sick like I did before—just tired, fatigued."

"Well, it's good you're checking it out. Can I go with you?"

"That is not necessary, Amy. It's a simple blood draw, not chemo."

I locked her eyes and formed the next question, then put it aside. I didn't believe her. Blood draws were seldom 'simple'. "Well, OK, I guess, but if you change your mind ...."

She nodded. We chatted about the kids and the latest People magazine gossip for another half hour.

Saturday morning as I stepped from the shower, the phone rang. The caller ID lit up with Luke's name and number. I wrapped the towel around my naked body and tucked in a corner to hold it in place. "Hello?" I made it sound like I had no idea who was calling.

"Amy ... Luke."

I almost laughed; could he possibly forget I had caller ID. I waited a second. "Oh, hi," I chirped.

"Do you have plans for tomorrow?"

"Well, I'm not sure. What did you have in mind?"

He told me about a downtown Phoenix event that included live bands, food trucks, wine and beer. It actually sounded like fun. It was hotter than Hades, but the park he mentioned had mature trees for shade, and I hadn't done anything fun in so long. England had been interesting and very enjoyable, but fun was different.

"I guess I could do that," I said. After all, it was during the day; no harm done.

"Great, I'll pick you up at noon."

The minute I hung up, I knew I should have driven and met him there. But I wasn't going to call him back to try to change it. He'd only argue with me anyway.

Sunday morning, I spent nearly an hour and a half on hair and make-up and tried on every item of clothing in my closet. I never primped. Instead of my usual which consisted of moisturizer, a little slapped-on foundation and eyeliner, I tweezed and plucked, exfoliated, moisturized, and carefully applied foundation with a damp sponge. I used a magnifying mirror to make certain my blush looked exactly like it said—a blush.

I used a lip liner and a lipstick brush to apply it from the tube. I found an old curling iron, and after I blew out my hair, I actually created some tendrils of curls around my ears. I checked my bathroom closet and found my old bottle of Channel #5 at the back of a shelf. I used a cotton ball to run the perfume lightly along my neckline; just enough to give off a hint of scent.

As I stood in front of the mirror, I assessed my body in panties and bra. I had lost ten pounds, and I didn't look bad for an old lady. I slipped on a new black and white print sundress and threw a white cardigan around my shoulders. Chose a pair of silver hoops and a simple silver necklace. Black sandals and a straw purse. In the full length mirror, I asked myself what the hell I was doing! It was too late to turn back.

The doorbell rang five minutes before noon, and I opened it, knowing that I looked damned good. I enjoyed Luke's face as his lips parted slightly, and his eyes opened wider.

"Wow," he said. He was dressed casually in khaki shorts and a light cream polo but was clean shaven and not a hair out of place.

"You too," I said, admiring him as he stood in the doorway. I had my purse on my arm, ready to go.

"OK, well; let's go, then."

He held the door for me as I climbed up and into his Chevy truck. He'd always been good at those small things.

"You cold?" he asked. "I can turn down the AC."

"No, fine," I said and smiled. He looked so nervous I almost felt guilty. Because I felt no sense of anxiety at all. It just felt like old times, and I chatted as he drove along the freeways and into the city.

Luke parallel parked several blocks from the event; the closest spot he could find. He reached behind me into the space between the seats and the bed of the truck. "Oh," I gasped. "Luke, how thoughtful."

He handed me the black and white polka dot parasol and smiled. "To keep the sun off, my lady." He was teasing, but it felt nice. And it was thoughtful. I had to give him credit.

"Thank you," I said as I took it and reached for the door handle.

"Wait," he said sharply, and he jumped from the truck and arrived outside my passenger door in two seconds. He opened the door, helped me down onto the running board and then the curb and handed me my purse.

As he grabbed a blanket from the backseat and locked the truck, I looked at the umbrella again; then pressed the button and pushed up to open it. It was small; just the right size for a summer day instead of rain. Where had he found it? I wondered. It was adorable. The polka dots fit my personality to a tee, and the fact that he thought of that made my eyes moist. He really could be a good guy. Had been the first year together. He had it within him. That's why I had hung on so many years. Hoping that guy would reappear. And now here he was—or seemed to be.

We walked around awhile to scope out the action. Several bands were playing at each end of the park. Reggae, country and pop.

"Which truck food do you want?"

"I may want one of everything."

He threw back his head in laughter and nodded. "Way to go. Me too."

I took his hand as we walked toward the first trailer, and we stood and read the menu top to bottom before ordering. "Let's get one thing from each cart and share," I said.

After we had our hands full, we walked toward the country music. "Let's go sit down," he said and pointed to a vacant grassy spot.

He placed the plaid cotton blanket on the ground. "I'll go get us a couple of beers? Is that OK with you? Coors, right?"

"As you well know," I said. It would be good to drink a good old pale American beer. I lowered the umbrella and laid it beside me. I leaned back onto my elbows and let my face rise to the sun. A few more freckles and a little color would do me good before heading to cloudy Oxford. The country band was playing an old favorite of Luke's. He hated to dance, but we often went to a country western bar and restaurant a few miles from my house. I quietly mouthed the words of the song, and then I heard a deep baritone humming the tune along with me. I turned quickly.

He grinned broadly and handed me a plastic cup of beer. "Clear," he said and shook his head. "Don't they know about red Solo cups?"

"Gauche," I said. "Everyone knows you put beer in red plastic."

We laughed together. It felt wonderful. Warm sunshine, cold beer, a lovely parasol and a blanket on the grass. It felt like heaven. And for the second time that afternoon I thought about cloudy, wet and cold England.

He pulled french fries from the paper container and held one to my lips. I opened my mouth. "Don't you dare," he said, and he laughed as I pretended to bite his fingers.

"Needs ketchup," I said in a joking tone.

"Give me that," he said, and he grabbed for the entire bar b q rib sandwich.

"No way," I said and turned away just as he grabbed for air.

"I love you, Amy," he said suddenly.

I stopped laughing and held my breath. All I could see were the clouds above his head, the blue sky and the crinkles around his eyes.

"I love you, too," I whispered. He took the two paper plates from my hands and placed them on the blanket along with our cups. He stood and took my hands to pull me up; then took me in his arms. The band was playing, "And We Danced." He held me tightly; his right arm around my waist and his left hand holding my right. My left arm went around his neck, and we danced.

When the song was over, my heart had melted. "I thought you never danced," I said. "You would never dance with me," I reminded him.

"I know," he said and nodded. "But I do now."

I smiled and took his face in both my hands and pulled him to me. The kiss was warm and soft, and I remembered the fullness of those lips on mine as if it were yesterday. Luke had a way of stretching a kiss into tomorrow, and he did so now. When we came up for air, I released a sharp gasp. I didn't want to mislead him. And I just had.

We finished eating, then walked around and people-watched; then had one more beer. The evening was settling in, and the heat was dissipating slightly. Luke spread out the blanket at the fringe of the dwindling crowd, and we laid back and shared a Coke and sobered up before he had to drive home. "Amy," he said.

I had my eyes closed and didn't open them. But I felt his right hand take my left and squeeze. My lips turned upward into a smile before I could stop them. "Yes?" I asked as I slit my eyes slightly open.

He lifted himself over me and leaned down to kiss me. No full body contact in public. I knew that about him too. But a slow gentle kiss that grew deeper with each passing moment. I let him take my lips into his mouth to gently bite them; felt his tongue probing; felt myself responding.

He pulled back and looked into my eyes. "Let's go home," he said. He made home sound like *home*, as in our home, not your house. But I didn't argue. I wanted to feel his big hands on my body again; wanted to have him undress me slowly as he relished every inch of my skin; wanted to feel his mouth doing things I'd never dreamed of before Luke. That's how I thought of it sometimes. B.L. (before Luke) and A.L. (after Luke). Those years with him I had grown into a woman though I'd been nearing forty and had been married at one time. I had never experienced the places Luke took me. And suddenly it all came rushing back. And if we had been alone in the park, I'd have let him take me right then and there.

On the ride home, Luke turned on the radio and hummed along as he drove. I closed my eyes and bent my head to his shoulder; my left hand on his bare leg, slowly running my finger along his skin to feel the softness. At one point he lifted my hand away and I knew why. I grinned at him.

He looked over at me. "What?" he said. I knew that "what" so well. That innocent what did I do?

"Too hot to handle?" I asked.

"Maybe," he said, and he grinned back. "Wait till I get you home."

I pursed my lips into a surprised look and raised my eyebrows. "Really?" I said. "What's going to happen then?"

"You just wait," he said. His right hand went up the skirt of my sundress.

"Oh, my God, Luke, stop!"

"Serves you right," he said and pulled his hand away. "Don't be rubbing my leg like that?"

We laughed, and I turned up the radio and sang the rest of the way home.

After I let us into the house, it took about two minutes before we laid down on my bed and all my earlier fantasies came to life.

After we were sated, he put his arms around me and spooned. A first time for everything I thought. He never wanted physical contact after we'd finished. This time his arms wrapped around me, and I heard him snoring within moments. I laid there wide awake. I could never sleep after sex. I could not believe what I was hearing and seeing and experiencing with him. Had he truly changed? It had been over a year; time enough for anyone to make change if they really wanted to. I just never thought he'd want to. Could I trust this? I didn't think so, but I wasn't sure now.

Chapter 34

When Jennifer phoned the next afternoon, we talked about everything under the sun except the two most important issues on my plate. Luke phoned every evening on his way home from work, and Roger called early in the day due to the time difference. The first time he phoned following my evening with Luke, I felt waves of guilt. As each day passed, I felt more comfortable with the situation. After all, I was not in a committed relationship with either of them. And I had learned the hard way that there is nothing to be gained by confessions that only ease the tension of the confessor.

When Luke called from work on Friday, he asked about my weekend plans. I told him I was doing a movie with Jennifer and also having dinner with my kids—both lies. It didn't dissuade him. "You can't be busy the entire weekend, Amy. How about Sunday?"

I swallowed hard. If I was going to develop any trust, I would have to go further down the rabbit hole. But the pain of finding out he wasn't to be trusted; that he hadn't in fact changed; was a pain I really didn't want to feel again. It had been too devastating in the past. His record was one of attempts and failures when it came to long-term change. I finally agreed to lunch just to appease him.

In order to avoid being a liar, I planned an early Saturday afternoon movie with Jenn and an early evening dinner with Chris and Sarah. Not a great model of honesty, I told myself. But at least I could look in the mirror.

At ten o'clock Sunday, it was already pushing 106 degrees. I texted Luke to make final plans. He suggested an indoor restaurant at one of the local farmers markets which sounded like a nice blend of both outdoors and in. I tried on a new sundress that required a strapless bra and then covered it with a light-weight sweater; white sandals and simple gold earrings completed the look. As I lined my lips and applied make-up I had to question why I didn't expend a little more energy on a daily basis. The results were damned good.

I had insisted on meeting him at the restaurant to avoid another roll in the hay—afternoon delight, they call it. Not that he couldn't follow me home, but it made it less inviting and less likely to occur. The road was dusty as I drove on a narrow dirt path past rows of vegetable gardens and fruit trees. The outdoor cafe looked packed, but I pulled clear to the rear of the property and parked behind the glassed-in sunroom of the white-table-cloth restaurant.

I knew he'd already be seated. For the first time I realized that he enjoyed being punctual because he could sit and observe me as I walked through the door.

Sure enough Luke sat in front of a bay window off to the right. "What are you smiling about?" he said when I reached the table. He had noticed.

"Just reminiscing," I said.

"Oh, really? About us?"

I shrugged my shoulders to keep him guessing. "You or someone else; I can't recall."

He changed the subject by offering me the menu. The waitress filled our water glasses while I glanced at the day's fresh offerings. "Give us a few," Luke told her, and she left us alone.

I looked up from the four page menu to find him gazing at me. "Have you already decided?"

"I looked earlier," he said.

"Well, stop staring at me so I can do the same," I teased.

He purposely turned to look out the window, and I shook my head and laughed.

"Well, I could have them put a TV behind you and stare at that." He turned to face me again and grinned.

I ignored the remark. "Everything looks delicious; but Luke, these prices." I knew he was on a very tight budget. "Can we split the tab, at least?"

"Absolutely not," he said as he turned back to me and took my right hand in both of his. He brought my fingers to his lips, kissed them lightly and then sucked my index finger for a quick moment.

"Luke," I said, "stop that." I pulled my hand back. "Let's order."

The waitress brought me a white wine and Luke a beer and topped off our water glasses. We sat and talked as we waited for our meals. About five minutes later, the waitress approached the table with a large bouquet of roses wrapped in green tissue, tied with a pink satin ribbon. "Would you like for me to bring a vase to put them in?" she inquired.

I gaped at the huge arrangement. There must have been at least eighteen fresh red blooms. I saw my amazement reflected in his eyes. "For me?" I was shocked. Never, in all our years together, had he ever brought flowers or gifts.

Luke answered since I couldn't manage another word. "That would be wonderful for the time-being. Just bring back the tissue, and we can re-wrap them later."

I held the bouquet and buried my nose inside their fragrance. "Oh, Luke; they are beautiful. Thank you." I wanted to really let him know how much this meant to me, but it was a fine line to balance between appreciation and accusation. I didn't want to dwell on the past any longer. This was today; a fresh start.

The thorny stems fit perfectly in the large round crystal vase. The server placed our food in front of us as the waitress placed the flowers in the center of the table.

I managed to keep our conversation light throughout the meal. He shared his week at work and his evenings with his kids.

"I swear, if I have to replace one more A.P., I'm going to retire early."

High school administration was one frustration after another. I had lived that life myself. I'd been an assistant principal and understood why he was losing them.

"How many teaching positions are still unfilled?" I asked. It was routine in Arizona schools. Half of the openings would remain that way throughout the school year, with substitutes changing every few days.

"Two science, one math, and German,"

I laughed. "German? In Arizona? Why, for heaven's sake?"

"Well, French didn't make last year, so the head shed thought we'd try German. Surprisingly I have enough for two sections, if I can find a teacher."

"In some ways I miss it," I said.

"School?" he said. "Seriously? I thought you were done with the BS."

"With the BS, yes; with the kids, no."

"Well, you'll have your own classroom soon enough, right? What is your start date again?"

"August 12th. But I leave for England in ten days." It suddenly felt like the days were flying too fast. I wanted more time. I wanted to see how this played out. I was suddenly invested in trying this relationship one more time. My thoughts must have shown on my face.

"Are you sad you're going back?" he asked. "You could call and tell them you've changed your mind, you know."

I shook my head. "Weren't you just saying how hard it is to fill positions? You wouldn't want a teacher to renege on a contract this late in the game."

He put his napkin on the table beside his near empty plate. "No, you're right." His voice was quiet, and I almost had to lean forward to hear him. When he looked up, I saw that his eyes were wet.

I was the one reaching for his hand this time. "Oh, Luke," I said. The words squeezed through the tightness in my throat, and I choked back tears of my own.

"Ten days," he said again. "Wow. We have to make the most of it, Amy. Somehow I have to convince you before you leave that we are meant to be together. Please say you'll try."

I nodded a silent yes and found that I meant it this time. I did want to believe him.

We were interrupted by the waitress. "Dessert?" she asked. She had dessert menus in her hand, and I shook my head. "I'm stuffed," I said, but I gave Luke a look that said go ahead.

"How about we split something chocolate?" he asked.

"You hate chocolate." How often had we had that fight as well?

"The brownie with ice cream and two plates please," he said and handed the menu back to her. "Coffee?" he asked me.

"Sure." As she walked away, I pushed my chair back from the table and sat staring into his brown eyes. We didn't need words for several minutes. When the waitress returned with an extra plate, I picked up the small fork and took a bite of the warm sweetness of melted vanilla on warm chocolate. It made me think of us. My Caucasian whiteness next to his dark velvet skin. My coldness melting into his warm eyes. "Do you want to come back to the house?" I asked.

Early Monday morning, I phoned Jennifer, and we met for coffee at 9:00. "I have a confession to make," I told her. "But before you yell at me, please know that I have to talk this through with someone, and I need you to not be mad."

She laughed. "I probably know where this is going, don't I?" she asked.

I nodded. "Probably."

"Luke." That's all she said. She scrunched her mouth sideways and frowned; then let it go with a deep breath. "Forget the confessional guilt," she said. "Tell me everything."

Which is what I proceeded to do over the next forty minutes, two cups of coffee and a Danish. I hardly took a breath as I shared the past two weeks with both Luke and Roger.

"Wow," she finally said. "That is one big decision."

"Aren't you going to ask me how I could possibly trust Luke again? Aren't you going to tell me what a bastard he always turns into once he hooks me back in? Really? You're just going silent?"

"Not silent," she said. "I just agreed with you. It's a big decision."

"So let me get this straight. You aren't going to tell me I'm crazy? You aren't going to tell me to get back to Oxford and enjoy a year with Roger? What good are you?" I laughed then.

Jennifer smiled at me. "I know; strange of me, huh? But seriously, Amy, you have two men in love with you and that's a pretty great thing, girlfriend. It may be a tough decision, but what a hell of a decision to have to make. I haven't had a date since Paul left fifteen months ago."

"So you think Luke might have changed?" I asked. I was totally confused. She had hated Luke for years; every time he had screwed me over, she had picked up the pieces until she was the one who said 'enough.'

"I honestly never thought he would or could do it, Amy; you know that. But what you just told me about this week? I just don't know what to say. Maybe he loves you enough that he made the effort this time. Will he switch right back to his old patterns? Who the hell knows? I'd love to yell at you; accuse you of being out of your ever loving mind! That would give me great pleasure." She shook her head and shrugged. "I just don't know. Who the hell knows?" she repeated.

So no help from my best friend. I could talk to my daughter or my son. I could go to church and pray. I could make long lists of pros and cons. I could re-read my old diaries from the past ten years of ups and downs, of love and hate, of forgiveness and starting over, only to be let down one more time. I could do any of those things, but there seemed to be no point in all that energy.

"I can't resign. It's too late for that. I don't break contracts or commitments."

Jenn agreed. "So that gives you nine months to make the decision, and it seems to me that should be plenty of time for Luke to show his true colors or prove he's changed for you. And it gives you time to date Roger and see how you feel about him."

Time was on my side. I'd be far enough from Luke not to get sucked into a trap. I'd have enough time to get to know Roger and discover all his rough edges and flaws. But could I sustain two relationships at the same time and remain sane? For bad or for good, I had always been monogamous; serially monogamous. This was suddenly new territory for me. And it felt rather risqué and exciting. Maybe I was growing up at forty-eight.

Chapter 35

When Roger called mid-day, I sat at the breakfast table and talked with him as I smelled one rose after another. I pulled the petals from two that hung their wilted heads and placed them in a small bowl. I loved laughing with Roger. He had been to the meadow and followed the wild horses we'd spotted so many times. He walked for over thirty minutes into the grassland, eaten up with gnats and mosquitoes, until he managed to reach what turned out to be a herd of grazing cattle. I had been there so recently, I visualized the entire episode, and I nearly cried with laughter.

"Oh, my God," I said. "How funny!" I hesitated for a moment. We'd been on international calling for nearly five minutes, and I needed to let him go. "I miss you." As soon as I said it, I knew my voice sounded weepy and needy. I never wanted to be needy. "I just mean … I'm anxious to do some of those things again … with you." Now I was stuttering like a teenager.

Roger quickly saved me. "I know what you mean. I can't wait to see you again. We'll go to the meadow before it starts to cool off. Hey, have you found an apartment yet?"

It was a wonderful way to switch subjects, and I thanked him silently. "Yes. Dean Montrose found a one bedroom, but it has a large living area and kitchen. Not too far from you actually. I think it will be fine, and it's in my budget. Plus they accept pets."

"That's great, can't wait to see it. Well, I'd better get off before my phone bill looks like the national debit, and England's is pretty high." We both chuckled.

I told him I'd send him my flight information and would take the earliest bus to Oxford once I arrived.

"Can you manage all that luggage, Amy? Let me meet you in London."

I assured him that I'd pay a baggage handler to get my bags from the terminal onto the bus and grab a taxi to the apartment.

"Well, let me know if you change your mind."

As I sat at the computer, typing out my itinerary, my mind took me back

Connie Wesala

to June--how nervous I had been about traveling alone, those two jerks on the bus, and my uncertainty about meeting the students at the conference. This time it would be old-hat to me. I was beginning to think that this year in Oxford would be a breeze.

That thought lasted several minutes until another thought gripped my gut—teaching again after being retired for so long. A classroom of college students facing me at the lectern. Holy crap, what was I getting myself into? I had to stop worrying about packing and get to the syllabus and book list; plan a few lectures to get ahead of the game. I was suddenly more nervous than I had been in June.

The next ten days flew by. I had lunch with Jennifer, spent two evenings with the kids, and managed to see Luke outside the bedroom and away from the house four more times. We met close to his work twice for lunch, and beers at a local pub not far from me the other two times. There were kisses and hand-holding, but no sex. Though it remained unspoken, I realized that both of us were being cautious, counting the days until I left, and knowing that the distance would be great for the next nine months. Perhaps too distant to maintain what we had started.

Plus Luke knew I'd be seeing Roger while I was over there, and I assumed—possibly a wrong assumption—he knew that the other man would have two things going for him: proximity and novelty. I was at the beginning of a relationship with Roger when you see what you want to see and ignore the rest. At the start there is something new to learn daily; there is passion that fuels the flames with a new partner; plus the most important—no past history to overcome. I knew all of this.

On the other hand, Luke and I knew each other inside out. It was comfortable; we didn't have to entertain or impress; didn't have to prove ourselves; didn't have to guess or try too hard. So in some ways, Luke had the edge. But I didn't know if he saw it that way.

Two days before my departure, I drove Hermione to the airport where she would be quarantined till our flight. "Sorry, girl," I said softly as I stroked her.

The woman in charge assured me she'd be well cared for and showed me around the facility. "Good news," she said. "They've agreed to quarantine her in Oxford instead of London."

I thanked her profusely. It made leaving Herm just a bit easier.

On our final evening I drank three beers instead of one. Luke ordered nachos and another round about nine o'clock. If I kept going, I'd succumb to the physical desires – the sparks in our eyes could grow into a fire quite easily. But I suddenly didn't care. If it happened, it happened. It would be months before I saw him again—if then. Maybe this year away would create another wedge, larger than the one of not seeing him for over a year.

"So, is it OK if I plan a trip to Oxford over my fall break?" he asked.

It was out of the blue, and I wasn't prepared to answer. Fall break was mid-October in his district. "Can you afford that," I asked, knowing full well that he honestly could not.

"I'll find a way," he said. He took my hand and patted the bench beside him. "Come over here," he whispered.

I complied. As I slid across the leather, he pulled me closer and put his left arm around my shoulders. I nuzzled his neck for a quick moment but pulled away again. No displays of public affection—PDA; he had always been firm about that.

This time was different. I felt his left hand move to my waist and then lower until he cupped my left cheek. I grinned up at him. "Stop that."

He laughed out loud, raised his arm to my shoulder again and pulled me toward him. He kissed me softly, and his lips felt like pillows on mine. He released me, though he didn't move further away on the bench. But we continued to eat and drink and talk about mundane things, avoiding what neither of us wanted to say. I could not say good-bye to Luke again. It would feel too much like that final day. If I'd been heading to France, I'd have said au revoir'. I laughed at that thought. Luke mistook my humor and pulled away. "Are you laughing at me?" he asked.

"Of course not … never!" I insisted. I went ahead and told him my thoughts.

"I don't want to say good-bye either actually. So let's not, OK? Can I take you to the airport next Tuesday?"

"Oh, Luke, that would really require a good-bye. I've asked Jennifer, and if she can't, Chris will."

His sad eyes met mine, and I felt sorrier for him than myself. I was the one heading out on an adventure; he was the one left behind. I knew how that felt.

I hadn't answered his earlier question. I moved back to my side of the table so I could see his face. He didn't try to stop me.

"Fall break would be lovely," I said. It sounded formal; I didn't like that. "I can meet you in London and take the bus back to Oxford with you. Or we could stay overnight in the city. Would you like to see the city?"

"I don't care to even fly. My idea of Paris is Paris, Texas as you well know." He grinned.

I shook my head. He was such a Texan. "Yes, I know—no place like the U.S. How long can you stay? That will probably determine what we do."

"Not more than a week," he said. "So you plan it and tell me. But yes, I would appreciate you meeting me at the airport."

He walked me to my car. I was reminded of the night six weeks ago when I'd met him in Oxford for the first time in a year and a half. Now I just felt sad. And torn. Part of me wanted him to go back to the house with me, but I knew how foolish that would be; how much harder it would be to leave him. No, it was best to do it this way.

He didn't offer to follow me home, and I didn't bring it up. After I closed the door, he placed his hand on the open window and kissed me one last time. As I started the car, I felt a tear slide down my right cheek and flicked it away. "See you in October!" I said too loudly. I calmed my voice before speaking again. "Oh, and Luke, please answer my emails this time, OK?" He was terrible at personal email—hated the computer. But we couldn't talk on the phone without going broke.

He smiled. "I will … honest."

I chose to believe him. On the way home, I felt like a magnet with two opposing forces. One pulling me forward to Oxford and Roger, and the other pulling me back to home and Luke. I let myself stay in the center, avoiding my feelings.

The next morning as I opened my eyes, the stronger magnet tugged me forward. I had the opportunity of a life-time. Oxford, England for a year. So many new people to meet. So many places to see. So much to learn. And Roger waiting.

As it turned out, Sarah took the morning off, and both she and Chris drove me to the airport. I had two large suitcases this time; had shipped two boxes the week before; and had my additional over-night bag and my purse. Chris loaded up a cart to take to check-in, and Sarah grabbed my carry-on.

"You are not hanging around for three hours," I said. "Let's grab a quick coffee upstairs, and then you guys head out."

The kids agreed. We had breakfast and coffee at a café on the second level of the terminal. After a tearful good-bye, I walked toward the security area. I turned one last time and waved. They were still watching, as I had known they would. I threw a kiss. "Love you," I mouthed. They waved and turned to leave, and I stepped up to the x-ray machine.

When I landed at Heathrow, I couldn't help but remember my first day in the U.K. three months ago. Now, I was here for a full year. I grabbed my luggage and Herm's cat carrier, then found a porter. I caught the bus to Oxford, dropped the cat at the ticket office at Glouster Green; then gave the cab driver directions to my new apartment to meet the super. I had rented it sight unseen, although Dean Montrose had sent a couple dozen photos. It looked nice enough—nothing fancy, but clean with high ceilings that gave the illusion of more space.

Wow, I thought as I walked through the apartment and back to the super who stood waiting just inside the door. *I'm really here*. He gave a few directions but handed me a typed list of instructions regarding everything inside the unit as well as local places near-by. The train station wasn't far, and I had Google Mapped to see that I was within walking distance of Roger's apartment complex.

He rang the bell an hour later as I unpacked clothing and personal items. It would be another week or two before the rest of my possessions arrived. I opened the door; he leaned in for a quick kiss; then closed the door behind him and pulled me into his arms for the real thing. I stood breathless when he released me. I smiled up at him warmly. "God, I've missed you." This phrase was becoming a habit lately.

Ten minutes later, after a brief perusal of my new living quarters, he excused himself to return to campus. He was already up to his eyeballs in lesson plans and textbook orders. "You'll be the same way by this time tomorrow," he reminded me. "But I'll pick you up around six for dinner if you want."

"That would be wonderful. I'm jetlagged so I think I'll just climb into bed for a few hours. If I don't answer when you ring the bell, knock loudly." I gave a slight laugh.

"Maybe I should have a key," he said, but he smiled mischievously to show he was teasing.

"Yeah, well; let me think about that," I replied.

Connie Wesala

When I closed the door and drew the dead-bolt, I placed her forehead against the coldness of the wood door. "No," I said aloud. "No, Luke, don't you dare intrude on my thoughts right now."

My nap did wonders, and I was showered and had on fresh jeans and a gray T-shirt when Roger arrived.

"Old place or new?" he asked.

"You choose," I said. "I'm too tired to care."

"Then old it is. Let's go to the first pub we went to when we met in June."

It was only a fifteen minute walk, so we chose not to waste an ounce of precious gasoline. Roger's car was saved for excursions outside the city only. On a part-time professor's salary, $8.00 for a gallon of gas was a luxury.

After the waiter delivered our dinner plates—a salad for me and a burger and fries for Roger, the conversation turned to practical matters.

"Which days will you be working?" he asked. "Do you have a set schedule yet?"

I nodded. "Tentative, although at Oxford you don't have students dropping out of classes last minute like we do in the states. So it looks like Monday and Wednesday mornings and Tuesday and Thursday afternoons."

"No Friday classes?" he said. "Aren't you the lucky one!"

"Office hours most all day, so don't be getting jealous of that just yet."

"But still—we can maybe take some three day weekend trips around England."

I had to smile at his apparent confidence in our relationship, but it pleased me that he felt that way.

When he grew silent, I watched his face as it clearly expressed his conflicting thoughts. I watched as he started to ask me a question, stopped himself, started to begin a different topic, back to the original question. I was fairly certain I knew the question. Should I bring it up first and get it over with? On the other hand, it was kind of cute to watch his mind churning. Out of kindness, I spoke up.

"You haven't asked but yes, I did see Luke a few times when I was back home. It's complicated in a way because he wants to make things work between us. But we had dinner a few times to talk, and I basically told him what I have for a couple of months."

"Which is?"

"That we simply do not work as a couple. If we can have a friendship, that's fine, but anything more is out of the question."

"But he doesn't take 'no' for an answer, does he?"

I shook my head. "No, unfortunately he does not."

Roger seemed to accept my assurances and changed the subject once again. I was glad he didn't ask more. While everything I'd said was true, I'd left out a few things like kisses and feelings and that one night I'd given in … and wishing things could be different with Luke. I truly did wish that. I also didn't mention the fact that Luke would be coming to Oxford in October. That date would come up before we knew it, so I couldn't wait too long. Otherwise, he'd think I'd been lying all along. I'd find the right time.

When we reached my apartment, he took me in his arms and hugged me. He kissed my ear and neck, and his hands wandered beneath my untucked blouse. I felt an urgency and desire to ask him in.

"You're jet-lagged and exhausted. I won't stay tonight." He grinned as he said, "But … tomorrow night will be a different matter."

I touched his face and kissed him again—gently with no passion but full of love and appreciation for his thoughtfulness. He was so kind and generous—so un-Luke. Well, unlike the old Luke, anyway. This was the man I should concentrate on while we had the time. Because if it did become serious—if I truly loved him—we'd have a lot of difficult decisions to make together. But it was just the first day back; we had nine months to figure it out.

I could not have been more confused, and I knew I was leading them both on; something I hated in other women. I didn't like this new *me*.

Chapter 36

I glanced in the mirror at 9:00 the next morning, and the bags under my eyes attested to my fatigue and the fact I was still on Phoenix time. I'd slept well though … eleven hours. I wanted to look fresh for my meeting with Dean Montrose at 10:30, but there was little I could do except cover it with make-up and try to sound alert and cogent.

Dean Montrose stood quickly and walked around her desk to give me a cordial hug. "So good to see you," she said. "I'm so excited that you're back. We have a lot to cover in the next day or two."

I would need to meet with Human Resources, of course, for all the paper-work. There were forms for my work visa to keep me legal. The university would handle all of that for me luckily. There was the syllabi for my two courses—two sections of each, a choice of textbooks and my student lists. The technology person would meet me at my own office tomorrow at 8:00 to get everything up and running, including the student computer system the university used for attendance, grades, etc.

"On Wednesday, I'd like to schedule with you to go over your class lists. I know most of these students pretty well and have some notes to give you on each." She glanced at the open notebook-style calendar on her desk. "Would one o'clock work for you?"

"Of course," I said. I wished I could think that far ahead, but my body was sending cues that I needed more sleep. It was obvious I would have no down time before classes started a week from today. I'd just have to pull it together and 'man-up' as we said in the states.

Dean Montrose walked me downstairs to the first floor, down a long windowless corridor and opened the door to a small janitor-closet-sized office. There was no window, and when she flipped the switch, the dim ceiling light barely illuminated the room. The wood desk had seen better days. There was just room for a metal filing cabinet in the left corner and a waist-high three-shelf bookcase. Whoever used the room last had left piles of notebooks and papers on the desktop and the book shelves. I'd need to go through those, and how would I know what to toss and what I shouldn't. Maybe I'd drag Roger over tomorrow to help sort through the mess. He'd been on campus for two weeks; he'd probably already organized everything and could advise me.

"Shall we go see your classroom?" Dean Montrose sounded excited for me.

I nodded. "Absolutely. Can't wait to see it." And I couldn't wait to see it after touring my tiny office space. I had no clue what to expect. The distance between the administrative building to the English classroom was six buildings away and took us about fifteen minutes to walk. I was thankful my classes were back to back both morning and afternoon, so I'd only have to make the trek across campus twice a day if I was lucky.

The lecture hall was enormous. I glanced around at the clearly new facility. I gazed up at the twenty or so steep rows that ended at the rear exit, high above. There were probably fifteen seats on each side of a center aisle. Like the room we'd used this summer, each cloth-covered seat was roomy and had a swinging arm desk for note-taking. How many students would I have each hour? I wondered. I remembered Dean Montrose saying classes were small. Perhaps I should have clarified that. *Guess I'll find out on Wednesday*, I thought.

I felt my gut clench. It had been years since I'd taught an English class. What the hell was I thinking when I said 'yes' to the invitation. I ran my hands nervously through my hair, pulling it behind my ears. When I spoke, my voice gave away the anxiousness I was feeling.

Dean Montrose sensed my discomfort and patted me on the back. "You'll be fine. I'm a good judge of character, and I've never hired anyone who regretted it."

I forced a smile and nodded. "I sure hope you're right," was all I could manage.

"Tell you what, Amy, after you finish with the tech guy tomorrow, come by my office for a quick minute, and I'll get you started on lesson plans and computer stuff. We don't usually give out class lists till Friday, but we'll still meet Wednesday to go over yours. Relax, you'll love it. See you tomorrow."

Dean Montrose turned and walked back through the door to the left of the lectern where we'd entered. I stepped onto the raised dais and tapped on the microphone which, of course, was turned off. I imagined myself next

Monday facing dozens of young people who expected me to have something to teach them. My hands felt clammy, and I bit my lip hard enough to draw blood. It was all I could do to curtail the tears as I fled up the steps and through the rear exit, down a hallway and through a set of glass doors leading to the quad. The walk home seemed like miles, and when I unlocked the apartment, it looked bare and strange and unwelcoming. Where were my large over-sized rooms and my back yard and my personal things that made a house a home? I slammed the door shut and without bothering to lock it, I threw myself onto the uncomfortable leather sofa and sobbed until I fell asleep.

A tap on the door woke me around seven. "Come in," I called as I lifted myself from the couch.

"The door isn't locked?" Roger asked as he let himself in. I could see his look of concern. "Are you OK?" He walked over and sat down beside me, pulling me against his chest.

I thought I was all cried out, but tears streamed once again, and I clung to him like a small child. "Oh, Roger, what have I done?" I managed through sobs.

We sat wound together for a few minutes until I contained myself enough to pull away.

"You're tired, off-kilter. Let's go get some food in you and another night's sleep and you'll feel like a new person." He grinned. "And maybe some beer and sex."

"I can't go out like this," I glanced down at my wrinkled clothes and knew how puffy my face must be after so much crying.

"Then we'll cook in," he offered. "Go take a shower, throw on something comfortable—preferably without bra or panties—and I'll run down the street to get a few groceries. Is steak OK?"

I nodded and followed his directions once I locked the door behind him. Thank God for this man, I thought. I can't do this without him. The water from the hot shower eased each and every tight muscle, and I felt myself relax into its warmth. By the time I dressed and blew my hair dry, I heard a tap and opened the door to a gorgeous man with big blue eyes and three large bags of much needed food.

I fell asleep in his arms that night and slept soundly until morning. When I opened my eyes, I smelled his usual breakfast of bacon and heard the splatter of eggs frying in its remains. The aroma of coffee woke me instantly. I stretched out my full length of nakedness and smiled. Then I remembered my meeting with the tech department guy, and the day turned just a little bit gray.

Roger had to be in his office at eight as well, but he promised to help organize mine right after lunch. We walked to campus under an unusual blue sky, and he stopped just behind a massive oak tree to give me a peck on the cheek. "Don't want to be seen too cozy … at least yet," he explained. We had talked about this at length, and I agreed that rumors of a campus romance was not in our best interests. Maybe by Christmas we could be seen together, but not before. As small as Oxford was, that might prove difficult, but we had to do it.

The tech guy was pleasant enough, in a nerdy way, and he had me up and running within a half hour. The phone and computer both worked; he had the software update completed within minutes, and taught me a few basics about the operating system. While he'd been working at my desk, I had removed all of the books and papers from the bookshelves and placed them in a couple of computer paper boxes that I shoved into a corner behind the door.

When he left, I locked the door and went directly to Dean Montrose's office where we spent another half hour at a round conference table making lesson plans around the first few chapters of the text. I felt better as I shook the dean's hand and thanked her. It was still early, but I didn't feel like sitting in a bare office, so I used my phone GPS feature to locate Broad Street where I knew I'd find the corner bookstore with all the supplies I would need. I picked out colorful file folders, a decorative desk set with stapler, paperclip holder, and a round paper-covered pen and pencil cup; then spotted a poster that I'd always admired. A favorite Monet painting with red poppies and sunshine would brighten the dark, water-stained almond-colored wall behind my desk. I'd stop at a different store this evening for a desk lamp.

Roger came at one o'clock as promised, tapped on the outside of my open doorway and laughed out loud. I had now stacked the papers on top of my desk and had to peek around the piles to see him. "Wow, do we have work to do," he said.

"Did you bring lunch?" I asked.

"In fact, I did," he said as he held up the white paper bag he'd been hiding behind his back. "But I have no idea where we're going to eat it!"

I laughed and shoved aside one of the piles until it nearly fell to the floor. In two hours, he helped me assign a place for half of the items, keeping books I might need and large three-ring binders full of lesson plans and bibliographies related to my subject matter. Even if the text was different this year, much of the paperwork would relate. We put those in my new colored folders and filled all of the hanging files in the cabinet. The rest went to the recycling bin.

Late afternoon I headed to Gloucester Green to welcome Hermione to our new home. Poor thing! She attached herself to my side for the evening.

Chapter 37

On Wednesday, Dean Montrose greeted me as I stepped into her office. I nodded at the large cup of hot coffee on the same table we'd used the day before. Spread out before us were the four class lists with an individual file for each student, already color coded and ready for use.

My surprise must have shown on my face, as Dean Montrose smiled and acknowledged my appreciation. "We can't have you feeling stressed before you even get started, now can we?" Her British accent made everything she said seem so official and proper.

I sat and took a sip of coffee.

"OK, let's get started," she said, and for the next hour we covered the background of each of my eighty-five students. I mentally placed twenty-two students in each class and filled up about four rows if they all sat toward the center. My stress level plummeted.

By Monday, I had read half of the text book, located some handouts in my file cabinet to pad my lecture notes, and created lesson plans for a full month. I made certain they covered the content required by the university and added depth to the text. I, as much as anyone, hated to sit through a lecture where the teacher re-read the assigned chapter to students who had spent their precious time reading the same material the night before. That was a sure way to put them to sleep and make them hate you as well. By the end of next week, I planned to hit the internet for additional in-depth articles that fit the subject content.

This was basically a freshman English Literature class and a sophomore composition course. Even so, these were Oxford students. The university was highly selective and accepted only the best and brightest. I knew these kids were going to challenge me, but I felt better prepared to face them than I ever thought possible.

"Will you go clothes shopping with me tomorrow?" I asked Roger Friday afternoon when he dropped by the apartment.

He groaned. "Seriously?" But then he gave a bright smile and said he would. "But I have to warn you, I don't go for this drab gray and brown British attire."

"But that's what they all wear," I countered.

"You're from America. That's one of the reasons they chose you. So look it! The kids will love you for it."

"And I'm to find American clothes where in Oxford?" I frowned at him. "Are you serious?"

But on Saturday as we shopped the mall and Debenham's, Roger picked out three lovely cashmere sweaters in royal blue, a deep ruby red and a forest green, and I matched them with a couple pair of gray and black wool pants and a navy blue plaid pleated skirt just for fun. A few scarves and a trench would complete my wardrobe.

Roger met me at the register and handed me a T-shirt … "Mickey Mouse?" I was horrified.

"How about Hello Kitty?" He pulled it from behind him and laughed.

"Roger!"

"Brits love American stuff. It will be great under a blazer."

I shook my head as he insisted on buying Mickey.

My first two lectures on Monday afternoon went well—composed mostly of reading and signing the syllabus, briefly discussing the text book, and having each student introduce themselves to the class. I spent a short amount of time giving them my personal background and welcoming them to freshman English and to Oxford. By the end of the day, I felt like a professor.

Roger treated me to an early dinner, but he was too busy with the first week of classes for anything more. It was obvious our time together would be considerably less than it had been in June. We were both working professors, and Roger had an extra load of "independent studies" students in their senior year.

I was thankful I had the younger college kids, and except for meetings, an occasional visit with the dean, reading, grading essays and prepping for the next day, my days should flow at an easy pace.

That evening, as I checked messages from my kids and Jennifer, I realized I'd been in Oxford since early Sunday and hadn't heard from Luke. As glad as I was about that, I also recognized a bead of irritation. He was certainly hot to trot back in Phoenix. So …out of sight, out of mind? I convinced myself I didn't care.

Sure enough when I checked my phone Tuesday morning, I had a text message. That was it … typical Luke— no emotion, to the point, man of few words. I typed a quick reply. "Trip uneventful. Hoping things arrive this week for apartment. Only taught 2 classes – good so far." I tapped Send. There you go—woman of few words.

The weeks began to fly quickly. Luke established a routine of texting every other day. And for the past three Saturdays he had paid for international calling in order to talk in person. No matter how much I explained Skype and the money he would save, his reply was the same as always: "I hate technology." End of story. So I let him pay the fees and spent a half hour filling him in on the week's activities and asking about his kids and his life when we had time. Each time we hung up, he hesitated for a moment and then said quickly, "I miss you, Amy. I love you."

The first week I'd repeated it before realizing I had said the L word. The next Saturday I was prepared and carefully said, "I miss you too." I wasn't going to start the love talk again with this man. He could say it as often as he chose. This past week he had reminded me that he had scheduled his flights for October as planned. I still hadn't told Roger about this visit. In fact, I hadn't mentioned Luke's phone calls or texts either. That fact was beginning to eat at me. I knew how I'd feel is he were keeping things from me.

But somehow the right time never presented itself, and I let time pass. Maybe I was hoping Luke would back out. He hated to fly, even in the states. Always drove straight through when he went home to Texas or on any other trip; not that he made many of those. He was a home body.

It was mid-September before I realized it. A pattern had emerged. Roger and I spoke roughly twice a day; time permitting, he came over for dinner Wednesday evenings, and two weeks into the semester, he began sleeping over Friday night through mid-afternoon Sunday.

I had finally convinced Luke to use email instead of phone calls and apparently his first cell phone bill had been a doozy because he had willingly agreed. He was busy with his school calendar so they were few and far between. But each Sunday evening, after Roger went back to his apartment to do laundry and plan his week, I sat and wrote a lengthy letter via email. He seemed to appreciate it, though he didn't reciprocate.

He was looking forward to his October trip and had even bought a new jacket to bring with him. It would still be in the 90's in Arizona. It seldom cooled off until after Halloween. But he had thought ahead and knew he'd need it in England. He was quite proud of himself. "Hey, guess what?" he wrote. "Not leaving everything to last minute for a change. Will I need wool slacks and jacket or will my khakis be OK? Week was slow but football practice taking 2 nights a week now. Love you, LB"

I replied, "Hi there yourself! If you bought a fairly warm jacket, I think you'll be fine without wool. But you have to remember, this is my first year here as well, so what do I know? I've been shopping also. It's sort of fun buying sweaters and wool skirts for a change. We have no winter in Arizona as you know! You won't believe what I've done with my hair these days? Yep, went curly. Don't scream. I think our trip will be so much fun … yada yada yada for a full page.

I went on to tell him about this week's teaching schedule, which kids were not making the mark and how Oxford treated "slackers" compared to the universities in the U.S. Dean Montrose had told me to up the ante on several of them and hold them accountable, and I was trying everything I could. Did he have any suggestions for strategies that work with higher level learners?

I told Roger I kept in contact with Luke, of course. I wasn't a total liar. I just didn't happen to mention the regularity of the messages or how much time I spent writing to Luke. I told him we discussed education much of the time. Every contact from Luke ended in "Love you." I did not do the same. Always: take care, thinking of you, or something else innocuous. Was I leading on both men? I asked myself that quite often these days. I didn't want to be honest with myself, but my best friend didn't pull any punches.

I texted Jennifer daily and Skyped when we could. On a Monday morning before class, I checked to see if Jennifer was online and when I saw that she was, I pressed the blue bubble with S in the center.

"Hey, girl, how's your morning going?" Jennifer said.

"Remind me what time it is there?"

"Noon," Jennifer replied.

"Oh, good; I thought so. You'd think by now I'd have this down. Good to hear your voice."

"You too, hon. How's the working girl?"

"Pretty good actually. This college schedule is great compared to what we used to go through working 50 hours a week! I probably should be in my office by now, but I didn't have anyone scheduled so why sit there? What are you doing today?"

"Doctor appointment and meeting Susan for our old people's college class." She laughed loudly.

"You're crazy. You said you liked it last time we talked. World Religions should be fascinating. Tell Susan hi."

"Will do."

"What doctor appointment is this, Jenn?" I asked, but she brushed it off.

"The usual . . ." was all she said.

I decided to let it pass for the moment. "I have to get going, but I have to ask your opinion on something."

"You haven't told Roger about Luke's visit again this week? Right? Amy, I'm going to throttle you. Why would you risk a relationship with a really great guy by keeping a big secret? Are you trying to lose him?"

I hesitated. My face flushed with both embarrassment and pride. Damn it, Jennifer was right, of course. I whispered, "I know . . . ."

"What?" Jennifer said. "Amy, are you there?"

I took a deep breath. "I'm here ... sorry. I said, I know. You're right. I promise to do it this evening, or Wednesday evening when he's here is better actually."

"Well, make it soon. He's going to be royally pissed—that's a pun—royal as in British?" Jennifer could always take a situation and lighten it which made me smile with appreciation.

"I promise no later than Wednesday. Can I tell him this was unplanned and unexpected at least?"

"I'll leave that up to you. You're not being very honest if you lie; but I guess it's better than hurting his feelings. I don't know what to say about that, Amy. You've kind of gotten yourself in a bind here. And while we're at it ...."

"Yes?" I said when I heard the hesitation.

"Have you really thought about what it is you're doing with Luke? Why would you let him back into your life after all he's put you through the past ten years? I just don't want to see you get hurt again. Plus you've got this really great guy now ... I mean, I just don't get it, but I've never understood your feelings for Luke. He can be so mean, Amy."

"I know he has ... was... but I'm getting the vibe that he really has changed this time. He's really trying hard, and I really did love him as you know. I guess I'm not sure what I'm doing. I can't seem to sort it out. That's why I hoped to wait until after this visit in October to make a firm decision about what to do."

"Well, I wouldn't let it drag on too long. When Roger knows Luke is coming over there again, after last time when he was practically having you stalked … well, I just don't think Roger is going to hang around if he sees you reconnecting with him, that's all. And I think you are going to be very sorry in the long run. And now I will shut up. Go teach those kids something, will you?"

I had a half hour to kill before leaving the apartment. I took a fresh cup of coffee into the living room and sat on the couch with my journal. I'd try writing out my feelings and see if I could sort them out. I wasn't going to cancel on Luke; that I was sure of. Not this late; not after he'd paid for plane tickets. That just wouldn't be fair. Here I was being fair to Luke and not to Roger. I really should be shot; maybe I'd tell Jennifer to get the bullets.

When I got to my office, I gathered my materials and my power point for my first class which started at 1:00. I headed toward the lecture hall. The leaves were changing into fall hues, and many were beginning to fall in the wind. I walked ten minutes across campus to Roger's office building hoping to find him in. He was between morning and afternoon classes and hopefully he'd be there working. I didn't bother to call. If he wasn't in, I'd just head back to my own class and call later.

Inside the 1850's building where his office was housed, I climbed the ancient stone steps and envied his luck. The Rothmere where I taught had been built in the 70's and had none of the charm of the rest of the campus. It was nice, of course, except for my janitor closet office, but I'd love to be housed here. On the third floor, I walked down the long hallway observing people at work in nearly every one of the spacious offices. Fourth door from the end on the right, I could see Roger talking on the phone with papers spread out in front of him. He looked like he was grading as he talked, and I grinned and tapped on the door.

He put his hand over the mouthpiece of the phone and motioned for me to come in. "Yes, that's great. Thanks. Talk soon."

"Amy, what a surprise. I'd give you a sloppy kiss, but we're at work, huh?" He grinned.

"Oh, darn," I said. "I was going to jump over your desk and attack you."

"Hmm, maybe I need to rethink this …"

I laughed. "May I shut the door? Or is that a no-no?"

"Uh, sure … go ahead."

I quietly pushed the door shut and sat down.

His look held all the questions I knew he'd ask so I jumped right in.

"I heard from Luke recently, Roger. You know; we text and email occasionally?"

"Yes …" he strung out the word and ended it with a question mark.

"Well, thing is … I guess he's made reservations to come to England during his fall break. Take advantage of having a free place to stay and see something of the world."

Roger lowered his head and looked down at his desk. I knew he was thinking about his response. "I see," was all he could muster.

"Roger, it's no big deal. Honestly. I told you I'm not interested in starting up with Luke again, and I meant that. I really don't. But he has his reservations paid for, and I don't see the harm in a short visit. He won't be here long. No more than 4 or 5 days max." I stopped before it sounded like begging. Let it lie, I thought. Just stop now and let it go.

Roger pursed his lips and looked around for a moment before speaking. I waited. Was he going to end it right here and now? Was he going to be OK with this?

I was practically holding my breath.

Finally he made eye contact. "I'm not going to give you permission to see Luke and me at the same time, Amy; if that's what you're asking. That would be ludicrous. If you want to see him, see him, but I won't make this into a ménage a trois."

"Oh, Roger, I never suggested that. I'd never think of it that way. You must surely know me better than that by now?" My lip quivered, and I was afraid I'd start to cry if I didn't keep talking. "I really care about you, Roger. Luke … well, it's strictly plutonic. I hope you believe me. You see Melissa occasionally, right?"

"She's my ex-wife but no, we don't communicate, as you know, and not at all since I started seeing you—since our last visit to Cambridge together in June, in fact."

"All I'm saying is … I need for you to trust me. I want you to trust my feelings for you. I want you to believe that I'm really into our relationship, and I won't do anything to jeopardize it. I promise." Now I really did sound like I was begging. I needed to be strong about this.

"Can we talk about this later, then?" he asked. "I have a class in fifteen minutes, and I think you do as well, right?"

I nodded. "Yeah, I do. I just wanted to tell you. We can talk about it more later."

I stood to leave, but before I could reach the door, he walked around his desk and pulled my arm to draw me closer. His voice had softened.

"Come here," he whispered, as he pulled me into his arms. "I do trust you, Amy. And I've told you before I'm certain about us. I hope you feel the same. I thought you did."

I laid my head against his chest and looked up into his clear, honest blue eyes. "I do feel the same. In fact, I think I'm falling in love with you." I'd never said those words out loud before, but they felt right. And Jennifer was right as well. What in the hell was I doing messing around with Luke again and jeopardizing this.

Roger opened the door and pretended to shove me out. He was teasing. "Get to class, young lady. We'll talk later."

I smiled and scrunched my nose at him. "See ya."

As I walked to class I questioned my ethics. Other people dated more than one person at a time. And you didn't share sexual exploits with either one, did you? Of course not. So how did other people handle this? I wasn't sure if I could much longer.

Chapter 38

The rest of that day and all day Tuesday, I could think of little besides Luke's upcoming visit. I had given no thought to sleeping arrangements or anything else. I'd need to borrow a futon or some type of extra bed for the living room. Maybe someone had a pull-out sofa they'd lend me. I'd be in classes that week as his school-year was on a different schedule. What would he do while I was working? I had Fridays off except for a few office hours, but would Dean Montrose allow me to lessen my hours that week? I'd have to ask. It was exactly a month away. I needed to begin planning. I'd like to show him around the countryside. But with no car ... we could take busses but that was slow going. I had to laugh at myself. Perhaps Roger could drive us around the Cotswolds. I did laugh out loud at that thought. Right ...

On Wednesday evening Roger rang the bell just as I was taking a roast out of the oven. I'd cooked the potatoes and carrots with onion and herbs like I did back home. The smell was inviting, and I knew he liked red meat. Was I trying to placate him? We hadn't really talked about Monday's conversation the past few days, but I knew it would come up again tonight.

As it turned out, Roger didn't mention it and neither did I. He stayed later than normal for a work night. He usually headed home by nine, but he poured a third glass of wine for both of us and took my hand.

"What?" I said.

He pulled me along behind him into the bedroom, placed the two wine glasses on the night stand and gently pushed me down onto the too soft mattress. I sank into its comfort. All thoughts of Luke or work or conversation flew out the window. I let myself fall deeply into the release of everything except this very physical reaction.

By mid-October, the nights were growing cooler. If the sun came out, the afternoons were pleasant enough. But most of the time the gray skies made everything dull, including the spires along the campus. I hoped that snow would make everything sparkle again and was almost looking forward to the change of season.

Connie Wesala

Luke would arrive next week, and I had begun to question what I was doing. I had spent days assuring Roger I wasn't letting Luke back into my life, but how could I expect him to believe that when I didn't. Roger was not the type to cause a scene. His Cambridge and Oxford upbringing made him a stoic Brit. I knew that about him. I also knew his tender, gentle side—the man who still checked on his ex-wife through her parents. I had no doubt that Roger cared for me, and I knew my feelings were growing toward love.

The night before Luke's arrival, he insisted on treating me to dinner at his place.

"Wear lace and perfume," he teased.

"Anything on top of that?"

"Not for me, but if you feel it necessary for the bus ride, I'll understand."

I found my laciest and slipped a simple black sheath over it. I dabbed less than a drop of Chanel #5 at my cleavage and the pulse point on my wrist and fastened my gold chain with the simple pearl that fell at just the right place to be kissed later.

Delicious," I said as I dabbed my lips with my napkin. I leaned back. "Well done, sir. I'm stuffed." I patted my stomach.

"Not too full for dessert, right?" He cleared our plates into the sink and returned with wine. As he leaned over me from behind, he kissed my ear as he poured. When he lifted the bottle to walk away, I turned and grabbed his right wrist.

"Yes?" he said.

I stood and took the bottle from his hand, placed it on the table and picked up my wine glass by its stem. He pushed me gently into the bedroom, placed my glass on the nightstand, and gave me no time to object. This time he was less than gentle. He took charge, but he made certain I was also satisfied.

I hadn't intended to sleep over, but I woke the next morning in one of Roger's blue button-down shirts and nothing else. I lay facing the ceiling, listening to him in the kitchen. This morning I realized he had meant to take me—to claim me.

Chapter 39

I had just enough time to shower and dress to meet Luke's bus. He'd finally insisted I not go to Heathrow to meet him. "Not much of a traveler, but I've made that trip once." I could hear him grin. World traveler—right—anywhere between Arizona and Texas.

I had made up the couch with sheets and an extra duvet. I wasn't ready to sleep with two men at the same time—a few weeks apart maybe, but not this soon. I'd take the sofa. I had gotten three personal days approved, but I would teach one Wednesday morning class and one Thursday afternoon.

I watched his bus pull into the bay and waited as dozens of people scrambled down the steps to retrieve luggage. I began to wonder if his flight had been late enough to miss the morning bus to Oxford. A few moments later, I saw him emerge with a large leather duffel. His brown eyes sparked when he spotted me, and I moved forward to greet him with a hug.

"Mind if we walk to the apartment?" I said. "It isn't far."

"That's right; you moved since I was here last. Sure, I need to stretch the legs after so many hours of sitting. Man, those flights are long."

I asked if he'd like to stop for a bite to eat, but he declined. "You know; I think a hot shower and a nap might be good for now. Then maybe I can actually stay awake when we eat."

He made a big issue of my sleeping on the couch, but I insisted. I was much smaller and it fit me fairly well actually.

I let him sleep for two hours, then tapped on the bedroom door and peeked in. Hermione was curled at his feet and looked up when she saw me. I smiled. I tapped again, just enough to wake him this time. "Come on, sleepy head," I said. "We need to get some food in you."

As we walked to a nearby diner, Luke said, "Some of these streets look pretty familiar."

I nodded. "You stayed not too far from here, as I recall."

We both ordered burgers and Coke for a late lunch. "I'll fix a meal this evening," I said. "We can stop at the grocery store on the way back."

We caught up on the past few days though there was little news. I began to list a few possibilities for day trips and sights in the city itself.

"That one palace sounds interesting since you said it's not too far by bus. And I like the idea of the castle that used to be a prison. That should be enough castles for me." He laughed. "I just want to spend time with you. You plan whatever you want."

I nodded. "OK, we'll keep it simple and not try to do too much. You can always just head out on your own to investigate when I'm in class. There are so many parks and museums, you could stay busy for a full week or more."

He took my hand as we walked to the nearby market and insisted on paying for the items I bought for dinner. "I'm fixing something that can sit awhile, just in case you feel like falling asleep again. I don't care when we eat."

We filled the evening with casual talk; then he insisted on another short walk to campus and back. I pointed out specific stores, the pedestrian only street where he would find most anything, and told him about the Indoor Market. I thought it might interest him. As we walked past the building that housed Rothmere College, I pointed further north and told him about the large city park just a few blocks beyond. "I can sit in there for hours sometimes," I said.

He turned and held my face up to his. His kiss was gentle and sweet. "Anywhere you love; I'm sure I'll love it too."

I tilted my head and smiled. "You're just saying that to make me feel good."

He laughed. "I would never do that, and you know that."

I slept off and on, waking to the sound of Luke snoring in the next room several times. I wasn't exactly rested when I got up to make coffee. I tiptoed in to shower and dress for work, and he never woke. I wrote a brief note and left it on the counter. "Headed to class. Walk over or just meet me back here. I'll be back in about two and a half hours. Hope you slept well." I drew a small heart beside my first initial.

I walked out the double doors to the quad around noon with two of my freshmen students who had asked to speak with me. I answered their questions and smiled as I told them I'd see them in two days. As I turned toward the street, I spotted Luke leaning against the tallest of the Chestnut trees, a bottle of water in one hand and a bunch of brochures and pamphlets in the other.

Timing's Everything

I met him half-way. "You must have found the visitor center?"

"I did." He seemed quite proud of himself. We sat on a nearby bench and looked through them. I pointed out what was a waste of time and what I thought he might enjoy. Two were museum brochures that I knew would interest him, and I pulled those out.

"Well, we can eat a bite and grab the bus to Blenheim Palace. Even if we don't tour it, you'll enjoy the grounds."

"Sounds good."

We grabbed the #6 bus; then paid the driver an additional fee to take us on to Woodstock, the closest town to the palace. I remembered my day at Blenheim last June when I'd fallen asleep on a park bench and dreamed of Luke so intensely that I had to call Jennifer. And now here I was walking beside him on the half-mile gravel road to the Palace. We decided to pay for the tour and headed inside. "We can grab a snack in a while since we didn't eat much for lunch," I said.

As we followed the guide, I remembered the history of this place and knew immediately we'd made a wise decision. Luke was a history major. When he learned this was the birthplace of Winston Churchill, his eyes lit up. "No way," he said. "Why didn't you tell me?"

I didn't want to admit that I'd forgotten. We toured for over two hours. Luke took a few photos with his phone and stopped to read every description card. We laughed when we walked into the darkened room where an interactive display took place. I jumped when some king entered the room and screamed at his wife who was in bed with some other royal. True fact, though, was that King Henry II had his mistress Rosamund living there in secret for years. The palace held a lot of intrigue and affairs and bastards in its time. "Pretty common, I hear," Luke joked. "The Brits and the French …."

"And American Presidents?" I added.

We walked through the gift shop, and Luke picked up a couple of small items for his kids. I fingered a lovely replica of a necklace worn by Queen Anne; then put it down. I waited for him at the door and decided I was hungry enough to eat again.

The cafeteria wasn't packed this time of day, so we walked straight through and ordered a dessert to share and two coffees. He returned the tray and came back to the table with a broad grin on his face.

"What?" I said.

He stirred sugar and cream into his coffee. I took mine black. I cut the dessert into two pieces and grabbed a fork to try it.

Suddenly I saw a tiny box inching toward me. Luke pushed it with his pointer finger until it sat beside my saucer. I questioned him with my look, but he didn't say anything.

"What did you …?" I opened the small white plastic jewelry box to find the necklace I'd been admiring earlier. "Oh, Luke …."

He pushed his chair back, stood and walked behind me to fasten the clasp as I held it in place at my neckline. "It's so beautiful, but you shouldn't have."

He sat again and sipped his coffee. He looked like the Cheshire cat; quite pleased with himself. It made me smile. The smallest things pleased Luke. I remembered that about him now. A home-made meal, a thoughtful baked good placed on his desk at work, an inexpensive present for his birthday. I also remembered a few of his birthdays when he'd reacted with anger at the attention I had given the day. I still didn't understand his reactions and maybe never would.

For the next two hours we walked the lavish gardens and along the edge of the 2000 acres of woods. Several peacocks came out to greet us, and we took photos of each other with their large turquoise plumes behind us. We made it look like we were closer than we were to the large birds. It was a fun afternoon, and we grew tired of walking and sat near a fountain to rest awhile. "You enjoying yourself?" I asked.

"Absolutely," he said. "Of course I'd enjoy anything with you."

I shook my head.

"I mean it. But this is a fantastic place. I can see why you suggested it. A perfect day. History, a forest, obscenely lavish palace." He spread his hands wide to exaggerate. "Peacocks."

He stopped suddenly, and I followed his gaze.

Just then a mother deer stepped from the foliage with a small baby behind her. "Shh…" he said. I sat completely still and watched as the female looked around, then nudged the little one onto the grassy area not ten feet from us. We didn't move a muscle. Then she stood in front of the baby and stared directly at us before they slid smoothly into the woods.

I looked at Luke. He was smiling broadly; then turned and pulled me to him. We kissed deeply but not passionately; a kiss of love, not lust.

I felt complete love for this man at this moment. I fingered my necklace and smiled up at him. "Thank you for coming."

The next day was Tuesday, and I had to work for an hour or two that afternoon. Luke walked with me to campus, and I left him with directions to the History of Science Museum.

"It's right up your alley," I told him. And I knew it was. He'd spend the two hours and more if I knew him.

Sure enough when I entered the museum and walked up the creaky ancient stairs, I saw him leaned over a glass case full of astrolabes. I tried to sneak up on him, but the uneven slope of the wood floor cracked with my weight and gave me away. He turned and smiled when he saw me. I had my arms out trying to balance my weight and looked like a stork getting ready for take-off.

"Interesting," he said as he pointed at my wing spread. "Hawk? Ostrich? Stork!"

"Fine," I said, "Last time I creep up on you."

"Good." He walked toward me and gave me a quick hug. "Wow, what a place."

"I knew you'd love it." I glanced at my watch. 3:30. "Are you up for a walk?"

"Sure—whatever you want."

I knew just the place. We walked straight north from the museum, crossed between St. Luke's College and Trinity College, and came out on the street that would lead to the Museum of Natural History. We walked up a set of stairs and turned left to find ourselves in a glass-domed room full of life size dinosaurs. Their skeletons stood, hung and flew from the three-story high ceilings. I loved how it made you feel so inconsequential, and I could tell Luke was thrilled. A science and history buff … it was a perfect day for him. We stayed until 5:00, and I promised to bring him back before my morning classes the next day.

We stopped at Turf Tavern for a beer that turned into three each. At 7:00 I put my mug down and said, "We need to eat!"

I ordered fish and chips at the bar—extra fries for him and another pint.

I saw him watching me as I returned to the table. His eyes seemed to be assessing my every move. He saw that I saw and smiled. I let my hips sway more than normal. A female soliciting attention. He smiled as I walked to him and stretched out his arms to envelope me. I nearly fell into his lap. We both laughed out loud. I was growing tipsy from the beer. I slid onto the chair beside him instead of across from him where I had been sitting. He moved his bar stool closer, put his arm around me and pulled me into a kiss.

I had made promises to Roger regarding this visit, but I had also made them to myself, and I knew that promise was going down in flames tonight. The sober part of me resisted, but unfortunately that part was too small to fight off the rest of me. The waiter interrupted a kiss to serve us, and he slid the plates quickly onto the table and left.

Chapter 40

On Wednesday I kept an hour of office time before my morning classes. I had left very specific directions for Luke for his trip back to the museums. Not that he needed them. The man had a photographic memory. He'd be fine. I didn't expect any students to stop in since I'd been gone all week and had made no appointments. But I thought it looked professional, and I had to be there for my ten o'clock class anyway.

I was a little hung over from our evening at the pub and the night that followed. The sofa bed was still intact from the day before. I knew Luke would make the bed we'd slept in—he was anal about those things. If I'd had a window I'd be staring out of it as I rotated my desk chair left to right to left and thought about what last night meant. The memory was getting very intense when the phone jangled, and I startled back to the present.

"Hello, Amy Crawford's office."

"Hi," the thick male voice whispered. "It's me."

"Roger … why are we whispering?" I whispered in response.

"In the office – door open."

"Ahh …"

"Thought I'd just check in before I got my day started. I gave you space all week."

He had to make that clear, I thought. "But I knew you were in the office for the morning."

"I am," I said without adding more. I knew I was leaving him hung out to dry, but he had called.

"So, well—how's the week going? Luke enjoying the visit? I mean Oxford and all?"

"He is," I said. "Loved the museums and is revisiting them while I teach today."

"Ahh, I see. Well, I mean, that's good really. Makes sense. I mean—that he'd enjoy the museums."

He was practically stuttering, and I began to feel sorry for him.

"Yes, he's a history and science buff," I said and kept it light. "How is your week going?"

"Fine—just fine. Same old. Same old—you know."

"Yes, I do."

"Well, I'd better sign off—get to work. Cheerio and all that."

I laughed. "British this morning, are we?"

The man was sweating blood, and I was certain he wished he'd never called.

"Roger," I said, "Thanks for ringing me. Good to hear your voice. I'll call when company leaves, OK?"

"Sure, yeah, that'd be great." Then the line went still, but I knew he hadn't hung up. I could hear light breathing.

"I miss you, Amy," he said. "Is everything OK over there?"

"Yes, it is—pleasant— just busy. Roger, its fine. We're fine. You and me I mean." That could be taken the wrong way. I was more confused than I'd ever been.

I waited for Luke outside my office building after class. We could tour Christ Church. We'd spent a fortune the previous night at the pub, so I was fixing a simple pasta and salad for dinner. No drinking I told myself.

By five o'clock we were tired and headed home. "I see why you love it here, Amy," he said. We were walking hand in hand, and it reminded me of our very first date. I vividly recalled the first time he ever took my hand, and later that same night, in his car, his soft lips and the way he had slipped his arm around my shoulders and pulled me to him. I remembered the scent of his cologne and the laundry-pressed blue shirt he'd worn.

His hand was familiar and felt right as did his slower gait which mimicked mine so well, and our bodies matched like fabric cut to fit without seams. I suddenly didn't want him to leave.

I stopped quickly which threw us off kilter. He looked surprised. "I'm so glad you came," I said. "I wanted to share this place with you."

"Me, too," his eyes bored into mine with questions unasked. And I had no answers to give.

We let the moment slide.

We ate in my small dining area with the telly on in the background. Luke had enjoyed Christ Church as much as I had. There was nothing not to love. It was spectacular in every way. I poured hot tea as a chill had formed inside my apartment. We were well into fall and coming upon winter very soon. I grabbed a sweater from the closet and returned to the living area. Luke stood and pulled me to him. "I know you don't want to sleep together tonight. I just wanted to get that out of the way."

I smiled as I pulled away. "Thoughtful of you," I said.

"Generous is more like it," he said. "I know you still see this Roger guy, Amy, even though we haven't talked about it.

I didn't want to talk about it now either. I put up a hand to stop the conversation. It didn't work.

"I want you all to myself, Ame ... all to myself. I don't like knowing that you're with him." He hung his head, and his tone turned serious. Then he peeked up at me. "That's what I want. I don't know what you want."

The tension grew as I hesitated for what I knew was too long. I had to say something. "Roger means a lot to me. He's been a fun friend to have in a strange place. I'm not going to lie to you. Just give me a little while longer, OK?" I pleaded with him with my eyes.

Luke sat back in his chair. He sipped his tea and grimaced. "How about some coffee instead?" It lightened the mood immediately.

I laughed. "Coming up." I stood and walked to the kitchen—just a few feet from where he sat. I talked to him as I filled the pot with water and found the coffee and filters. "Luke, it isn't that I don't want to talk about Roger; but honestly, I don't talk to him about you either. It's just too awkward."

"And you're not ready to make a choice?" His question startled me.

"I ... I don't know what to say to that. I don't want this to be a competition. I don't want it to be a decision between two men. I want it to simply be about reaching a place where I know my own heart."

I didn't know if that made any sense to the male thought process, but it was all I had to give him for now.

He walked to the counter and stood for a moment. He didn't say a word. Then he did his Luke thing and turned back to the living room sofa and turned up the television. He found a sports channel and sprawled out on the couch placing a throw pillow behind his back. I served his coffee and brought sugar and cream to the coffee table.

After I cleaned up the dining table and filled the dishwasher, I returned and sat down beside him and opened a magazine.

I had a substitute teacher for Thursday, so the next morning, I slept late while Roger headed out on his own. I heard the door creak and lifted up on one elbow. "Come back by noon, and we'll do Oxford Castle. Get ready for some ghosts." I grinned, and he did the same.

I insisted on paying the entrance fee. Oxford Castle was right in the city of Oxford, only a mile southwest of the apartment. I'd been going to tour it but hadn't taken the time. Our guide was a typical actor, but he knew his history. Dressed in Victorian prison garb, he started our journey by warning us of the narrow circular stone staircase with 100 steps. I didn't know if he was warning because of my age or not, but I took it that way and was determined not to sweat … or pass out.

By the time we reached the top, my breathing was labored and shallow. I touched my chest and smiled. "OK," I said. "I'm fine." I looked at Luke. His wide athletic shoulders barely squeezed along the walls of the stairwell and the wrought iron banister, but he was in much better shape. He smiled at me and patted me on the back. "Good for you," he teased.

I punched his left arm. "I made it, didn't I?"

"Yes, you did." He smiled and gave me a hug. Then he whispered into my ear so no one could hear. "You might want to use the university gym a bit this winter."

I punched him even harder in his gut. We both laughed.

The history might have been made up, but neither Luke nor I was certain. We decided to believe the guide as he took us through one century after another, one tall tale after another, to the top where he shared his own personal sighting of ghosts in the cold dank room. It would be too cold in another month to even enjoy this excursion. I pulled my sweater closer around me and wished for a jacket.

On the top of the tower we had a view of the entire city. The famous spires lit up when the sun peeked from the clouds. It was an incredible place, and I felt an inner joy and peace. How lucky to be here, I thought once again. Whether I wound up with either man, it didn't matter at that very moment. I was simply happy on my own.

The next day was Friday. I had the entire day free, and we discussed options over breakfast. Luke had seemed satisfied with all of our excursions, but I wanted the last two days to be special as well. A day trip by train seemed like a lot, though nothing was very far. At the last minute, I suggested renting a car though neither of us could easily drive on the wrong side of the road.

"Or we could take the train to Stratford upon Avon." It was something I wanted to do, but I left it to Luke.

"Well, I could probably get the hang of this driving thing as long as we weren't on major highways. It sounds like the Cotswolds are tiny two-lane roads where you don't drive very fast anyway. What do you think?"

I considered for a moment. It would be a nice excursion, and Luke was right. There were few things he couldn't do well. We'd probably be fine.

Luke noticed I was taking my time deciding. "Seems like you'd really like to go to Stratford. You are a Shakespeare person, after all. English major, right?"

I nodded.

"How long is the train ride?"

"Two hours," I told him.

He glanced at the time. "If we leave now, is there a train going there within the half hour?"

I got onto my laptop to check the train schedule. One would be leaving at 9:50 a.m.. It was 9:15. We could make it. I checked returns and found one back to Oxford at 8:00 p.m., but we wouldn't be home before 10:00 or 11:00

He pulled me into his arms and looked down at me. His brown eyes still mesmerized me. "I know you can go anytime. You're here the rest of the year. But I'd like to watch you enjoy it."

It was a statement so unlike Luke, I actually gasped with surprise. Never, in my wildest dreams did I ever think I would hear him say something so generous and thoughtful. My heart caught for a second, and I kissed him.

"That is the loveliest thing you've ever said to me." In fact it was one of the loveliest things I'd ever heard from anyone.

"Grab your coat," I said, "It may get cold along the river." We gathered our belongings and pushed them into a deep canvas shoulder bag. I threw in a few granola bars and a couple bottles of water. We were both in jeans and tennis shoes. I locked the door, and we headed out. On the train ride, I pointed out sites to pass the time.

It was fun seeing Stratford through Luke's eyes. While I was the English major and Shakespeare buff, he enjoyed the historical tour we took on the Hop On - Hop Off bus during the afternoon. I chose Anne Hathaway's house as our first stop.

"What do you want to see next?" I asked. We were on top of the double-decker bus even though the wind was cold and rain was threatening.

"Well, we have to see his birthplace and where he's buried, right?"

I agreed. "But those are right in town, and we can walk. We have time for one more stop."

He thought looked at the guidebook again. "Mary what's-her-name's farm," he said. He grinned. I shook my head.

"Mary Arden. Shakespeare's mother, for heaven's sake."

It turned out to be a good choice. It was still a working farm, and we wandered among horse barns and pens of chickens, goats, and sheep. Geese waddled along the dirt paths. The house was open to tour, and Luke hit his head more than once.

"I'm not even tall," he said when I laughed the second time he hit the door frame.

He glanced at the guide book one more time. "Hey, there's an aviary show starting." He led me over to where a group of people were standing in a large circle. I groaned. "Hey, it'll be fun," he assured me. His right arm went around my shoulders and pulled me closer.

When the show began, I watched his face. He was mesmerized by the costumed, white-haired gentleman who exhibited the talents of the trained falcon perched on his left arm. The bird flew when commanded and swooped down as he returned to his trainer. I cringed as it got too close for comfort. Luke laughed.

When the falconer asked for a volunteer, I watched in shock as Luke stepped forward. I'd never seen him in this kind of situation. He was so serious and even touchy back in the states. Who is this man? I thought. But I had to admit, it was a nice change.

Luke raised his left arm straight out, and the trainer covered his forearm with a piece of heavy leather. The man whistled sharply and the large bird took off, soared above the crowd as he circled and returned to perch on Luke's arm. I was more than nervous, but it was a show, right?

When he walked back to the outer circle to my side, he grinned from ear to ear. "You'd think you were the show bird," I said, and I laughed. "Anyone can stand still and hold their arm out," I teased.

Just then we heard a clap of thunder. We turned to each other with raised eyebrows and headed for the entrance where we hoped to catch the next bus.

"No umbrella in that big bag?" he teased.

"Darn," I said. "I have an apple."

As the rain began in earnest, we raced each other to the gift shop and ticket office. The skies literally opened up, and we were drenched before we reached the entrance. We were laughing loudly as we rushed through the door, dripping onto the checkered vinyl floor. I asked when the next bus would arrive and was told fifteen minutes.

"Do you have anything hot to drink?" Luke asked the woman behind the desk. She pointed to some large beverage containers sitting on a table near the entrance.

"Hot water and coffee," she said. "Two?"

Luke nodded and dug in his pocket for some coins, while I poured us each a hot coffee. The bus ride back to Stratford was long enough for the skies to clear. Luke took my picture as I posed in front of Shakespeare's birthplace.

We walked along the River Avon, ate dinner at a nice restaurant with a patio facing the water and headed back to the train station at 7:30. I had booked us First Class, so we had nice comfy seats, and both of us nodded off about 45 minutes into the trip.

I woke to find my head on his shoulder and his left hand settled on my lap. I had known this man for ten years and had rarely experienced the relaxed, unself-conscious person I had been with this week. I had a sudden memory of another trip we had taken together, and it reminded me of this. I had commented when we returned home that year that he had been a totally different person those few days. I guess I did know we could have this, but I'd forgotten after so many years of tension and chaos. It felt nice.

Connie Wesala

Chapter 41

We had a slow day on Saturday to give Luke time to pack and to relax after our busy week. We walked into town so he could buy a gift for Tyler, and we went to the bookstore where he bought a novel for Sammie. It was rainy and cold, so we had hot tea and browsed in the market. I wound up falling asleep for an hour late afternoon, then cooked dinner while Luke caught up on some work-related emails. I could tell his mind was already back in the states. I did the same thing at the end of a vacation.

I was in the tiny narrow kitchen just placing the lasagna into the oven. The salad was chilling in the refrigerator. A baguette sliced and spread with butter and garlic. Luke was opening a bottle of wine for me and a bottled beer for himself.

When the doorbell rang.

Luke was closest to the door and looked toward me with the unspoken question of whether he should answer. I shrugged my shoulders and said, "Must be the super. No one else would come by. Go ahead."

I turned slightly to adjust the pan on the heated rack and glanced back to ask the guy what he needed, but what I saw made me gasp. Luke was shaking hands with Roger who stood just inside the doorway; obviously making his way on into the apartment.

What?

The two men were now conversing as I stood mute with disbelief and watched them. I heard the words, but I couldn't believe it. Things like: good to meet; Amy tells me … Yes, very much … Education ….

Then Luke invited Roger to sit down and offered him a beer. Roger declined, thank God, which I hoped meant he was leaving. But instead he walked toward the one comfortable arm chair—his usual perch—and sat down. That's when he saw me and waved.

The audacity! The least he could do was act apologetic or at least embarrassed. He should look guilty. Luke was now sitting on the sofa and took a swig from his bottle and continued to talk to Roger as if he were making a new friend. He patted the spot beside him, but I shook my head. Men … what the hell?

I poured myself a glass of wine and leaned against the door frame to support myself. Roger explained his second Master's degree and his position at the university. Luke mentioned his superintendents certification and the fact he was leading the largest high school in Phoenix with tons of kids on each side of the academic spectrum. It was more satisfying on a day to day basis than a desk job at the head shed. Roger expressed the academic rigor of Oxford and the level of student he was teaching. I wanted to start keeping score and announce their progress.

Right now it was a dead even heat. Rugby – Roger. Football – Luke. Published research – Roger. National recognition – Luke. Unbelievable. If I had any thoughts that they might actually fight for me, I was sadly mistaken. This was just an old fashioned pissing match. Leaving their scent in my lair. Claiming ownership of the female. I was disgusted with them both. *What children!* I thought.

I returned to the kitchen area to finish my preparations. If Luke invited Roger to stay for dinner, I would add arsenic and feed it to both of them. Neither had even acknowledged my presence, but I felt certain they wanted the audience. I stabbed the lasagna to check for doneness and slid the pan of bread into the oven. Took out dressings for the salad. I slammed silverware against the hard counter. When the talk slowed, I stuck my head back into the room.

"Dinner in ten," I chirped like Donna Billingsley on Father Knows Best.

They both looked at me like I was an apparition. I wanted to yell – Surprise, I'm here, but I smiled graciously while I fumed inside. *You son of a* … I thought.

Roger rose then. "I'd better be heading out," he announced. "Nice to meet you, Luke," he said as he shook his hand once again. He turned toward me and waved. No peck on the cheek, no arm around my shoulders; but his presence stated the obvious--I'll be here, Luke, and you won't.

"See you tomorrow night, hon," and to Luke he asked, "What time do you leave tomorrow? Well, have a good flight."

"Hey, you too, man. Be sure to visit if you come to the states. Amy and I would enjoy showing you around."

What the?? I shook my head and responded to Roger's good-bye. "Bye—later …."

When the door closed, I stood hands on hips and shook my head again.

"What was that?" I said.

Luke just grinned broadly and asked if dinner was ready.

"Sure …" Hmm, maybe the sword fight was later.

"Good, I'm starving." He settled himself across from me at the small table.

After dinner we settled on the sofa and cuddled while we watched nonsensical British TV. Luke chuckled while I basically tuned it out. It wasn't long before cuddling turned into fondling which turned into bedtime. Luke always fell asleep after we made love, at least for a short while. I laid there staring at the ceiling wondering who I had turned into. This has to stop. It had to be resolved. But I couldn't resolve this puzzle. I didn't want to have to choose, and I didn't want to lead this double life.

Luke woke enough to pull me into a spoon. "So you're really not coming home for Christmas?"

"The kids are coming." I knew he remembered.

"Not sure I can wait for spring, but I can't afford another trip, Amy."

"I know."

"Why don't you just come back with me tomorrow?"

"And break a contract, Mr. Principal?"

I was sure he was smiling. He'd fire anyone who even mentioned breaking a contract.

"We'll figure it out," he said, and in an instant he was out for the night.

As soon as Luke's bus turned the corner and headed toward London, the tears began. I didn't want to go back to the empty apartment, and I wasn't expected on campus. My closet office wasn't appealing anyway, and of course, I couldn't run to Roger crying over another man. The most peaceful place was the meadow, but the temperature had dropped even further overnight, and the wind felt blustery and harsh. So I headed toward Alice's neck of the woods. Christ Church meadow was small and had a wind break from the large sycamore trees. I stopped at Starbucks to get a large hot coffee on my way and warmed my hands as I walked. Entering through the St. Aldate's gate, I made my way to the River Cherwell and took an empty park bench. My Starbucks napkins served as tissue for my tears and runny nose, and I could visualize Luke's trip home. If he had come here for an answer, he had left without one which at the moment seemed cruel of me. Let the man go, my conscience told me. I didn't want to listen to that particular voice. so I counted backward on my fingers and called Jennifer anyway. Her voice sounded thick with sleep, but I needed her.

"Amy?"

"I know you're asleep. Just listen to me for a few. You don't have to say anything."

I heard the bed covers rustling and could tell she was fluffing pillows and flicking on a lamp. "Did Luke just leave?" she asked.

I blubbered the words. "Yez." I sobbed. "Oh, Jenn, I didn't tell him yes or no—neither one. He's still hanging. But I just can't." I sobbed again.

She took a moment and then said, "Well, first of all he probably didn't expect an answer. The goal was to see you, to let you know he cared enough to come and second, it's your life too, and you can take as much time as you need."

"He didn't push me," I said. "In fact, he didn't really talk about it at all."

"See? Like I say, and I hate saying it because as you know he's not one of my favorite people, but he's trying to prove himself—regain your trust. Pushing you would have done the exact opposite. He's not stupid. I'm sure he accomplished exactly what he intended—to get in your good graces and your bed." She laughed. "He did do that, right?"

"Oh, hush …" I said, but I chuckled. She knew.

"Where are you?"

"At the Christ Church meadow—on a bench …"

She interrupted. "Go home, take a shower, drink coffee and fill up your day with anything … museum, library, a movie, a good book. Get busy."

"You're always right," I said. "Hate you …"

"Love you too—now let me go back to sleep."

We said good-by, and I left the campus and found a bus back to the apartment. If Luke loved me and if he had changed as he said, he would wait. Jenn was right; he was not a stupid man. This trip was the start … at least in his mind. What was it for me?

Chapter 42

As stupid as Roger had been last night, he was smart enough to leave me alone all day and all evening. Luke texted as he boarded the plane.

When Roger did call the following day, he was soft spoken but acted as if we'd just seen each other. It had been a week, and I'd been with another man. I gave him credit for being a better person than I was. I'd have questioned him about another woman for hours—insisting on every damned detail—then wallow in it for weeks.

Men did get it right some times.

"Want to go see a movie this afternoon? How about a good action-packed Tom Cruise?"

"I'd actually like that."

"OK, meet me there; its half way between us on George. I'll be the one with popcorn and a drink in each hand."

He made me laugh, and it felt good.

Sure enough he was standing just inside the glass doors with full hands but motioned with his head to come on in. "I got tickets already. In my right pocket. His jeans were tight, and when I worked my hand into his pocket, the tickets were difficult to pull out, and my hand grazed an area he liked.

"Oh, that's right; it's the left pocket."

"Oh, no, you're not getting more than that little pleasure. They're right here,"

I held up two tickets. "Come on, Mr. Concession man ... follow me and don't spill that popcorn."

Once we were seated with drinks in our cup holders and the large bucket of popcorn between us, I said, "You know I hate Tom Cruise, right?"

His eyes widened, and he looked distressed until I laughed. He threw a piece of popcorn at me and put his arm around me.

It was a perfect way to reconnect, and I thanked my lucky stars for him. Other men might ... well, any number of things but this.

He whispered in my ear as the previews began. "Love you."

"Love you too," I said. And I did. I loved them both. I'd lived alone for over fifteen years, except for dating Luke, and now I was in two full blown relationships at the same time. Nothing this good could possibly last, I told myself.

Connie Wesala

Chapter 43

After Luke left in late October, Roger and I took several weekend excursions. When he said I didn't have to do a thing, I nearly fainted. "Where have you been all my life?" I exclaimed.

He laughed. "Here in the UK I guess. You should have made the trip sooner."

"Seriously, can I make some food? Arrange a hotel?"

"All taken care of, including a cooler of car snacks. Just pack a sexy nightie and your jeans and sneakers."

What a treat. That word struck me. To be treated was something I'd rarely experienced. He planned, organized and did all the work. All I had to do was show up. Amazing!

Bruce was always too busy, and except for coming up with an idea or two, he did nothing for any of our vacations or holidays. And Luke was too spontaneous to ever plan or decide a thing. His idea of a get-away was to throw an overnight bag together in five minutes and hit the road. Hotels would simply show up when you needed one; as would food and gas. I was an organizer and planner myself, so I'd done it all. I never thought to look for another planner. Always thought opposites attracted.

One weekend I asked if we could go back to Cambridge. It was where he'd grown up, and I wanted to know more about that part of his life. Our only trip there had been in June when we checked on Melissa and when I had been certain she was the one having me followed. Sometimes, especially when he was being so generous and thoughtful, I wondered why she had warned me not to get involved. Making it seem as if he had pushed her over the edge into whatever paranoid world she had fallen. It made no sense, but according to Roger, Melissa rarely made sense. I'd never shared her warning with him—never had a reason to.

We left after office hours on a Friday afternoon. Fall was in brilliant array, and it brought to mind my life before Arizona. "Fall is my favorite season," I said as we drove past mile after mile of Plane trees.

He looked at me in surprise. "Really? I'd never have guessed."

"I know—doesn't make much sense living in the desert with no such season. But…."

My mind wandered, and I didn't know if I had spoken aloud or not. I loved the sounds of fall; leaves skittering to the ground from high above. The crunch of shoe sole against the brittle dryness as they lay brown against the ground. As a child, I would gather large oak leaves and press them between pages of heavy books. Or place them under thin drawing paper and rub them with crayon dark enough for their veins and shapes to appear as a mirror image. The muted soft tones appealed to me even more than the colors of spring.

My life always felt like fall. Closing doors, but gathering as well. Gathering leaves, red sumac, pecans, bouquets of mums and apples right off the trees. Fall brought Halloween and children's costumes and upcoming plans for Thanksgiving and Christmas.

Fall was a busy time. Squirrels and other animals gathering winter stores of food. Harvest. Bounty. Pumpkin anything—bars, cakes, breads and pies. Hayrides. Gold, red, brown, rust. Fall seemed to be the color of life going into a quiet hibernation, slowing down.

Roger's voice brought me out of my reverie.

"What?" I asked.

"I said, 'where did you go?'" He laughed. "Must have been a lot to think about."

I felt myself blush. "Sorry. Did I really zone out?"

He took my hand and squeezed it. "That's OK. I'm good with quiet. Just curious what you were thinking about so intently."

"Oh, just silly stuff."

"About fall?"

"I loved school so much as a kid. I loved fall … brand new pencils, erasers that smelled of rubber and a fresh box of crayons with those perfect points and that new crayon smell."

"We always had fires in the fireplace as soon as there was a hint of fall," Roger said. "And bonfires not far from the house with all the kids in the neighborhood."

"Are we going to see your first house?" I asked.

"Yeah, we'll go past, though it looks nothing like it did in those days.

Connie Wesala

Lots of older people who never moved away. Very few kids. Whereas *we* filled the streets with American football and soccer, and when we were little … Foursquare and King of the Hill. At five o'clock when our mums yelled for us to come to dinner, it was like a swarm of ants emptying the streets.

"You know how it is when you leave and then come back and you expect nothing to have changed except you? But you were what made it that way in the first place, so how could it stay the same?"

I hadn't thought of it that way, but he was right. You can never separate a place or a time in your life from your part in it. Without you, it would have been an entirely different experience.

Even right now—this year—my life in Arizona would not be the same, because I wouldn't be there to touch it with my thoughts or my actions. My absence would change every waking hour for everyone back home.

"Not sure I like that thought," I said. "But you're right."

He took a left just past the center of town along streets that we'd call urban blight in the states. The Welcome to Cambridge sign had said population 100,000, but new housing must have been further from town. The streets were rutted with potholes and some disease had killed off the trees. He was right. His old neighborhood and primary school looked forlorn and in disrepair. I watched his face and saw a grimace of sadness.

His high school looked better, and then he cruised by Cambridge University where he had received both his Bachelors and his Master's.

"Beautiful," I commented as we drove around campus. "So you met Melissa here?" I couldn't recall what he had said, but I was pretty sure.

"We went to different secondary schools, but I actually met her once when she was fifteen."

"Lovely campus," I said. We were directly in front of the sports complex now.

He nodded. "I spent most of my time here," he said, pointing to the rugby and soccer fields. He laughed. "Might have been suma cum laude if I hadn't loved sports so much."

I laughed too. "I have a hunch you did quite well. You just got your second Master's from Oxford, and I'm sure Cambridge doesn't accept any slouches."

He nodded. "No, the two schools are pretty much the same caliber and in constant competition."

He circled around campus until we reached the main entrance once again. "Enough reminiscing," he said. "I'm bloody starving!"

After lunch I asked if he wanted to visit his parents' graves. He stopped at a small florist shop and bought a bouquet of mums and daisies; then drove straight north on Newmarket Road. We passed through an arched stone entry way onto dirt and gravel roads that wound among the cemetery.

When he stopped, I handed him the flowers I'd been holding. "I can wait in the car," I said.

He shook his head. "No, no need. Come with me."

We walked across the roadway from where he'd parked and down a curvy path. I pointed out a grave stone dated 1915.

"Not sure how you do it in the states, but British cemeteries have large family burial plots that date back to the late 1800's or early 1900's. It's not uncommon to see four generations in a small area."

When he stopped, I saw a few dozen head stones and room for more. Aunts and uncles, parents, grandparents, and great grandparents. Several rows of Reynolds.

"Will you and your sister be buried here as well?" I asked.

"The plots are here; whether we use them—I don't know. My sister's husband comes from a long line as well—over in that far corner." He pointed a distance away. "She'll probably be with his family instead. And I'd just as soon be cremated and ashes scattered. No kids—no future generation to come by and take care of the plot, you know."

He looked sad as he spoke.

"Well, I have two kids, and neither of them wants to take care of me either. So they can do as they wish with the remains I guess."

He nodded. "I suppose."

I knew he sometimes wished he and Melissa could have made it work—wished for a child or two with her. I did feel fortunate in that regard. I missed mine every day. I was used to daily contact and doing things with them every couple of weeks. That must be a huge void.

Before we left Cambridge, Roger drove along a narrow winding river. I asked which river it was, and he chuckled. "Cam," he said. "The Cam River ... Cambridge, get it?"

I laughed. "Ahh," I said. "Well, can we stretch our legs?"

He indicated the blanket in the backseat of the car, and I grabbed it.

He took my left hand as we walked along the banks of the river. The sun teased us off and on for the next hour. We settled on the blanket, and Roger laid his head in my lap and seemed to doze, though I wasn't certain if he was really asleep. Several punters approached from our left, and I woke him as I reached for my cell phone to take a picture.

"I want to do that before I go back home," I said.

"Punting? Sure, we can do that. I'm an excellent punter." He smiled.

"I'm sure you are; you're good at everything."

"Not sure about that. But let's wait till it's warmer—like maybe April."

"Today was perfect," I said. I leaned toward him and kissed him gently.

It had been a perfect day. It was good to see his roots. "I hope to meet your sister soon," I said once we were back in the car.

"Sure thing," he said. "Hey, guess what?"

I saw his eyes crinkle with humor. "What?"

"I'm starving. Let's get dinner and head back."

I laughed. "I've never known a time when you weren't starving. But I agree."

By mid-November, Oxford was into winter, though the temperature was more moderate than I'd expected. 30's at night; 40's during the day. I was missing both Sarah and Chris' birthdays, but they understood the cost of shipping. I told each of them to choose a nice gift of their choice and send me the bill.

Thanksgiving is no longer a sore-spot for most Brits which I found out by watching the grocery ads. Turkeys were selling like crazy as well as cranberry sauce and all the other essentials. The week before the holiday, I called Luke to see if he was headed to Texas.

"Of course; when have I ever *not* gone?" When he talked about his home state, his Texas accent became more pronounced than usual.

"I'm sure your mama is preparing a feast!"

"Sure is …." he hesitated. "Hoping next year you'll be there with me."

"Are you serious?" My tone was one of shock and disbelief. "Luke, you never once invited me to go with you—all those years." Now I felt an old anger seeping through layers to the surface. "Always a damned secret, Luke—always …." I stopped. It grew quiet on both ends of the line. Then he gently spoke my name.

"Amy … I know. But can you not believe I've changed? What is it going to take?"

"I don't know," I said, and I didn't. What would it take? And did I even want to believe it? Why not focus on Roger and put aside this past relationship with Luke?

"What are you doing this year?" he quickly changed the subject and segued into safe territory.

"I'm baking a turkey and fixing a traditional American Thanksgiving." I laughed. "The Brits can get over it."

"With Roger?" he asked. Luke never mentioned Roger's name—ever. It was as if he had no knowledge of the man. I was surprised. Lie? No …

"I invited him." I left it at that. I knew *he* knew. We moved on to safer topics: work, students, grades, end of semester which was approaching quickly.

"What week are your kids visiting?"

I reminded him.

"I have a three week break. I'll spend one at home, of course, but I wondered if …." He stopped.

"Are you serious? It's so expensive, Luke. You can't."

"Don't you want me to come?" His voice sounded hurt.

"It's not that … I'm just so surprised. You cannot afford another trip, Luke."

"That's what credit cards are for, right?"

I was speechless. Luke, here? Again? We had a great time in October but …

"I … that would be great, Luke. Just let me know." When I hung up I noted my shaking hands and feelings of … what? He's just teasing, I thought. He'd never do it.

I spent Thanksgiving in the kitchen of my tiny apartment. The oven was so small, I worried that the bird might not feed us all. I had to bake the dressing and pies the day before—one item at a time. I fixed yams but didn't bother making them into a casserole dish with butter and brown sugar. We would eat them like baked potatoes instead. Roger was most impressed with the pumpkin pie, as I'd made the crust from scratch.

At the last minute I had invited Dean Montrose and two of Roger's colleagues. They brought wine and beer and two lovely appetizers and seemed to enjoy seeing an American in action. They quizzed me on the specifics of the holiday, but had a hard time believing the Indians and Pilgrims sat down together after that first winter. "They jolly well would not have sat or shared corn with people intent on taking their lands," one said.

"The whole thing doesn't bloody add up. I mean, I get wild turkey and all, but yams and dressing and green beans and pumpkin pie? Come on … blimey," said another.

"Well, it's a lovely holiday and a great reason to gorge one's self," Dean Montrose said agreeably.

I could have used a third pie.

As everyone said their good-byes, I noticed Roger missing and called his name. He popped from behind the kitchen cabinets, a tea towel slung over one shoulder, and shook hands with everyone and thanked them for coming. Dean Montrose pecked me on the cheek. "Lovely dinner, my dear—just delicious. I'll see you tomorrow." I waved good-bye as I closed the door. Then turned to Roger.

"What are you doing in there?" I asked.

He looked sheepish. "Thought I'd get a head start. There's so many dishes, and you cooked for two days. He poured the last of the Chablis into a glass and walked me to the sofa. "Feet up—drink some wine, and let me do this."

"Oh, Rog…."

"No, no … not a word. Sit!"

I sat. I called after his back, "You're the best; you know that?"

From the kitchen I heard, "I know … I know."

By nine p.m. I couldn't move a finger. I wanted nothing but a shower and bed. The weather had turned dicey—strong north winds and the smell of snow in the air. 60% chance by morning they said on the evening news. I kissed Roger good-night as he lingered by the door. The kitchen was spotless, the living room back in order; folding chairs tucked in the corner ready to be returned to campus.

We spent ten minutes praising each other and arguing over who was the greatest catch. I finally gave in and accepted the honor. Fifteen minutes later I was ready for bed—in warm pj's, house slippers and my heavy chenille robe. The cell phone rang, and I grabbed for it. Sarah and Chris probably. With the time difference we hadn't had a chance to talk all day. "Hi, guys—Happy--"

Luke laughed. "It's me," he said. "Hope it isn't too late. Are you alone?" He was in Texas—an additional hour more than the norm between us. "Mama's gonna be calling us to the table in a few. Wanted to wish you Happy Thanksgiving. How was your party?"

I told him briefly and asked about his mom's health and the kids.

"Wish I were there to tuck you in," he whispered into his cell.

"Stop that! Your mother will hear you."

"I don't care. She knows me." He laughed heartily.

"Have you been drinking?"

"It's football season; of course I've been drinking. Just beer—I'm sober."

I started to ask another question, but he cut me off. "Gotta go--love you."

My "bye" got lost in the hang up.

But he had the advantage of being the last voice I heard, and I dreamed about him all night in one scenario after another—mostly in bed. I couldn't help but wonder if that had been his intent.

I had work the next morning. Even though I'd taken a day off for Thanksgiving, I didn't dare stretch it to two. I'd had to get coverage for my Thursday classes with a promise of reciprocating during Christmas holidays.

The kids would be here in two weeks, and possibly Luke the week immediately following their return. My tiny apartment was feeling even smaller, and I wished for the two bedroom apartment I'd turned down. We would manage, but I started questioning why I hadn't just flown home instead. I had a large house sitting empty, and Luke would not be spending money he didn't have. I suggested that option when Sarah called next, but she assured me they'd manage. They wanted to see Oxford and my life here, and, I was certain, meet Roger and weigh in. She was going to kill me when she found out Luke was flying over again, so I didn't mention it.

I'd been begging Jennifer to make the trip, and she'd tentatively said spring—April.

"That's a promise!" I told her. "And I'm holding you to it.

Chapter 44

As the semester drew to a close, the students worked their butts off to raise grades. No one missed a class or an assignment. If they'd taken the year lightly in September, they certainly weren't now. No one wanted to be on probation spring semester or risk the possibility of having to leave Oxford. I didn't have to say a word. The system was clear. I assigned study groups a week before exams and hoped the more advanced students could work magic on those falling behind. If not, my classes could be smaller come January.

Grades were due on a Thursday. The kids would arrive on Saturday. I raced home early Wednesday afternoon to frantically grade and turn in my assessments the next day. I had a few gifts still in shopping bags and tissue in my closet. I could put Sarah to work baking goodies and helping prepare a Christmas meal. Chris kept reminding me this was a holiday—a vacation—nothing had to be traditional.

As I stomped the snow off my boots and unwound my wool scarf, I noticed my front door open a few inches. Someone was inside. I listened for a moment; ready to bolt at the slightest movement. A curse word rang out, and my body tensed. Something metal struck the wood floor, and then I heard, "Bloody hell!" The voice I knew—Roger. But what the heck was he doing?

I swung open the door. A metal stand sat upside down and off to his left. The pine tree lay flat on the ground to his right. His face was red with anger that then turned a deeper shade of embarrassment when he spotted me. My mouth flew open. "Roger, what the ..." I wanted to laugh, but I could see that was unwelcome. "What can I ...?"

"Would you flip that damned stand upright and hold it while I wrestle with this tree?"

I threw my work bag to the floor and did as he asked. I stayed deathly silent as he lifted the tree to a standing position; then with both hands, hoisted the seven-foot pine high in the air and brought it down an inch from my fingers where I held the metal Christmas tree stand.

It slid into place, and he tightened the four bolts that held the trunk in place. I stood and applauded as he dusted his hands off on his jeans. "So much for the surprise," he said.

"No—it is a surprise—a wonderful surprise. Thank you! Thank you!"

He finally grinned "You're welcome."

On the sofa sat two paper bags filled with glass ornaments and a few strands of lights to decorate the tree. "It's a fir," he explained.

"It's just beautiful," I said as I walked toward him. I put my arms around his neck and pulled him to me in a kiss. His lips tasted soft and salty.

"Have you been eating?"

"Your pretzels ... yes."

"You deserve a beer. How about a buttered rum instead? No rum—lots of butter," I joked.

"Fine, a beer—a warm beer though; not that cold stuff in the fridge."

I returned from the kitchen with two open bottles and a bag of crackers.

"Thanks," he said, and he toasted my bottle with his. "I can't stay. These are for you and the kids." He pointed to the boxes of ornaments and lights. He held up a package of silver icicle strands.

"Oh, Roger, thank you. What a lovely gift. I'll remember this forever." My eyes welled with tears. "God, I love you," I said before I could halt the words.

His eyes showed his disbelief. "You do?"

You don't take back "I love you" once those words fly from your mouth. They hung in the air like the notes of Christmas songs. I took a deep breath and reminded myself to be quiet. Roger walked to me and held my face up to his; he pressed his lips softly on mine and held me like he owned me—firm and certain and possessive. "I love you too, Amy."

"Would he have said it if I hadn't?" I asked Jennifer later that night.

"Does it matter?"

"Maybe ...."

"Or maybe not. He doesn't sound the type to fake it, Amy. I'd go with he just hadn't found the courage until you opened the door."

"I hope you're right. I had no right to say that yet. But seeing that Christmas tree in the living room and all the thought he put into it. I mean ...."

"You don't have to explain. Hell, *I* love the man!" She teased. "You didn't ask him to marry you. You just said you loved him, Amy, it's OK!"

I hung up from our call feeling a little better but still wished I hadn't said

Connie Wesala

it. Once again I had failed to find time to tell Roger about Luke's upcoming visit. And now? I love you and oh, by the way, my other lover is coming in two weeks. What was wrong with me, for God's sake?

I stayed up till four a.m. grading exams, slept two hours, and woke at six. I completed the paperwork that was due to admin by 10:00 that morning. Roger called at 9:30 just as I was zipping my boots and pulling my coat collar up around my neck. I answered with one hand, wrapped a long heavy scarf around my neck and tugged on a knit beret with the other.

"I'm leaving a little something on your desk," he said. "Wish I could see you before I leave for Cambridge, but I promised my sister I'd take the eleven o'clock train."

They were catching a flight out of London to ski in the Alps for their holiday. No spouses, no kids—they were all the family they had, and I had yet to meet her.

"Wish you could go," he said.

"Well, I'd be a bloody boring hanger-on—I don't ski."

"And the kids arrive tomorrow."

"But, you'll be back before they leave, right?"

"Of course," he exclaimed.

"Roger," I said sheepishly. "Oh, my God, I was going to give you your gift last night and with the surprise of the tree, I simply forgot."

"Not to worry!"

"But, if you're at my office dropping off, can you just wait a few minutes? I'll be there in a half hour."

"I'd miss my train, Amy. I simply can't. Don't worry. We'll celebrate when I get back. Love you. Really gotta run." He hung up. And then it hit me.

Oh, shit, I was going to tell him about Luke's visit. I tried to ring him back—no answer. Shit. Shit. Shit.

Dean Montrose was in her office as I passed by on my way to admin with the first semester marks. "How did they do?" she asked. I knew she meant my first year students.

"Only two under an 85," I said. "Probation?"

"Most likely. I'll take a look and decide."

I nodded OK.

"Amy, have a wonderful Christmas and a great visit with your kids."

"You too," I said. "Don't work the whole break."

I knew she would though. I always had as an administrator. Too much to do before second semester began in January. I waved good-bye and headed to my office. When I turned on the light, I saw the small gift-wrapped box front and center on my desk. The paper was gold metallic with a red velvet bow tied neatly around it. It was too small to be anything but jewelry. Several scenarios flew through my head. I hadn't said the L word until last night. He'd obviously gotten the gift earlier this week. I picked it up and felt the lightness. I shook it slightly, but no sound. Bracelet, necklace, earrings? For some reason I sniffed it though I had no idea why. I would wait till he returned from holiday even though he had said not to wait. Then I raced home to start preparing for the kids.

That evening Jennifer called. Her doctor appointment was the following day. "It will be fine," she said.

"But I want to be there," I argued.

"Oh, for heaven's sake. Your kids are coming tomorrow. I'll be fine. Susan will take me. Quit worrying."

I felt somewhat betrayed—a foolish thought, of course. It was simply my need to be there. It had nothing to do with her. "But you'll call me with the results as soon as you know, right?"

"Of course, silly! Tell your kids hi and have a great Christmas. I'll call you later in the week."

"Merry Christmas!" I yelled into the phone. I was shaking as I clicked off the phone. Something didn't feel right about this.

Connie Wesala

Chapter 45

I waited outside Arrivals at Heathrow airport, and saw Sarah and Chris walk through the passport check. I nearly shrieked with excitement; I was ecstatic. It had been nearly five months since I'd seen them. "Here, let me help you," I said as I took a carry-on from Sarah. She was able to push her purse onto her shoulder as we hugged.

On the way to luggage, I talked with Chris about their flight and jet lag. "I'll let you sleep when we get back to the apartment if you need."

They both agreed with that scenario. We still had an hour bus ride to get to Oxford. Once we clambered aboard, they lasted twenty minutes before leaning their heads against the window and falling soundly asleep. I smiled.

For two days, we tromped about Oxford as I showed them the sights. I narrowed it to campus and planned to hit a couple of museums after Christmas.

Both of them laughed when they saw my office space, but I could tell they were proud. As we cooked meals, I shared my fall semester—classes, particular students, troubles and achievements.

"Here's to our Oxford professor mom," Sarah said as she raised her wine glass and clinked my beer mug and Chris's glass of water.

Chris had helped me finish decorate the tree that afternoon, while Sarah baked a small ham and made scalloped potatoes from scratch and fresh green beans. The bakery rolls were in the oven, and I could smell the yeast scent of warm bread.

"I am so glad you're here," I said, and suddenly tears were running down my cheeks.

"Ah, mom," Sarah said. "Here, let me get you a Kleenex." She came back with a box from the bath.

"It won't be much longer, Mom," Chris said. "You'll be home soon, plus we have a few more days, and you'll be ready to kick us out by then." He tried to lighten the mood, but all I could think about was seeing them fly off in just days. I felt I'd missed so much this fall and winter. Birthdays, Thanksgiving, Halloween. It added up.

Once I stopped blubbering and began to eat, Sarah made eye contact and said, "OK, when do we get to meet this Roger person?"

I had explained his ski trip with his sister and had told them there would be a one-day overlap when they could meet him. "We'll go out Friday night to a pub, and you can check him out," I said. My smile felt silly, and I figured it looked the same.

"Is this serious?" my son asked. His face told me he wanted the truth.

"I'm not sure what to say about that, honey. I mean … yes, it is, but whether there is a future together, I'm really not certain. We live in different countries; we've had such different experiences …." I waited a moment before continuing. I sighed out loud. "It's just so frustrating to meet someone I really care about and know it can't go much further."

He smiled and patted my hand. "Well, if it's meant to be, you'll figure out a way."

I nodded. I had a perfect opportunity to mention Luke's last visit and his upcoming trip to see me. "Do it," my mind screamed. "Just do it." If I didn't speak right now, the opportunity would pass.

"Oh, crap," Sarah said as she threw her napkin onto the table and ran over to the range. She grabbed for a pot holder and pulled the overly brown bread onto the top of the stove. "Damn it."

"It's fine … they don't look burnt," I said. The edges were tinged more than dark brown. "Scrape off the edges … they're fine."

She did as I suggested; took a knife and scraped off the blackened areas, threw them into a basket and brought them to the table. "Eat up," she said. I could tell she was upset with herself. My perfectionistic daughter.

Chris could care less. He reached for two pieces, buttered them quickly and popped them into his mouth one at a time. I laughed. "Well, they must be good."

Sarah laughed, and I was glad she was letting it go.

The next evening was Christmas Eve. We bundled ourselves into warm coats, boots and mittens. Wrapped wool scarves around our throats and tugged knitted caps on our heads to keep in the warmth. It was a fifteen minute walk to Christ Church, but I wanted to experience Christmas in that setting. I had planned on this event for weeks— double checking times, asking around to see how early we needed to arrive for a seat, and getting the kids ready a good half hour earlier than needed. As we sat half-way back in the worn wooden pew of the famous chapel, I took the hand of each of my children as I sat between them. I squeezed and tried not to cry again.

"I can't imagine a better Christmas," I said through a tight throat.

Chris squeezed my hand, and Sarah put one arm around my shoulders. "It's perfect," she said. When the organ began playing Silent Night, and the famous Christ Church choir began to sing, I felt angels everywhere in the high ceilinged chapel.

We sang one hymn after another, and when the service ended at 8:30, we held our lit candles as they illuminated the stain glass windows that surrounded us. Instead of extinguishing them as we did in the states, everyone began filing out of the chapel still holding their candles carefully away from each other as we wound ourselves outside into the famous Tom's Quad.

There were at least two hundred people, and we walked along the sidewalks filling three sides of the quad as we continued to sing. The centuries old stone gleamed in the candle light, stars glistened in a clear black sky, and suddenly a few light flakes of snow began to drop from nowhere like a gift from God. There were no clouds to produce them, but there they were melting on our clothing.

As we walked home in a quiet reverie, arms hooked together at the elbow, three of us astride, we hummed another hymn and then began to sing more lively Christmas songs. Chris began Grandma Got Run Over by a Reindeer, and I bumped him with my elbow.

"What?" he said. "It's better than the Chipmunks."

I had to agree. After cups of hot chocolate, I hugged them good-night and left the tree lights on so Santa could find his way. Sarah tucked herself into the far corner of the bed we were sharing. I could hear Chris plumping his pillow on the sofa bed and heard his iPod music low in the background.

"Thank you, God," I prayed. Whatever happened with these men in my life; it didn't matter really. This was what mattered. My family—my kids.

We spent Christmas day inside after unwrapping gifts and fixing breakfast. There was still a light dusting of snow on the ground though it was melting quickly. Hermione played in the bunched up wrapping paper, then found a piece of plastic to chew on before I caught her and took it away. We worked on a puzzle and took a short walk around the neighborhood.

I pulled the turkey out around two o'clock, and Sarah placed the potatoes, dressing and green bean casserole in for an additional twenty minutes.

Chris set the table and filled the water glasses. It reminded me of every other Christmas Day we had celebrated for the past twenty years. Except for the landscape outside the windows and the fact that we had three homes back in the states that were each twice as big as my miniscule apartment. I smiled as Chris pushed the sofa back against the window as far as it would go.

"You need a little more leg room, son?" I teased.

He laughed at me. "Seriously, Mom? This place is tiny. But I guess it's just you."

I wanted so badly to reply, but I kept it in. Yeah, I thought, except when Roger or Luke stays over. He saw me smiling.

"What?" he said. "What did I say?"

I just brushed it off with a swipe of my hand. "Put the salad dressing and butter on the table, please."

After dinner, Chris used my computer as a stereo by plugging in to the internet. He cleared the table, and I filled the dishwasher. We agreed on a board game and settled in for the remainder of the evening.

The day after Christmas arrived, and Roger called when he got into town. We arranged a time to meet at Tom's Tavern for fish and chips. I was not looking forward to introducing him to my grown children. I knew they were going to grill him just as I would if they brought home someone new. For the next three hours, they did just that. But Roger pulled it off beautifully.

Around 9:00 he suggested we walk to another pub around the corner and down a few blocks. It was ancient, and Chris was properly impressed. Inside we hung our coats on hooks, and Roger walked us to the rear where a large dart board hung. He and Sarah pulled out some bills and made a bet. Around 10:00 I walked back from the bathroom and saw the three of them laughing their heads off and throwing more pound notes into a large pot on the table beside them. Sarah pulled back her arm and let the dart soar – right into the bull's eye. "Yes," she yelled as she jumped into the air and high-fived her brother.

Roger was grinning from ear to ear, and I wondered if he had purposely blown his last shot. Either way, it was proving to be an enjoyable evening. I sighed as I walked toward them. What was I thinking even considering to add Luke into the picture? The kids hated him for some of our past history. They were obviously connecting with Roger just as I'd hoped. *Not now*, I thought, and I let it go.

Connie Wesala

The next day, Roger drove the three of us into London a few hours earlier than we needed for the airport. He took us to a couple of sights that could be easily seen from the car. Chris had visited London before, but Sarah had not, and Roger knew that. He was doing everything he could to please her, and, in fact, had brought along two gifts for them to take back to the states. He parked as I helped them with their luggage and headed to security where I would have to say a final good-bye. I refused to cry in front of them.

"Thanks for a wonderful week, Mom," Sarah said as she hugged me. Chris did the same.

Just before they turned to place their stuff on the security conveyor belt, she added. "He's a great guy, Mom. Don't blow it."

Chris laughed. "Great is a strong adjective," he said in all seriousness now. "But I do like him."

"Bring him home this spring," she called as she walked through the x ray machine.

They both waved and called out one last good-bye. Just then, an arm wrapped around me, and I felt Roger's warmth. I turned into his camel cashmere coat and let the tears flow.

I had barely walked into the apartment when my cell phone rang with Jenn's ringtone. I grabbed it from my purse and answered. "What's going on?" I asked immediately. "How are things? Did you get the test results?"

There was quiet on the line for a moment which frightened me further.

"Hello to you, too." She gave a laugh. "Amy, it's probably nothing, but they want additional tests. And maybe a genetic screening."

My heart stopped. No, not again. She had been through too much already. This would not be fair.

"I should come home, Jenn."

"You should not," she insisted. "It's just cautionary, honestly. It will turn out to be nothing; you'll see."

"But Jenn …."

"No buts. You're teaching. You're needed there. You can't just fly home on a whim, for heaven's sake. At least let me get these next tests done before you start packing, OK?" I knew she was teasing me; trying to keep things light.

"Jenn," I said with tears in my eyes. "Whatever happens, you know I'll be there for you, OK?"

"I know, Amy, you always have been. Now let's talk about your holiday, OK?"

There was no way to change the subject back to her. I knew her too well. So I gave her the rundown of my week with the kids."

Chapter 46

Luke was due in four days, but on Monday morning my phone woke me out of a dead sleep around 4:30 a.m. I saw his name on the screen before I answered.

"Luke?" I said. "Is everything OK?"

I could hear the tightness in his voice and a sadness when he spoke. "My mother …."

It went silent. "Your mother, Luke?" I said. "What's wrong?"

He took in a deep breath and managed to continue. She'd been fine during Christmas. He had returned to Arizona to pack for his trip to England and to check in at work, and got the call late last night. A heart attack, rushed to the hospital by his older sister, and pronounced dead around midnight.

I couldn't believe what I was hearing. "Oh, my God, Luke. I am so sorry!" I wanted to put my arms around him and hold him to me and let him cry. I wanted to be there with him, instead of a thousand miles away. What good was I to him this far away?

I could hear him trying to sniffle away his tears, and I gave him some time. There was nothing I could say that would mean a damned thing anyway. So I finally asked, "Are you headed to Texas now?"

He was leaving within the hour; driving the long trip to south Texas again just days after getting back. He was going to bury the woman he loved more than anyone else on earth. I had teased him often about being a mama's boy. It seemed cruel now, but at the time it seemed to sum it up.

He spent every holiday and every vacation taking care of her needs—the old house he'd grown up in, a summer garden, huge family events, and her health. What would he do now? I felt sick with sadness.

"Luke, what can I do?" I asked, knowing the answer as I said it.

"Come back," he said. "Amy, please come back. Get on a plane. I need you."

His words startled me. He had never pleaded with me like this. I knew it was grief but I also sensed his desperate need.

"Oh, Luke," I said. My thoughts were churning. "I'm not …"

This time he was sobbing. "Amy, please … I can't get through this without you."

I didn't know what to say. I needed time to think this through. "May I call you in the morning?"

"Sure," he said.

"Let me know the arrangements. I wish I could be there with you," I said, and I truly meant it. I wished I could sit in the passenger seat of the truck, hold his hand, put an arm around him; anything to make it better. But I was here … in Oxford, England, and there was nothing I could do but pray, as he said.

We said our good-byes, and I told him I'd phone around midnight his time—early morning for me. I hung up and laid my head back on the pillow. Tears wet the pillow case, and I sobbed not only with grief for him, but with my own sense of aloneness. I wanted nothing more than to hop a plane tomorrow and be there before the funeral. I wanted to be with my kids and my best friend who needed me right now. I missed home.

I fell asleep thinking through my options and how I could arrange for a substitute teacher for the beginning of the spring semester. I knew Dean Montrose would grant me the leave. It was a family emergency. Or was it? I wondered. It wasn't my own family. Maybe she would not be able to grant me that. Plus it was a huge expense I really couldn't afford. I dreamed dark bizarre dreams the rest of the night and woke up exhausted.

Roger woke me around 10:00 the next morning. He rapped on the door, and I startled awake, grabbed my robe and pushed my feet into my slippers. The wood floors were freezing, and I had wished for carpet more than once. I glanced in the mirror on the way to the door—eyes swollen, hair disheveled … I looked like I'd pulled an all-nighter.

I opened the door to let him in, then excused myself and went back to the bedroom to throw on some clothes. Jeans and a heavy wool sweater with my bedroom slippers.

When I returned to the living area, I smelled coffee. Roger had his back turned to me, and I watched as he opened a bag of bread and popped two pieces into the toaster, then turned to the refrigerator where he pulled out a butter dish and a jar of jam.

I smiled to myself. He really was a wonder. I bumped into the end table as I made my way toward him. "Damn!" I swore, as my hip caught the sharp edge. That would bruise.

My cursing startled Roger, and he turned quickly. "You OK?"

"Yeah, just clumsy," I said. "Thanks for making coffee."

"It's almost finished perking," he said. "Do you have tea?"

I pointed to the upper cabinet to his right. "There … further back."

I rubbed my hipbone and cursed again.

Roger put a tea bag into a large mug, turned on the electric kettle and walked to me. "Do you need some ice on that?"

"God, no," I said, "It's freezing in here already."

"Well, maybe some heat instead?" He smiled. "I could kiss it and make it better."

I gave a vague smile. It just wasn't the right day for this. All I could think about was Luke driving to Texas to plan a funeral for his mother. Even the coffee and toast wasn't enough to make me feel better.

"You seem out of sorts. Were you up all night or something?" he said.

"I had a phone call that woke me and couldn't go back to sleep," I explained.

He walked back to the kitchen, poured a cup of coffee, placed the buttered toast onto a plate and told me to sit down on the sofa. After he served me, he returned to the kitchen, poured hot water over his tea bag and came back to sit beside me.

"Anything I can do?" he said. He didn't ask who had called. Sometimes his English manners were too much for me. I drank my coffee and wished he would ask so I didn't have to open up the topic. He waited me out.

I finally sighed loudly and turned to face him. "Roger, Luke's mother died last night. I'm considering going home to help him with the funeral."

His face tightened into a mask.

"He has a large family, right?" he said. I knew what he was thinking. He was right; there was no reason for me to fly back to the states for this unless …."

I didn't answer right away, and he sat somewhat rigid and sipped his hot tea. "Do you have any honey?" he finally said. I knew he was avoiding an argument.

"In the pantry," I said. He walked into the kitchen again, and his demeanor felt cold and distant.

"Roger," I said. "Luke needs me. No matter how big his family is, he needs me right now."

I knew that was no explanation, but there was none that would satisfy him. He had been kind enough when I'd finally told him about Luke's trip to Oxford—his second trip in four months, but I knew he was not happy about it. And now ... here I was running off to the states because he couldn't come here. I was sure that was how Roger saw this.

He stirred the teaspoon around his mug and sat back down. When he turned to face me straight on, he didn't hesitate any longer.

"Amy, what's this all about? First you forget to tell me he's coming over here again, and I tried to be gracious and not question you. But I have to question this decision. He has a large family; his own kids. I get that you guys are friends, but obviously he means a lot more to you than that if you're willing to just pick up and fly over there right when a new semester is starting. Not to mention the expense of a last minute flight."

I looked down at the floor. I couldn't meet his eyes. Had I made the decision to go? When had I made that decision? In the brief five minutes since I'd awaken? Even though he'd begged me to come, Luke would be fine once he got with his large extended family. He wouldn't expect me to just pick up and go at the last minute. I was certain of that. I was the one wanting to go, and I knew it.

I'd only met Luke's mother once, but several times I'd sent Christmas gifts to her post office box, and a few times I'd called and talked to him as he sat in her kitchen right next to her. I knew she knew about me, and I'd always felt her to be a kindred spirit. Another woman who could see through Luke's hard shell; who loved him in spite of his tendency to run away and hide.

I knew her through his eyes—a generous, kind hearted woman who had raised eight children in a tiny two bedroom house. A woman who had insisted he speak no Spanish at home despite it being her native tongue. A woman who protected him from his father's anger and alcoholism. At some deeper level, I loved her for loving him and for making him the man he was today. With all his faults, Luke was loyal and caring and hard-working. He was sensitive and intelligent and wise. I credited her for that, and I grieved the loss of her.

I finally looked at Roger and placed a hand on his fore-arm. "Roger, I know you don't understand. There's no way I can explain it to you, either. But

I'm going as soon as I can make a reservation and call Dean Montrose to get a replacement."

"You're coming back though? Right?" His tone expressed his uncertainty.

"I don't know …." my voice trailed off. But I suddenly knew that I probably wasn't. I'd be back to pack up and ship everything home, of course. But it might be some time before I even did that. Even I was surprised at this decision. And even though I knew I was hurting him, I couldn't think about Roger right now. Maybe later I would. I didn't know about that either.

"I see." He picked up his mug and walked to the kitchen sink, rinsed it out and placed it on the counter. He slipped on his full-length cashmere coat and pulled his gloves from the pockets. He didn't say another word, and he didn't come near me.

"Roger …."

At the door, he turned the knob, then looked back at me one last time. "I'm sorry it turned out this way," he said. There were tears in his eyes. "Let me know what you decide."

He slipped out the door, and I listened as the locking mechanism caught.

I ran to the bedroom to grab my cell phone, left a message for Dean Montrose on her office machine, dialed American Airlines reservations; then called Luke's number.

When he answered, I said, "I'm coming home."

THE END

Proof

Made in the USA
Charleston, SC
29 October 2016